I0527674

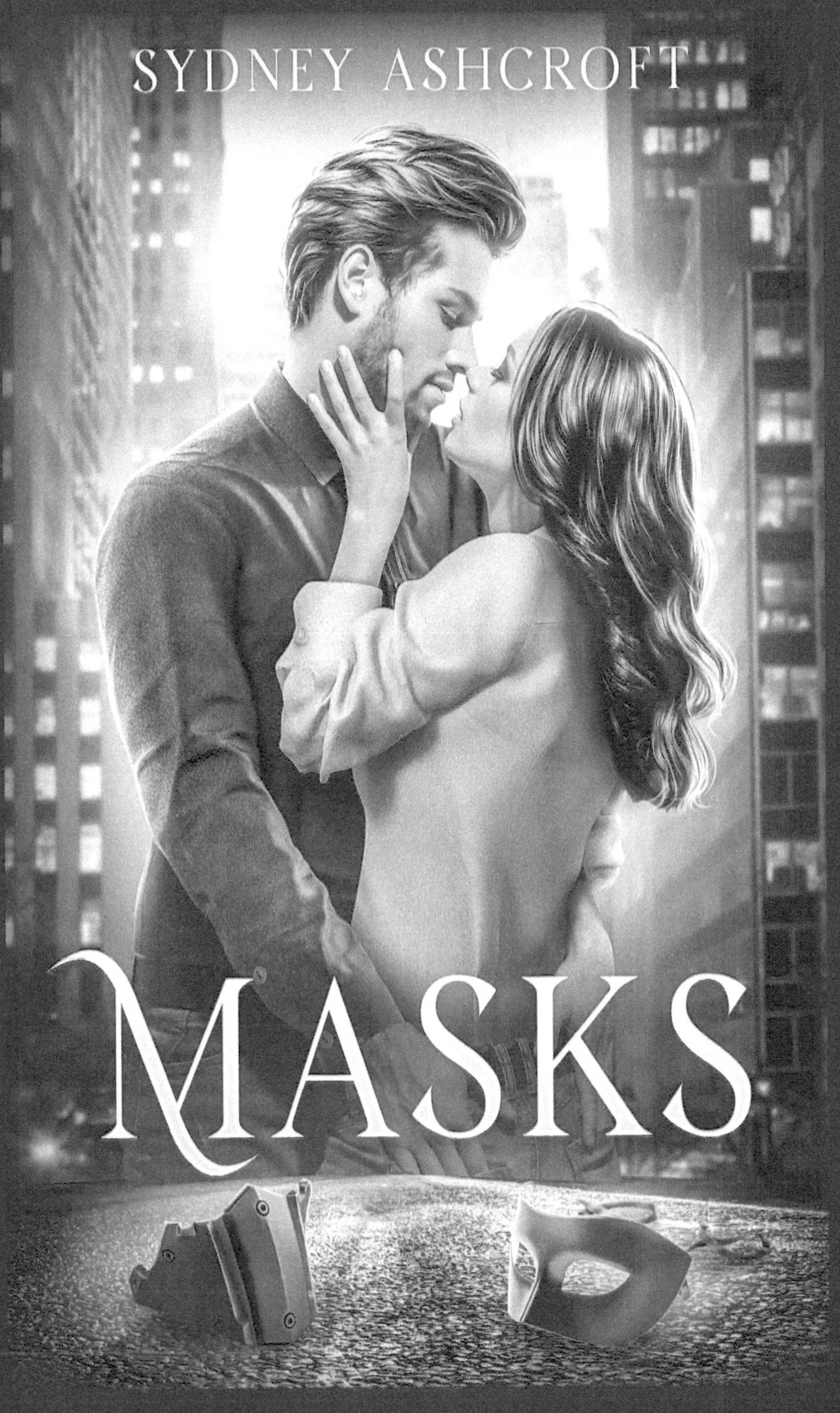

SYDNEY ASHCROFT

MASKS

MASKS

SYDNEY ASHCROFT

CITY OWL
PRESS

This book is a work of fiction. Names, characters, places, and incidents either are products of the author's imagination or are used fictitiously. Any resemblance to actual events or locales or persons, living or dead, is entirely coincidental and not intended by the author.

MASKS

CITY OWL PRESS
www.cityowlpress.com

All Rights reserved. Except as permitted under the U.S. Copyright Act of 1976, no part of this publication may be reproduced, distributed, or transmitted in any form or by any means, or stored in a database or retrieval system, without the prior consent and permission of the publisher.

Copyright © 2024 by Sydney Ashcroft.

Cover Design by MiblArt. All stock photos licensed appropriately.

Edited by Tee Tate.

For information on subsidiary rights, please contact the publisher at info@cityowlpress.com.

Print Edition ISBN: 978-1-64898-452-5

Digital Edition ISBN: 978-1-64898-451-8

Printed in the United States of America

For Jeff. You were gone way too soon.
For the women who walk their own path in life.

CHAPTER ONE

Light reflected off the steel blade of a knife for a split second before it slashed across Maria Grayson's upper arm. The knife tore through the thick material of her Balestra costume and bit into flesh. She cried out and jumped back, almost stumbling over the uneven sidewalk.

"Bastard," she growled at him, but she was angrier at herself. She missed the fact that he carried a knife and paid for it. She was never this sloppy when out on patrol and blamed it on her mind being elsewhere.

An unholy grin appeared on his face, and he lashed out with the knife. Expecting it this time, Maria ducked under the strike and the knife whooshed through the air above her head. She didn't give the man time to recover by driving her shoulder into his stomach. He doubled over and Maria drove forward, shoving him backward until she heard the dull thump of him colliding with a light pole.

She straightened and delivered a right hook with as much power as she could put into it to his face before he could react. His eyes rolled back, and he slumped over, sliding down the pole into a heap on the ground. A heavy sigh escaped her, and she looked at her wounded arm. Blood seeped through the gash in her costume and glistened on the black material. Thankfully, it would heal within a short time.

Maria nudged the knife away from the man's reach with the toe of her boot and picked it up. The last thing she needed or wanted was for him to wake up, grab the knife, and take more swings at her. She grabbed the blade and bent it back, rendering the knife useless. She shook her head and pulled out a burner phone she used for crime fighting. She sent a quick text to Detective Rollins, her contact with the NYPD, with her location. Now all she had to do was wait for him to arrive. Thankfully, a fight on New York City sidewalks at night didn't attract much attention.

Maria took a moment to catch her breath. The man proved to be a tougher opponent than she had believed he would be. She had scored a few hits on him, which should have brought him down with her enhanced strength, but he had remained on his feet longer than the average person. She bent over and leaned in toward his face. White powder lined the rim of his nostrils. She'd bet money it was Boost, the newest drug to appear on the streets of New York. It seemed to be everywhere lately, and it explained why the fight had taken more effort than normal. It gave a regular human abilities on par with hers when taken, and it gave powered folks a huge increase in their powers. It was bad news all around.

Sighing, she straightened and looked at the black duffel bag sitting a few feet away. Rollins would lecture her if she opened it, but it didn't stop her from wanting to. She didn't need to. She observed the man sell packets of white powder out of it before she engaged with him. Maria wished Rollins would hurry up.

Her personal phone vibrated, and she yanked it out of a pocket. *Where are you? You're late!* Of course, Gayle would be texting her to admonish her for being late.

The two women met in kindergarten at the ultra-exclusive private school their parents sent them to and were fast friends.

The two remained inseparable since. Maria was an only child, but Gayle Simon was her sister.

"See that," she said, holding the phone toward the unconscious man, screen toward him. "You've made me late."

I'll be there as soon as I can, she replied.

You better be. Your grandfather has noticed your absence.

"Shit." At any other time, being late wouldn't be a big deal, but tonight there was a charity event her grandfather expected her to attend. Maria pushed a lot of limits in her life, but she rarely pushed them with her grandfather.

Ten minutes later, Rollins pulled up and climbed out of the car. Maria offered him a smile. Rollins had acted as the police liaison for her for the past few years. Maria liked the soft-spoken, brown-haired, brown-eyed officer. Maria met him during her early costume days, and the two worked well together.

"Balestra." He nodded in greeting.

"Detective."

"How are—"

Maria held up a hand, cutting him off. "While I normally enjoy our little chats, I gotta be somewhere like ten minutes ago. Drug dealer." She nodded toward the unconscious man. "Most likely Boost. He's on it and the duffel bag is full of it."

Rollins nodded. "Anything else?"

"Not really. I promise we'll talk more next time."

"Uh huh." He grabbed Maria's wrist of her wounded arm. "You okay?"

Maria looked at the wound and then at Rollins. "Yeah. It's just a scratch."

"You probably need stitches."

"Naw. It'll be fine."

He shook his head and released her. "Have a good one."

"You too," she said. She pulled her phone out while she walked away. *On my way. Be ready* she sent to Gayle. Maria reached her bike and climbed on. The engine came to life, and she pulled out, opening the throttle to speed through the streets.

Fifteen minutes later, Maria pulled into the parking garage of the American Museum of Natural History and parked next to the elevators on the lowest level. Gayle stood there with a black bag in her hand. The scene had played out a few times over the years when crime-fighting clashed with familial obligations.

While Gayle's family wasn't as rich as Maria's, they were wealthy enough to afford luxuries and run in the same circles as the Graysons. Gayle wore a dark blue dress trimmed in silver and her red hair was in an updo. Her green eyes sparkled.

"You're a lifesaver, and I love you," Maria said as she killed the engine and climbed off the bike.

"And you're late. As usual." Gayle tossed the bag to Maria.

"Drug dealers are so inconsiderate." Maria grinned and caught the bag. She placed a kiss on Gayle's cheek. "I owe you."

"You could've skipped playing hero tonight." Gayle shook her head. "I'll add it to the long list."

Maria placed the duffel on the seat of the motorcycle and opened it. Maria removed her mask and unzipped her costume to her waist.

"You could do this in a restroom," Gayle pointed out.

"I know." She flashed Gayle a grin and removed a dress from the duffel. She pulled it over her head and let it fall to her waist. She slipped off her boots and her costume.

A deep sigh escaped Gayle, and Maria chuckled as she smoothed out the dark purple dress. It fit like a second skin and accentuated her curves. She pulled a pair of one-inch heels out of the bag and slid her feet into them. She grabbed her costume and boots and shoved them in the duffel.

"Can you put this in your car?" Maria asked, holding out the duffel for Gayle.

"Of course." Gayle took the duffel and handed Maria a small

clutch in the same shade of purple as her dress. Gayle gasped. "What happened to your arm?"

"Guy had a knife." Maria glanced at the wound. It was now a thin red line across her pale skin. In an hour or two, it would be gone completely. She only needed to wipe the dried blood off. Along with enhanced strength and greater durability, increase healing was part of the power package. While she didn't win the jackpot of powers, they were the ones she had been born with. "And he was on Boost. Had the strength to cut through the costume and me." She opened the clutch and removed a diamond and amethyst necklace and matching earrings. She noticed a coat check claim ticket in there for later. Gayle thought of everything.

While she put the earrings on, Gayle removed a wet wipe from her clutch and cleaned Maria's arm. "You're always a hot mess."

"But you love me." Maria held up the necklace to Gayle. "A little help?"

"I do," Gayle said and accepted the necklace. Maria held her hair up while Gayle fastened the necklace. "All set."

Maria let her hair fall and turned to face her best friend. "Thank you."

"Of course," Gayle said with a little wave of her left hand.

The sparkle of a ring caught Maria's eyes and a broad smile appeared on her face. "It's about time! I thought Charlene would never get around to proposing." Gayle turned a shade of red and showed off a sparkling princess cut diamond. Maria pulled her in and gave her a tight hug. "I'm so happy for you two. Congrats!"

"Thank you." Gayle released Maria. "Wait. You knew?"

Maria grinned. "I helped her pick out the ring."

Gayle threw her hands in the air. "I should've known."

"I love Charlene, but if she hurts you, there's no place she can hide."

"I know, and I know you'll always have my back."

"Damn right I do." Maria would do anything to protect

members of her family, and she counted Gayle as family. "I better be your maid of honor."

"I wouldn't have anyone else. One day I'll be your maid of honor."

Maria blinked, and a loud laugh escaped her. "Getting married is never going to happen for me"." Marriage, relationships, and dating weren't in her vocabulary and never would be. She was quite content being single and never wanted to get entangled in a relationship. She didn't need any extra complications in her life and that's all relationships were.

"Never say never," Gayle said. "One day, someone, male or female, is going to sweep you off your feet, and you'll be walking down the aisle. You'll get your inheritance as well."

Never trust a prophet in a party dress.

"It's cute you still have dreams for me. You're as bad as my grandmother was."

Her grandmother, rest her soul, wanted Maria to find a husband, settle down, and pop out kids as expected of a woman. Maria stepped off the path her grandmother envisioned for her to walk and forged her own way ahead. Maria stayed true to herself and what she wanted out of life, not adhering to other's expectations.

"And one day I'll be saying I told you so. C'mon. Your grandfather's expecting to see you." Gayle grabbed Maria's wrist and pulled her toward the elevator.

Maria went along with Gayle. "I know. I'd rather be at a club. There's a better chance of finding someone for some fun later." Mr. Right may not exist for her, but she never minded meeting a Mr. Right Now once in a while.

"You're incorrigible," Gayle grumbled, hitting the call button for the elevator. "Contacts."

"But you love me. Oh!" Maria removed the purple contacts she wore, tucked them in their case, and tossed them in her clutch.

"Thanks." The elevator doors opened, and the two women entered.

MARIA FINISHED OFF THE LAST OF HER CHAMPAGNE and looked forlornly at her glass. Drinks never lasted long enough, especially at functions like this. Champagne flowed freely and a string quartet filled the Milstein Hall of Ocean Life as the New York elite moved around the room. The wealthy dressed up, pretended they cared about a specific cause, threw money at it, and got drunk. Repeat a dozen or so times a year. Some cared about the causes the events raised money for, but most saw it as an opportunity to socialize with others in their circle.

It was all quite tedious. Maria would rather be wearing her costume and kicking bad guy ass at night on the streets. It was far more entertaining, even with all the bruises or broken bones she received. Occasionally, the temptation to beat some of the people attending events like this seeped in and it would certainly make these parties livelier.

Maria placed her empty glass on the tray of a passing waiter and walked to the edge of the crowd. She loved being at the center of attention at times, but she loved watching from the edges. One learned more when they watched and listened, a lesson Maria learned at a very early age. She looked up at the ninety-four-foot blue whale suspended from the ceiling. It never failed to impress her, and she loved this exhibit hall and its marine life.

Maria scanned the room out of habit. Her next one-night stand could be in here, but she doubted it. Handsome men filled the room, some even around her age, but Maria had most likely slept with most of them. She never made her flings anything longer than one night, and she avoided dating and relationships. Having a full-time day job and a full-time night job didn't leave much time for much else, including relationships. Some men wanted more than one night, but she set them straight and on their way. She didn't need them getting close and uncovering her nighttime activities.

The married ones were never given consideration. She didn't poach on another woman's territory even though rumors and tabloid articles persisted despite all her efforts to stop them. Maria had standards, and she followed them. She couldn't say the same for nearly half of the other women in the room. Rumors about who was sleeping with whom flew around her social circle, and most of them were probably true. New York may be the city that never slept, but its wealthy sure slept around.

A glass of champagne appeared in her line of vision, and her eyes traveled up the length of the arm to the face of the person offering the drink. Maria managed to keep from rolling her eyes when she saw his face.

"You look thirsty," Devon Cargill said with a smile.

"Thank you," she said, accepting the glass from him, but not drinking from it. Her mother taught her to never accept drinks from men right before giving her the talk on birth control and masturbation.

"You look positively stunning tonight."

Maria forced a smile. "Thank you. You're looking quite good tonight yourself. Then again, we all are. Shame that we're here."

He smiled, and his crystal blue eyes sparkled. Oh, he was nice to look at with his chiseled features, perfect white smile, and sandy-colored hair. He sipped his champagne. "Thank you. No date this evening??" he asked as he glanced down at the glass in her hand.

Maria figured he was wondering if anyone would miss Maria after drinking the spiked champagne, and he escorted her out. She wanted to hit him and send him flying across the room but clenched a fist behind her instead. She dug her nails into her palm and the pain helped center her. She didn't want to hear the lecture she would get from her grandfather if she beat him senseless.

"I'm with my grandfather, of course," she replied as she searched the room for her grandfather. She found him in the middle of a small group of men. Wayne Grayson possessed a presence not diminished by a wheelchair and people gravitated to him. "Why do you ask?"

"I was going to offer you a ride home," Devon said.

"How generous of you," she said.

"Something wrong?" he asked with the weight of his penetrating gaze coming to bear on her.

Maria smiled and leaned in close. "I know what you try to do to women when they're too drunk to fight back," she said into his ear.

Devon pulled back, and he managed a look of outrage. She gave him props for his acting skills.

"Pardon me?"

Maria smiled. "You heard me."

"I was cleared of those charges," he said in a low voice.

"I wasn't talking about the charges," she explained. "I know what happened a year ago. I heard about that girl you tried to rape in an alley behind a bar. I also heard you got your ass kicked by Balestra." She smiled at him. "Word gets around."

The color drained from his face, and his eyes darted around the room. "Whatever you heard was a lie."

Maria resisted the urge to laugh and tell him she gave him the beating of his life. "Of course."

"Let's go somewhere to talk about this," he suggested, putting his hand on her upper arm.

"No thanks," she said. She jerked away from him, slipping out of his grasp.

"Maria, you've known me since we were kids. Come on. We can go find a quiet spot and talk. Like we used to do at events like this."

"I said *no*. I get that you haven't been told that many times in your life, but I'm saying it to you now. No."

His face flushed.

Maria moved and put her face an inch away from his. "If I ever hear about you raping or *trying* to rape anyone, I'll give Balestra my entire trust fund to make sure that only a DNA test could identify you. That's *if* they find any pieces of you." Maria pulled back and smiled at him. "Now, if you'll excuse me, my grandfather is waving me over, and one mustn't keep Wayne Grayson waiting." She walked away, not waiting for him to respond. Her grandfather did no such thing, but the excuse always worked for getting her out of an unwanted situation.

Maria dumped the likely spiked champagne into a nearby potted plant and placed the empty glass on the tray of a passing waiter. She approached her grandfather where he was holding court.

Wayne Grayson's blue eyes matched her own, and gray dominated his dark hair. Wrinkles lined his face, clustering around the corners of his mouth and the corners of his eyes. He was in his mid-seventies and hadn't slowed down or missed a thing.

"Gentlemen," she said with a nod as she reached them.

"Maria," her grandfather said with a nod. "How are you enjoying the party?"

She knew most of the men surrounding her grandfather, but there were one or two unfamiliar faces. "It's been interesting," she said, going with a safe answer. She grabbed a glass of champagne, not spiked, from a passing waiter and took a long drink from it under the scrutinizing eyes of her grandfather and the men around him.

"The goal is to make them last longer," her grandfather told her.

Maria smiled. "No, the trick is to drink as many as I can and as fast as I can to make this party far more interesting."

Her grandfather sighed. "Of course," he said. The men around him chuckled a little, one of them being Devon's father.

Like her parents, her grandfather held no illusions about

Maria. They all knew about the copious amounts of alcohol she consumed when she went out, the one-night stands, and her costumed night job. Hell, her grandfather and both parents had all held costumed night jobs at some point in their lives. She was only living up to the family legacy of being powered and cleaning up the streets at night.

"Devon was looking for you," Devon's father told her.

"I saw him," Maria said, forcing a neutral expression on her face and bit her tongue to keep from telling the man exactly what she thought about his son. This man kept his son out of jail, and, in Maria's book, he was as guilty as Devon.

"We were discussing how last quarter, the comp—"

Maria held a hand up, cutting her grandfather off. A few of the men gasped at her audacity. "I don't want to hear work talk tonight. I'm trying to have fun. You gentlemen can talk work all you want; I'm going to go see what trouble I can get into." She grinned at her grandfather and winked. He shook his head a little, but he smiled. "If you'll excuse me, gentlemen." They nodded, and Maria slipped away from the small circle.

Maria loved working for Grayson Industries, and her grandfather did all he could to get her to take more of an active role, but Maria didn't want to talk work tonight unless it was about beating up bad guys. She'd always talk about that, given the chance she could do it without revealing her secret. Some of her fondest memories included her grandfather telling her stories about his time in costume. Her father as well. They were her favorite bedtime stories.

She polished off the remaining champagne and looked around for a waiter with an empty tray. The hairs on the back of her neck stood on end, and a tingle ran down her spine. Someone had her in their sights, and instinct told her it was more than a casual glance.

Maria spun around and saw *him*.

She drank in the sight of him, and her heart beat a little faster.

Moisture in her mouth evaporated, leaving her mouth drier than the Sahara. The tuxedo fit him perfectly, especially across his broad chest. She wondered what it would be like to run her hands across the hard muscles lurking beneath the tux. His dark hair was on the long side and combed back. Dark eyes studied her, and she walked toward him. Was he tanned, or was that his natural skin tone? Either way, she wanted to see more of it. All of it.

Hello, tonight's wrong, Mr. Right. Maybe she did have someone to take home tonight. She smiled and walked toward the mysterious man. Love at first sight didn't exist, but lust at first sight did.

CHAPTER TWO

Tomas Dorrance tugged at the bow tie of his custom-fitted tuxedo to keep it from strangling him. No such luck. He sipped champagne as he slowly walked around the cavernous room. He wanted to see more of the museum, but ropes blocked off the exhibit halls. He made a mental note to visit the museum during the day.

He wasn't a party person; however, work brought him to New York City. He took the time to get the lay of the land and get to know the right people. His family's company was doing more and more business in New York, and he expected to spend more time in the city.

He glanced at his watch. The night moved too slowly for his taste. He mingled and chatted with various folks, even Wayne Grayson, for some time, but his interest diminished. His father, also in attendance, busied himself talking to the mayor and other New York elites, leaving Tomas to entertain himself. Even his twin sister abandoned him to go mingle, though he doubted she mingled. She was more of the watching type. He finished off the last of his champagne and thought about leaving.

Purple silk and perfect curves entered his field of vision and the breath stayed in his chest. Black hair and pale skin accompanied the tight dress. The noise of the room drained away, and the people around him disappeared. Nothing else existed except the vision in purple. He stole a glance at her left hand and didn't see a wedding ring or a diamond on her finger. All thoughts of leaving evaporated. If luck was with him, he'd get to know her better tonight.

She walked toward him with her head held high. She possessed the confidence and walk of a warrior about to go into battle. The temperature in the room rose a few degrees, and his bow tie strangled him even more. He swallowed and then offered her a smile.

"You look like you'd rather be anywhere else," she said, her blue eyes sparkling. "Maria Grayson," she said, extending a well-manicured hand.

A trophy wife, just not wearing a wedding ring? His hopes died a quick and brutal death. He didn't know much about Wayne Grayson's personal life, but it wasn't uncommon for old men to have a beautiful young wife. "Until now, yes. A pleasure, señora," he greeted as he took the offered hand. Instead of shaking it, he placed a soft kiss on her knuckles. Lingering perfume on her wrist tickled his nose. He wondered where else she may have applied perfume. "I am Tomas Dorrance. Grayson as in—"

"Wayne Grayson," she finished for him, flashing him a smile. "He's my grandfather."

Tomas smiled as hope sprang to life inside of him. It thrilled him that she wasn't Grayson's trophy wife. There could be risks about her being Grayson's granddaughter, but she looked worth taking them. Tomas nodded. "Of course, señorita," he said.

"New to the city? I don't recall seeing you at any previous charity events."

Tomas nodded. "I am."

"What brings you here?"

"Business," he replied. "Though I hope to see some of the

sights of New York that I keep hearing so much about." He enjoyed the sights so far, especially the one standing before him. He wanted the chance to see if her skin was as soft as her silk dress.

Maria smiled, and his heart rate increased. "Lucky for you, I happen to be a great tour guide."

He arched a brow, his interest piqued. "Is that so?"

"It is," she said with a grin.

"It appears to be my lucky night." Spending time with her became a much better idea than this party.

"Tomas, who is this lovely lady?"

Tomas turned to face his father.

Like Tomas, his father wore a custom-fitted, black tux. Brown eyes observed everything and looked into Tomas's soul. Gray feathered through dark hair at the temples, and his skin showed the love of the outdoors. His father held a love of boats and the ocean.

"Father, this is Maria Grayson. Maria, this is my father, Antonio Dorrance."

Maria held out a hand and smiled. "A pleasure."

"The pleasure is mine, Miss Grayson," his father said, taking Maria's hand and placed a kiss on her knuckles, mirroring Tomas's earlier actions. "Your grandfather speaks highly of you." His father smiled.

Maria smiled, and Tomas's mouth dried out, and his stomach somersaulted. It had been some time since a woman affected him the way she did. "Well, it's easy to earn his praise and devotion when you're the only grandchild."

"He mentioned you working for the company," his father said. Inwardly, Tomas groaned. One night without talking about business was too much to ask for. Tomas couldn't remember the last conversation he had with his father that wasn't about business. He missed the old conversations about life, girls, and other things.

"I am," she replied. "Learning the ropes rights now. My grandfather hopes I'll one day run the company."

"I'm sure you will," Tomas said.

His father nodded. "Just as Tomas will run my company one day."

"As if I had a choice in the matter," Tomas joked. Since he was old enough to understand, his father's plans for him included running the company, getting married, and having kids. Someone had to run the company after Tomas. Tomas wasn't sure he wanted any of it, or what he wanted out of life in general. One thing he knew for certain was that he would be himself and not what others wanted him to be.

Maria chuckled, and his father scowled. Tomas would never say his father had a sense of humor.

"What does your company do?" Maria asked.

"Private security," his father answered. "We have one of the largest private security firms in the world."

"We're in the process of negotiating a contract with the NYPD," Tomas added.

"Oh?"

"Yes," his father answered. "It seems the drug problem is getting too much for the NYPD, and we're going to help."

Maria smiled, and Tomas sensed she forced it. "That's interesting."

"We also have some other business in the city," Tomas added.

"Well, the city has to do something about the drugs pouring in," his father continued, as if Tomas hadn't spoken. "I hear Boost is becoming a major problem. The police don't have enough manpower, and those so-called-vigilantes cause more problems than they solve."

"I don't know about that," Maria said. "I think they do some good. Some work with the police to keep things from getting too far out of hand. I can't imagine what the city would be like if it weren't for the costumed set helping out."

"Maria has offered to play tour guide for me while I'm here in New York," Tomas said before his father could reply to her comments about costumed heroes. The man held a strong opinion on the costume set, and Tomas didn't want to see an argument arise if Maria held the opposite viewpoint.

"That's very generous of her," his father said. "I'm sure you will be in excellent hands."

"Of course he will."

"If you'll excuse me," his father said with a nod and slowly walked away.

"I'm sorry," Tomas said once his father was out of earshot. Antonio Dorrance wasn't the easiest person to get to know or impress. Not that Maria had to impress his father. She had already made an impression on Tomas.

"You have nothing to be sorry about or apologize for," she assured him. "Everyone has an opinion on the heroes." She smiled and light sparkled in her blue eyes. The temperature in the room climbed another few degrees. "And some of them are wrong."

Tomas laughed. "Well, I'm sure they'd be happy to know they have a supporter in you."

The smile faded from her face and a seriousness settled in. "What about you? What are your thoughts on them?" she asked.

He shrugged. "I do see the benefit of the costumes working with law enforcement, but I do see the potential problems with them getting involved."

"So, you're neutral on it?"

"Maybe." He had only heard of the costumed vigilantes in New York through the media and had never met one. He didn't trust mainstream media and would form his own opinion when he finally met one.

"This party stopped being interesting five minutes after it started," she said as she looked around.

"I hadn't noticed," he admitted. He had spent the time studying the people in attendance and their interactions with their peers. One never knew when the little things would be necessary. He chatted a little bit, but he stuck to the periphery, observing. "If there's something else you'd rather do, I'm at your service."

She laughed. Her dimples burned themselves into his brain along with her smile. Sure, he noticed the way her breasts strained against the purple material and the way it hugged her ass, but the dimples and the smile made more of an impression.

"That sounds like an invitation to get into trouble. I excel at getting into trouble."

Tomas grinned, and his interest rose along with his heart rate. "Señorita, I excel at trouble. If you're of a mind, consider yourself invited."

"Now that's an offer I can't refuse," she said and put a hand on his arm.

As much as he wanted to scout out New York's rich and powerful, getting to know just one better counted. Right? Besides, this one promised to be much more exciting and seemed like his type. "Shall we go see what kind of trouble we can get into?" she asked.

He stared into Maria's blue eyes, letting himself fall under their spell. "I'm at your mercy."

"You may regret saying that," she warned and waggled her eyebrows. She hooked an arm through his.

He laughed, a real laugh. "Maybe. I guess we'll just have to see."

"Do you have any other family members in town?" she asked as they made their way toward the hall exit.

"I have a twin sister," he said. "She's here somewhere." Tomas looked around but didn't spot Carolyn in the crowd of people.

"What about in Brazil?" she asked.

He glanced over at her. "How'd you know I'm from Brazil?" he asked.

"Your accent," she answered. "I've been there quite a few times on business trips with my grandfather."

He nodded. "A mother back home. I hope you enjoyed my country," he said as they neared the doors. He steered her toward the coat check. He handed the attendant his claim ticket, and she removed hers from her clutch. She handed it to the attendant.

"I loved it. Beautiful country, and the food is amazing," Maria said, turning to face him.

"What about you? Any siblings?" he asked, then regretted it. She had already told his father that she was the only grandchild. It probably wouldn't be the first time he'd feel like an idiot tonight. There was still a good deal of night to go.

The attendant returned and handed him a long overcoat. Mid-October in New York was undoubtedly colder than back home, and he slipped on the heavy overcoat. He accepted her overcoat from the attendant and held it up. She slipped her arms in, and he settled it on her shoulders.

"Thank you," she said, flashing him a smile. Maria shook her head. "It's just me. I'm the result of a brief, torrid affair between my parents."

He smiled in return and put a hand on her elbow to guide her toward the main doors. "They weren't married?" he asked. He pushed the glass door open and held it for her.

"Does that bother you?" she asked before passing through the door.

"No," he said, following her through the door. "I'm not very religious, much to my mother's disappointment, but it seems odd that they're not married considering who your family is."

"You'd understand if you'd met my mother. She's not one to do what others expect her to do. She made my father see that marriage wasn't a good idea for them."

"Are they still together?" he asked as they reached the sidewalk at the bottom of the stairs.

"No. They knew they wouldn't work as a couple, but they're still good friends. Best friends, actually. The whole co-parenting thing worked great for them."

"That's great. Most couples aren't friends after the relationship is over. Let me hail a cab." He stepped to the curb and raised a hand.

"I have a car," she called after him.

Tomas lowered his hand and turned around. "What about your grandfather? How will he get home?" he asked when Maria reached him.

She stopped and patted his cheek. "He won't leave for a few more hours, and I'll send the car back as soon as it drops us off."

He nodded. "Where are we going?"

"Hungry? We may need some food if we're going to go find some trouble."

He grinned. He didn't know if Maria was talking about food or something else, but he didn't care either way. He could go for a bite to eat or other things. Or both. "Yes," he grinned. "I have tremendous appetites."

Her smile grew, and this wasn't just about food. She dropped subtle hints with the flirty smiles and looks. Here he thought the evening was going to be dull with a bunch of stuffy elites. She was a pleasant surprise, and he wanted to be surprised by her more often. "Is there anything in particular you're in the mood for?" she asked as a black limousine pulled up in front of them.

He opened the rear door and held it open for her. He climbed in after her and pulled the door closed. "Whatever you're in the mood for."

"How do you feel about diner food, or is there something else you'd prefer?"

"I prefer your company," he answered. "But if there's food as well, the more, the better."

Maria smiled and leaned forward. "The diner, please."

"Certainly, Ms. Grayson," the driver said, and the divider went up, giving Tomas and Maria some privacy.

Tomas looked at her and tilted his head. "Joseph knows my favorite diner," she explained.

"Ah. That explains why you didn't specify which diner," Tomas said.

"Joseph has been our driver since I was a child. He knows all my favorite places."

"I bet it's nice having someone who's been around for quite a while," he said. "My father rotates staff, so we never have someone in our employ for a long time."

"That's...strange and unfortunate."

He shrugged. "Maybe compared to what you're used to, but my father doesn't like staff getting too familiar. I never understood it."

She nodded. "Okay, no more comparing lives," she said. "We're going to live in the moment, and right now, we're going to go get one of the best burgers in New York."

"It's that good?" he asked.

"It is. Trust me."

He smiled. "I do."

Fifteen minutes later, the limo came to a stop outside the Pearl Diner. Tomas climbed out and offered a hand to Maria. She placed her hand in his and looked up at him. The breath stayed in his chest as the crystal blue eyes looked into his soul. She couldn't know how her looking at him that way affected him. Or maybe she did.

CHAPTER THREE

Tomas gave her a fierce kiss and Maria kicked her apartment door closed. She'd been waiting for this part since she first laid eyes on him. The long looks into each other's eyes, the light touches as their fingers brushed as they reached for fries, and the innuendos tossed back and forth all led to this moment, and she couldn't be happier.

Maria pressed her body against his, her head reeling from the feel of the hard muscles under his tux. He wrapped his arms around her, and she moaned into his mouth. Dizziness washed over her, and she put her hands flat on his firm pectorals as he moved his hands down to her ass. He squeezed and pulled her hips against his. It didn't even cross her mind to resist. She wanted him, and judging by the hardness in his pants, he wanted her.

Maria ran her hands across his chest and shoulders, pushing the tuxedo coat along with them. Her movements were careful and deliberate. Restraint could be challenging, but she never wanted to hurt a partner.

The garment slid down his arms and to the floor. For the briefest of seconds, Maria thought about picking it up so it wouldn't get ruined, but the thought disappeared under the searing hot kisses he dropped along her jaw. He reached her ear and gently bit down on the fleshy lobe. She gasped, and a shiver raced through her as she worked on the buttons of his shirt.

She fumbled with the buttons, and she would have pulled on Tomas's shirt to pop them off, but she wasn't that desperate. *Yet.* The shirt slid off and thankfully he ditched his bow tie earlier. She wouldn't have managed to remove it in her current lust-filled state.

He moved his hands up from her ass to the middle of her back and fumbled around. Maria had to smile at his attempts to find the zipper on her dress. She pulled away far enough to turn around and unzipped her dress, the silk whooshed as it slid down to the floor. She turned back around and stood in front of him in nothing but a purple thong.

"You, sir, are severely overdressed, and I need to do something about that," Maria said as she took a moment to appreciate the view in front of her. Someone frequented the gym. His well-defined muscles moved under skin, and dark hair shadowed his chest. She hummed with appreciation and bit her bottom lip. She loved a man with chest hair. To be honest, she would have pegged him as a manscaping kind of guy. She loved being wrong.

He pulled his mouth back into a sly grin. "Yes, you do," he said. He cupped each breast with a hand and rubbed her pert nipples with his thumbs.

Maria smiled and reached out for the front of his pants, trying to focus on the task at hand while he fondled her breasts. She took her time unbuttoning and unzipping his pants to avoid looking like a clumsy, desperate schoolgirl. The button quickly came undone, as did the zipper. The black pants fell to the floor, and he stepped out of them. Maria bit her lower lip as she watched him move.

Well-defined legs were covered in dark hair. He wore a pair of black boxer briefs. He moved with the sureness of a predator, and Maria was quite happy being his meal tonight.

"Oh Santa, you shouldn't have," she whispered as the breath she had been holding slipped out. "And it's not even Christmas."

He laughed and reached out, grabbing her by the waist and pulling her in. Maria pressed her mostly naked body against the length of him. She closed her eyes as skin pressed against skin. In her book, there was no better feeling in the world. He captured her mouth in a fierce kiss, and she returned it in kind. Right now, nothing mattered except the feel of him, and all thoughts evaporated like mist.

"Bedroom?" he asked during the few seconds his mouth left hers.

"And here I thought you were going to do me right here against the wall," she muttered against his lips.

He gripped the straps of her thong and yanked it down. Cold air rushed in between them for a few moments while Tomas slid his boxer briefs down and kicked them off. Tomas fished a condom out of his pants and slipped it on. He put his hands on her upper arms and pushed her against the wall with his body. Maria groaned. God, she loved a forceful man. She savored every second of being trapped between him and the wall. He slid his hands down to her thighs, and Maria jumped while he lifted. He pressed her against the wall for leverage as he settled her body on his erection.

Maria gasped as he entered her, and his mouth came down hard on hers, swallowing her reaction. For a brief second, she thought he was too big for her, but her body adjusted to him. He slid in and buried himself to the hilt. She didn't know where her body ended, and his began. She put her arms around his neck and wrapped her legs around his waist.

He moaned as he moved in her. Maria echoed his groan as he went deeper. Maria held on and moved her body with his.

He settled into a rhythm of powerful thrusts, and Maria

couldn't get enough of him. Deep enough and hard enough didn't exist. She wanted as much of him as she could get. She tore her mouth away from his and dropped hungry kisses along his jaw and down his neck. She moved along his neck and shoulder. A hard thrust caught her off guard, and she bit him in response. He increased the speed of his thrusts.

Blood pounded in her ears, drowning out the sound of his grunts and her gasps. Tension coiled snake-like inside of her, ratcheting up to the inevitable conclusion. She wanted to race there, and he sensed her urgency. He pushed her harder against the wall and increased his speed and the force of his thrusts. The tension inside of her tightened and snapped with a hard thrust. Tenderness and love didn't exist. Only pure animalistic lust existed. She'd never complain in a million years.

She unwound around him, her body shuddering as waves of pleasure washed over her. She screamed her climax, and he covered her mouth with his, swallowing the sound. Maria couldn't do anything but hold on as each new thrust amplified the ripples of ecstasy coursing through her. She gasped for air during the brief seconds his mouth left hers, and her heart pounded in her chest.

After a few more thrusts, his body shuddered as his climax poured into her. His mouth left hers, and he tilted his head backward and released a deep grunt. Maria curled her fingers, and her nails dug into the flesh of his back. She kissed the tip of his chin. Salty sweat remained on her lips after the kiss, and she licked it away.

"Mmmmm," she purred.

He straightened and looked at her. He smiled, and she returned it. A thin layer of sweat covered both of their bodies, and his heart pounded against her chest. It had to be her imagination, but she'd swear hers beat in time with his. Maria shivered as the cool air of her apartment chilled the parts of her that weren't plastered against him.

"Mmmm is right," he said in a hoarse whisper. "Where's your bedroom?"

"To the right," she said. He tightened his hold on her and pulled her away from the wall. Shivers chased over her back, and she melted against him, and she soaked up the heat his body produced.

He almost tripped a few times on the way to her bedroom. She forgot to warn him she was something of a slob and her housekeeping skills were non-existent. Thankfully, he didn't trip as he navigated the minefield of clothes and shoes. He reached the bedroom and turned around when he got into the bed. He slowly sat down and then laid back without separating their bodies, leaving Maria on top. Her favorite position.

He read her mind. Oh God, she hoped he wasn't a telepath. She despised the idea of someone being able to read her thoughts and sex with a telepath involved intimacy on a level she never wanted. Then again, her brain-to-mouth filter didn't really exist, so he probably wouldn't discover anything new in her head.

Maria ended the kiss and sat upright on top of him. She looked down at him and smiled as she slowly moved her hips forward and then back. He groaned, and Maria took it as a sign of encouragement. She moved a little faster and rose a little off him as she moved forward and then down as her hips moved backward. She placed her hands on his chest for leverage and increased her speed.

Her head fell back as tension built inside of her once more. He covered her breasts with his hands and slightly pinched each nipple between his thumb and index finger. The small points of pain enhanced her pleasure and increased the tightness inside her. He thrust his hips up. All thoughts fled from her mind, and she focused on the feeling of their joined bodies.

She rode him fast and hard until she reached the breaking point. Her climax hit her, and she came undone around him, calling out his name as pleasure rushed through her. She kept moving, hoping to have him follow her into oblivion. He groaned and surged upward with her hips, and Maria smiled, knowing he had just peaked as well. She collapsed on top of him, their bodies pressed together with only a thin layer of sweat between them. Maria dropped a kiss on his lips and slowly eased off him. Despite being in shape for the nights of kicking ass, she needed a breather.

Maria rolled to the side, intending to put some space between them to cool off, but he reached out and pulled her against his side. She looked at him for a long moment, a little confused, before resting her head on his chest and intertwining her legs with his. Were they cuddling?

It had been so long since she cuddled with anyone that she didn't remember it. Cuddling led to closeness, and that led to other unspeakable and unthinkable things. Her brain told her to pull away and put some space between them, but a small part of her enjoyed the closeness.

His heart pounded in her ear, and she imagined hers was beating as hard and fast. He sighed, his chest rising and falling with the action. It sounded like a contented sigh, and it made Maria smile. She dropped a kiss on his chest. Salt lingered on her lips, and she licked it off. He moved his hand to the curve of her hip and lightly caressed it.

Time ticked by, and neither of them moved. Maria enjoyed the quiet and pushed the intimacy to the back of her mind. It was too dangerous to think about it. He dropped a kiss on the top of her head. Thankfully, he didn't talk. Most of her one-night stands were getting out of bed to get dressed at this point. Maria didn't let partners linger in her bed in an effort to prevent any attachments from forming. Life was less complicated that way, and she didn't need any more difficulties in her life.

She slipped out of his embrace and rolled to the edge of the bed. She glanced at him and climbed out of the bed, heading to the bathroom. She used the toilet and then looked at herself in the mirror as she washed her hands.

Dark hair flew in every direction. Her makeup remained unblemished, and her lips were a little swollen from the hard kisses. She turned the water off and dried her hands. She stared at the door.

Maybe if she waited a little in the bathroom, Tomas would get dressed and leave. Post-sex interactions were not her strong point. Hell, they weren't even a point. Sex was for physical release and enjoying the moment. Purely transactional in her world. Emotions and attachments didn't play a part, and she didn't want them to.

She listened for signs that he was moving, but silence reigned on the other side of the door. Had he already dressed and left? No. No one could move that fast except for a speedster, and he didn't fit the type. He didn't appear to have the typical appetite, and he didn't have an issue with moving at an average pace.

How long should she wait? Five minutes? Ten? Fifteen? What was happening? Her partners got dressed and left within ten minutes. She put an ear to the door and didn't hear any signs of movement. She didn't have to tell her one-night stands to leave. They got the hint when she climbed out of bed as soon as they finished. Cuddling did this, and she made a mental note to never let it happen again.

Maybe she should come out and order him to get dressed and leave. She hoped he would get the hint on his own and leave. Goodbye, or see you later, weren't necessary. Maria wasn't the type for dragging out goodbyes, and there definitely wasn't going to be a see you later. Or again.

Sounds of movement drifted through the door, and Maria sighed with relief. Thank God he was leaving, and she didn't have to go out there and tell him to go.

"Are you okay?" he asked through the door.

"Fine," she called back. She took a deep breath and opened the door.

He stood there in all his naked glory, and Maria relished the view. He wore a concerned look on his face. "Are you okay?" he asked again.

"Yeah," she said. "Everything's fine."

"Good," he said and reached out to her. He put his hands on her hips and pulled her toward him. Maria didn't resist but knew she should pull away. He lowered his head and kissed her. Only this wasn't the passionate type of kiss from before, but softer and more tender. Way more dangerous.

Now Maria pulled away and took a step toward the bedroom. Wearing some clothing would help put some distance between them. Right now, she couldn't get far enough away.

He followed her into the bedroom and stopped. He looked at her and didn't get dressed. Maria stopped with a pair of underwear pulled halfway up her legs.

"What's wrong?" she asked, dreading the possible answers he could give.

"Nothing. I figured you'd be up for a few more rounds," he said with a shrug.

"You want more?" she asked, pulling her underwear up the remaining distance and settled them in place.

"If you do," he said. "Otherwise, we can sleep."

Sleep? As in sleep in her bed with the possibility of cuddling? He couldn't mean that, right? What did she do to give him the impression that she wanted cuddling and intimacy?

"Sure," she said after a brief pause. "I could go a few more rounds." She was satisfied, but she wouldn't say no to more. She didn't know the next time she'd have a guy in her bed again. The next few nights were scheduled for kicking ass. She felt guilty for taking a night off even it was for getting laid.

He smiled and climbed back into the bed.

Maria removed her underwear and slipped into the other side of the bed. As if on instinct, he reached over and pulled her close against his side. She didn't resist. This was for more sex, not intimacy, she reasoned. More sex was always a good thing.

She pushed up and rested on an elbow and kissed him. The kiss was demanding and hard, but his response wasn't what was expected. He resisted and returned it with a softer kiss. She pulled back and looked at him.

"I thought you wanted more rounds," she said, confusion settling in.

"I do," he answered. "Just not right this moment. I was enjoying having your body next to mine. We can get back to the naked fun time in a bit."

"Why not now?" she asked.

He smiled at her and kissed her. "So demanding. I like that about you, but I do like having you next to me. Is that such a bad thing?"

"I guess."

"You guess? Let me take a guess of my own. You aren't exactly the post-sex cuddling type, are you?"

Maria shook her head. "Nope. Not in the least bit."

He tilted his head. "If I may ask, is there some reason why?" he asked.

"I don't like getting close to my one-night stands," she replied without thinking.

"I see," he said. "Is that what this is, a one-night stand?"

"Yes," she answered. "What did you think it was?"

He shrugged, and his muscled shoulders moved with the motion. "I was hoping this could be a regular thing while I'm in town. I certainly enjoy your company in and out of clothes."

"I don't do more than one-night stands," she said with conviction. On the other hand, it could be nice to have a regular thing when she wasn't out beating up bad people on the streets. No, it was too risky even if it was for a limited time. She had a secret identity for a reason, and she couldn't let him even begin to suspect she had an alter ego. A mask not only protected her, but it also protected those she loved. If anyone discovered her secret, her parents, grandfather, Gayle, and anyone else close could be harmed or worse, to get to Maria. Relationships and heroing didn't mesh unless both people were in the hero life.

The one time she had been in a serious relationship and her partner knew her secret, he threatened to out her to the media when she confronted him about cheating. The number of people she had helped take off the streets added up over the years. She'd never risk the lives of the people she loved again.

"I'm sorry to hear that," he said. Silence settled over the room like a shroud, and awkwardness came along with it. "Do you want me to leave?"

"Only if we're done," she said.

"Are we?" he asked.

"No." She wanted more of him. It was greedy, but she only had tonight to get as much of him as she could.

He smiled and pulled her in for a deep kiss, his tongue invading her mouth and dueling with hers. When the kiss ended, he pulled back a little. "Good."

Maria smiled and kissed him. The kiss was deep and demanding, rekindling the fire and desire inside of her. She wanted him as much as she had the first time.

CHAPTER FOUR

A NONDESCRIPT WHITE VAN ROLLED TO A STOP OUTSIDE of a warehouse in the Bronx as Maria, dressed as Balestra, watched from her perch on the roof of the warehouse. One would think that criminals would get more creative about their pick-up locations and their choice of vehicles.

Maria adjusted the purple mask and double-checked her inventory of weapons. Two eskrima sticks. Check. Two tasers tucked into holsters on each thigh. Check. A knife tucked along the length of each forearm. Check. She held a small crossbow modified to shoot tranquilizer darts and aimed them at the white van below. A non-lethal approach to crime-fighting meant fewer complications with law enforcement and not stepping over a line. She could kill if it were the last recourse, but she preferred to leave the bad guys alive for law enforcement to deal with. There were costumes out there who used lethal force on a semi-regular basis, but how heroic was it for people with extra abilities to kill regular people?

Maria refocused on the van and watched two men in dark clothes emerge from each side. She rolled her eyes. If they picked a different location, any other vehicle, and regular clothes to blend in, they would be less likely to attract attention and get caught.

"Morons," she muttered under her breath as the two men walked to the rear of the van. They opened the two rear doors and reached in. They helped a gagged woman with bound hands out of the van and another woman after her. The two men helped eight women out of the back. All were gagged and bound.

Her blood boiled and red-hot rage consumed her. Drug dealers were bad enough, but human traffickers were the worst kind of scum. They were going to a special hell along with child molesters and people who talked at the theater. Maria took a step off the three-storied building and dropped to the ground, landing in front of the two men.

Maria landed with enough force to put a small depression in the concrete sidewalk. The city wouldn't appreciate having to fix the damage, but judging by the surrounding sidewalks' condition, they weren't too concerned about repairs. She slid the crossbow into its holder on her back and went in without weapons drawn. These assholes deserved fists.

"Hello, boys. Ready to get your asses kicked by a girl?"

They froze in place. A woman wrested away from a man's grasp and bolted down the road. One of the men chased after the fleeing woman, and the other man charged toward Maria. She lowered a shoulder and slammed into the man. The force lifted him off his feet and sent him flying backward through the air. He landed in front of the van with a loud thud.

The women remained still and watched. Maria turned and ran toward the man chasing the woman down. She reached him just as he reached the woman, and Maria grabbed him by the back of his shirt. She heaved and threw him into the side of the warehouse. He slammed into the concrete wall and slid down to the ground.

The warehouse door opened, and a man stepped out. Maria waited to see what he would do. The women stood between him and Maria, and she didn't want any of them to get hurt. Something dark flew straight toward the man as he came toward Maria. He stopped in his tracks and collapsed to the ground. The dark handle of a knife rose from his chest as blood soaked his shirt.

Maria frantically looked around for the person who threw the knife. No longer under the men's control, the women scattered and ran down the street away from the van and warehouse. A dark figure dropped down from above and landed next to Maria. Maria slowly drew one of her knives and cautiously approached. Friend or foe? The darkness made it difficult to tell.

The new guy stood around six-three and wore a dark costume that covered him from head to toe. It looked like it was made from the same bulletproof material as her own. The man wore dark gray and possessed no distinguishing features, and a dark mask covered his eyes and half his face.

He ignored her and moved toward the guy Maria had thrown against the warehouse. Light reflected off metal, and Maria's eyes went wide. She flung her hand out, and the knife sailed through the air and hit the man's hand. He grunted, and the knife dropped to the ground. He spun around and glared at Maria.

"Stay out of this," he growled.

"You stay out of it!" she shot back. "I don't know who you are, nor do I care, but no killing! The police will be called, and they will take care of him." She didn't mind the assist, but she did mind the killing. She did her best to never cross that line.

He glared at Maria. At this distance, in the dim light from nearby streetlights, she couldn't determine the color of his eyes. The man against the building gasped, and he gurgled as blood began to spill from a neck wound. She never saw him draw and throw the second knife.

Anger spiked, and she stepped toward him, but he didn't move. She clenched her fists and closed the distance between them. He didn't move an inch as she got in his face. "What the fuck did you do?" she yelled.

"Took care of the problem," he answered.

His voice was deep and unfamiliar. The casual tone in which he answered fueled her anger. She swung a fist aiming for his face, only it never reached its target. He caught it and held onto it, and Maria's eyes widened. He had to be powered to be able to catch and stop her punch without moving an inch. Her eyes narrowed. "Who are you?" she asked.

"No one you should worry about as long as you stay out of my way," he growled as he released her hand.

She would discover his identity before long. She knew almost all the costumes in New York on all levels. Maria latched onto mysteries like a fish to a hook. She couldn't help it.

She put her hands on her hips. "Stay out of your way? You're the intruder here."

"New York doesn't belong to you."

Maria never got territorial and welcomed help, just like she helped other costumes, but the killing. Killing folks drew unwanted attention from law enforcement and the costumes who worked closely with law enforcement.

The warehouse door burst open and four men carrying weapons poured out. Maria charged straight toward them, not giving them time to aim. She lowered a shoulder and plowed into one. She kept moving and pushed him back into the wall of the building. The man groaned with pain when he hit the wall. Maria released him and delivered a right hook to the side of his face. He crumpled to the ground.

Mysterious Costumed Man, MCM from now on, reacted as well. He grabbed the forearm of the man closest to him with one hand and the gun with the other. He yanked the weapon from the man's hand and pulled on the man's arm. The crack of a breaking bone echoed in the street, and the man screamed.

Maria focused on the two remaining men. One ran for the driver's door of the van while the other aimed his weapon at her. She ducked the second she saw his finger move, and the bullet whizzed over her head. She charged ahead and jumped, delivering a side kick to the man's head. His head snapped back, and he joined his fellow criminal on the ground.

The other man reached the van and climbed in. It started, and the tires squealed and smoked against the pavement as the van pulled out. MCM dropped the man he had been dealing with and ran after the van. It disappeared into the night.

Maria reached for the building's door and looked around. The place was empty of people, well, men anyway. A makeshift cage had been built in one corner and contained a few women. Four tables sat off to the side, and packages filled with white powder sat on the table. If there had been more people in here than the ones they fought outside, they disappeared. Maria clenched her fists and screamed.

"A temper tantrum?" MCM asked, striding into the room as if he owned the place.

"Go to hell," she growled and headed over to the cage with the women. She grabbed the lock and squeezed as hard as she could until the lock crumbled. She dropped the remains of the lock and opened the door. She motioned for the women to come out, but they huddled together in the corner. Maria sighed in frustration. Of course, they were too scared to move. "It's okay. We're not going to hurt you." At least she could say that about herself. He was a different story.

She glanced behind her and noticed that he still stood there. "You can leave now," she called over to him. "I'll wait for the police." And try to explain the corpses to them. This wasn't going to be fun.

"I'll wait until they're on the way," he said.

"I'd prefer it if you left. You've messed up enough tonight."

He scowled, but it had little effect on Maria. Her grandfather was the king of scowling. She had spent twenty-five years seeing his scowl and, hopefully, had many more years ahead of her.

"Excuse me?"

"You heard me," she said.

"How did I do that? I helped you."

"You killed two men," she said, "and you let some of them get away."

"Me? Your sloppy tactics allowed them to get away," he countered.

She only just met him, and she already hated him. She wanted him to go away and never cross her path again. "I had everything under control until you showed up. Now I won't be able to find out how they're bringing the women and drugs in." She looked at the tables and shook her head. She walked over to one of the tables and looked at a package.

"Didn't look like it from my vantage point," he said dryly.

"You're looking from the wrong point," she said, giving the package a closer inspection. Powder lingered on the table, and she ran a gloved fingertip through it. She tentatively touched her fingertip to her tongue. Boost. Worse than most drugs out there.

He laughed, and her anger rose even more. She wanted to punch him as hard as she could. She smiled, envisioning her fist meeting his face. And then a second time. Just the thought dissipated some of her anger.

She pulled out her burner cell phone and pressed the speed dial for Rollins. She helped the police, and they didn't question her methods too much. Tonight was a cluster fuck; she didn't know how she was going to explain it all. All thanks to him. She looked at him and glared.

He smirked and crossed his arms over his chest. God, she hated him more with each passing second. She continued to glare at him while she informed Rollins of the incident and where she was. She also requested he bring female officers to deal with the frightened women since Maria knew they wouldn't do well with male officers. She hung up and stuffed the burner cell away.

"They'll be here in four minutes," she told him, hoping he'd go away.

He nodded with the smirk still on his face. "I'll double-check the place and go."

Maria sighed with relief. With him gone, she could focus on the critical things. She glanced over at the women, and her stomach twisted. She had been born into a life of privilege and wealth, never knowing what hardships other women had to endure. Fate had been kind to her. One small change, and she could have ended up like the women in the cage. Hopefully, they would soon be reunited with their families wherever they were.

MCM turned and walked away. Maria watched him and had to admit that he had a nice ass. A very nice ass. She'd bet money she could bounce some quarters off it even without the armored costume—what a crazy night. As soon as the police took over, she could go home and fall into her bed. Alone. It was too late to go out and find a playmate for the night.

Her personal cell phone vibrated, and she removed it and looked at the ID of the person who texted. Tomas. She scrunched her forehead and wondered when she gave him her phone number. Maybe he got it from her phone while she had been in the bathroom. She wasn't sure if she should be angry over him prying and looking in her phone or not. Right now, she was going with not. She was already angry enough.

She glanced at the message. Tomas wanted to have dinner. Did he not get the message that she didn't see guys after one night? She wasn't the relationship type, even if it was for a limited time while he was in town. She sighed and shoved the phone in the pocket of her costume. She could deal with that later. Right now, she had to focus on working.

It took the police five minutes to get there along with Tomas's father's forces. Surprisingly enough, Mr. Dorrance himself was on the scene. He glared at Maria and scowled. His dislike for costumes was as plain as day. Thankfully, Maria was wearing a mask and purple contacts. He wouldn't be able to connect her costumed identity to her civilian one.

Maria explained what happened as best as she could while ignoring the glares from Tomas's father. She turned and glared at him; her eyes locked with his. She continued to stare, and he looked away first.

Female officers handled the women and ushered them into a police van. The drugs were collected by the police, bagged, tagged, and then put into one of the vans. Anger bubbled up while she watched them with the drugs. If he hadn't interfered, she may have been able to listen and find out where the drugs were coming from.

"BALESTRA!" A VOICE CALLED WHEN SHE WAS HALFWAY to her bike.

Maria stopped and turned to see Detective Rollins of the NYPD hurrying toward her. Maria sighed. She wanted to go home, shower, and crawl into bed. Her day job started in a few hours. Now she probably had questions to answer, and goodness knew how long it would take to answer them.

"Detective. What can I do for you?" She offered him a tired smile.

Rollins stopped in front of her. He nodded once.

Maria nodded in return. "You look tired."

"It's been a busy night. I'd like you to tell me what really happened back there."

"I see we're skipping the small talk again. It's good to see you too. I told you. I busted up the men running drugs and women."

"I'm sorry," he said with a deep sigh. "There's more. It's not like you to kill."

"I didn't kill them," Maria answered defensively.

"Then who did?" Rollins asked.

Maria tore her eyes away from his face and looked at a point just above his right shoulder. "I don't know," she answered. She looked back at his face, and his deep brown eyes bore into her.

If she had met him as Maria and not Balestra, she would have been interested in taking him to her bed. He was only five years older than she was, in decent shape, and a boy scout. He was one of the good guys.

"Are you sure?" he asked.

Maria bit back a snide reply. There was no reason to antagonize Rollins. She wanted to remain on his good side. She never knew when she'd need his help with something. "Just between you and me?"

Rollins looked at her for a long moment. She could almost see the gears turning in his head. Did he say yes and get information he couldn't officially use or say no and not get the information? He nodded. "Yeah, fine. Just between us."

"Some costumed guy," she said. "I don't know who he is, and he didn't give me a name. He killed those two men before I could stop him."

Maria kept the simmering anger from bubbling over. There was no reason to be angry with Rollins for the actions of another. Anger served no purpose here. She'd unleash it on the person who deserved it.

"Is that all?" he asked.

"Yeah," she said. "He helped me take care of the men and free the women."

"So you think he's on the side of the angels?"

"It seems that way," Maria answered. "Tonight's the first time I've seen him. I would've told you about him if I had run across him before." Maria wasn't sure what to make of the costumed man yet. She would be quite happy to never run across him again, but she knew she'd see him again.

"I know, and I appreciate everything you do, and everything you tell me," he said.

Maria nodded. "If I learn anything else about the costumed guy or the Boost, I'll let you know."

"Thank you."

"Have a good night, Rollins," Maria said.

"You too, Balestra," he said. Maria turned and walked to her bike. She climbed on, waved to Rollins, and took off.

The relatively late hour and lighter traffic allowed Maria to reach the Village in a short time. She pulled into the parking garage on the east side of the Village, not far from the NYU campus. The parking spot for the bike cost a small fortune, but it was New York City and any parking space in the city cost a small fortune. She climbed off the bike and headed toward the exit. For a brief second, she thought about walking back to her place, but a Friday night near NYU guaranteed people around. Even at one am. Hell, her favorite local pub was open until four am on Fridays and Saturdays.

Maria exited the building and crossed Mercer Street. She did a quick scan of the immediate area and launched herself up to the roof of the building that housed Josie Woods Pub. Maybe she'd get home, change, and come back for a few beers. It'd be a nice way to wind down.

She headed west along the rooftops, running along Waverly Place until she reached the next intersection with Greene Street. She looked down at the street, preparing to jump the distance across the street to the buildings on the other side, when she spotted a couple crossing the intersection and turning down Greene Street. Most likely coming from Josie's. A man had his arm around the woman, and the woman jerked away from the man with a yell. He grabbed her arm and pulled her toward him.

The woman yelled again, and the man put a hand over her mouth, using his body to push her up against a nearby car. She fought him, but he ignored her blows as he pressed his body against her. He shoved a hand between their bodies, and Maria knew what he was trying to do.

Maria took a deep breath and ran to the edge of the building, jumping down to the street. She landed in front of the sports car and recognition washed over her. Of course, it was Cargill. The perfect ending to an already rough night.

He didn't seem to notice her arrival as he continued to try to remove the woman's jeans as she struggled. Maria grabbed his jacket at the neck and, using all her strength, yanked him away from the woman. She tossed him against the building, and he grunted when he impacted the wall before sliding down to his feet. The woman pulled her jeans back into place and zipped them.

"Don't go anywhere. Call the police," Maria ordered and turned her attention to Devon. Maria smiled at him. A yell of pure rage erupted from him, and he rushed at Maria. She waited until the last second and stepped into the charge, turning into it. She hooked her arm and used her hip to toss him against his car. A spider web of cracks appeared in the glass, and Devon struggled to stay on his feet, using the car as support.

"Had enough?" Maria asked.

Devon lunged at Maria, swinging with a roundhouse right. Maria sidestepped the punch and drove her right fist into his stomach. He doubled over, groaning in pain. Maria grabbed a handful of hair and pulled, straightening him up. She released him and then grabbed him by the throat and squeezed.

Devon hit her hand and arm in vain efforts to get her to release her hold.

"I could squeeze just a little harder and end your pathetic life," she growled. He struggled to break her grasp. "I recently had a nice chat with Ms. Grayson." He stopped moving, and his eyes went wide. Fear radiated from him, and Maria smiled. "Lucky for you, I don't kill." She released him and he slumped, holding his throat.

"But you'd be amazed at what you can live through," she said, delivering a right to the side of his face. He fell over. Maria sighed and picked him up, setting him on his feet. He wobbled. Maria kneed him in the groin, and he doubled over, groaning in pain.

She glanced over at the woman. "Did you call the police?" The woman nodded. "Good."

Devon took two steps away from Maria, trying to escape, and stumbled. She grabbed his jacket and pulled, sending him crashing into the car again. "You're not going anywhere." She leaned in close to examine his face where she hit him. "That's not going to be pretty." She smiled and then hit him with a left on the other side of his face. "Now both sides will match." Devon looked up at her for a moment before his eyes rolled back, and he slipped unconscious. He fell to the ground.

Maria looked back at the woman. She couldn't have been more than twenty-one or twenty-two and probably a student at NYU. Josie's was popular with students. "You okay?"

She nodded. "Yeah," she answered, her voice shaky. "You stopped him before he could do anything."

Maria nodded. "Good." Maria resisted the urge to kick Devon. Kicking an unconscious man wasn't as enjoyable as it would be if he were conscious. Hopefully, this time, the charges would stick. Though daddy was certain to post bail for him. "What's your name?"

"Michele. Michele Stewart."

"When the police get here, Michele, we'll tell them what happened. I'm not going anywhere. You won't be alone."

She nodded. "Thank you."

"You're welcome," Maria said. It definitely had been a night.

CHAPTER FIVE

MARIA YAWNED AND LOOKED AT THE CLOCK. FIVE minutes had passed since she last looked at it. This day dragged like no other. Of course, staying up late at night and getting only a few hours of sleep didn't help much. Neither did dreams about Tomas and the man in the costume. Thankfully, coffee and espresso existed. Her blood had to be mostly caffeine by now, and Maria couldn't remember a time when she didn't run on coffee.

"Hey," a voice called, and Maria looked up and saw Gayle standing in the doorway.

"Hey yourself," Maria said and smiled. No matter how tired or cranky she was, she always had a smile for her best friend.

Gayle entered without being invited and sat down in the chair in front of Maria's desk. "How was your weekend?"

"It was a weekend," she answered, not giving Gayle the satisfaction of getting the answer she sought.

"Dish. Now."

"Sunday night sucked," Maria said. "I was busting up a drug and human trafficking ring, and some asshole got in the way." There wasn't a facet of Maria's life that Gayle didn't know about. Gayle even helped her crime-fighting by providing information that helped her bring down bad guys. The woman was a wizard when it came to computers and finding information.

"That's not what I was asking about, and you know it," Gayle chided. "Okay, first things first. What happened and what asshole?"

"I don't know his name, but he was in costume. He got in the way, and some of the drug dealers slash human traffickers got away. It would've been a clean bust if he hadn't gotten in the way. Then he had the nerve to accuse ME of getting in the way. As if."

Gayle laughed, and Maria scowled. "No wonder you're cranky this morning."

"Cranky doesn't even begin to describe it," Maria grumbled. Just talking about the strange man rekindled the anger. Anger and lack of sleep contributed to her bad mood. "He killed a few of them, and then I had to explain what happened to the police." Maria sighed. "Definitely not the highlight of my weekend."

"What did the police say?" Gayle leaned forward in the chair. Gayle wasn't an action kind of woman, but she loved hearing about Maria's adventures on the streets.

Maria shook her head and suppressed the rising anger. "Not much. I only mentioned him to Rollins."

Gayle's eyes went wide. "Rollins doesn't think you have anything to do with the killings, right?"

"No. Rollins knows I don't kill. I stopped Devon from sexually assaulting another woman."

Gayle looked at her and blinked. "Again? Was he arrested?"

"Yeah," she said. "But I'm sure his father already bailed him out. I guess we'll see what happens."

"Next time you should castrate him."

She'd hate to admit it, but Gayle had the right idea. "It's a thought. A good one."

Gayle grinned. "Okay, now that that's out of the way, tell me about the guy you left the party with. Don't think I didn't see who you left with. What's his name, and where is he from?"

There's the real news Gayle wanted to know. It was the same each morning after one of Maria's one-night stands. Gayle would ask questions Maria didn't want to answer. If they didn't go through this ritual, Maria would think there was something wrong with Gayle.

"Were you always so nosy?" Maria teased. "His name was Tomas Dorrance, and he's from Brazil."

"Nice to see you branching out and trying some international flavor," Gayle teased right back. She rested her arms on the desk. "What's he doing here in New York?"

"Business," Maria answered. "His family's company is in the private security business, and they have some work here."

"So, how was it?" Gayle grinned.

"Incredible," Maria answered and smiled. The night with Tomas would always be a happy memory. It would be a while before she found another guy who could compare to Tomas.

Gayle pulled back. "Now there's a word I haven't heard you use in some time. He must have made a *big* impression."

Maria shrugged. "It was."

"Going to see him again?" Gayle asked. Light twinkled in her green eyes, and the woman was hoping that this would be the one guy who would cause Maria to end her string of one-night stands. Gayle thought that of just about every person Maria slept with.

"Of course not." She scoffed at the thought. "You know my rules, and I'm not about to start breaking them now." Maria's rules kept her life as uncomplicated as possible.

Gayle nodded. "Never see them more than once and never get attached."

"Exactly. Why are you so obsessed with trying to get me into a relationship with someone?" Maria sat back in her chair and allowed herself a few moments to relax. With Gayle here, the risk of falling asleep didn't exist. Besides, if she did fall asleep, Gayle would wake her up in a way that was sure to annoy Maria. What were best friends for? "You've been trying harder to chain me to someone since you got involved with Charlene."

"I want to see you happy," Gayle said, leaning back in her chair.

"Who says I'm not happy?" Maria countered.

"Are you really content with a string of one-night stands and no real connection with someone?"

Maria sighed. They must have had this same exact conversation a million times and would probably have it a million more. "I am. I have real connections with people. You, my parents, my grandfather, family, and a few other friends. Why do you think I need a steady partner to have a connection with someone?"

"You know I'm going to give you a hard time about this. It's not healthy to have a string of one-night stands for years."

Maria would never sacrifice who she was to fit into someone else's idea of who she should be. Everyone in her circle, including Gayle, had their own idea of who Maria should be. Her grandfather wanted her to be the CEO of Grayson Industries one day. Even her deceased grandmother had thought she should be a wife. Her parents both held an idea of what she should be.

"Well, when Mr. Right, or Ms. Right, comes walking through the door, you can say I told you so," Maria said. "For now, I'll stay with my Mr. Right Nows and have some fun."

"I will," Gayle beamed.

A knock on the door interrupted them, and Maria tore her eyes away from Gayle. Tomas stood in the doorway. He wore a white dress shirt, a blue tie, and a pair of dark gray dress slacks. His gray suit jacket was casually tossed over his shoulder. Could he look any hotter? She didn't think so.

Her eyes widened at the sight of him, and she felt her heart beat a little faster. What the hell was he doing here?

"Am I interrupting?" he asked.

Gayle spun around in her seat and looked at him. She glanced back at Maria and winked. Maria scoffed. Tomas meeting Gayle was a recipe for disaster. Him being here was not a good idea. "Of course not!" Gayle flashed him a broad smile. She stood and walked toward Tomas. "I'm Gayle Simon, Maria's best friend since we were in diapers. Nice to meet you." She held out a hand, and he shook it.

"I'm Tomas Dorrance. A pleasure to meet you, señorita." He flashed Gayle a smile, and Maria wondered if he knew he wasted the smile on the woman.

"I'll leave you two to talk," she beamed. "I told you so," she said and left the office.

Maria glared daggers at her best friend's back as she left the office. She shook her head and turned her attention to Tomas. "To what do I owe the pleasure?" Maria asked.

"You offered to show me the sights of the city," he said, crossing the small space and taking the chair Gayle had vacated. "Or did you think you were going to be off the hook?" The slightest of smirks appeared on his face.

Maria opened her mouth to say something and closed it. He was right. She did offer to show him around the city, and she'd keep her word. It looked like she wasn't done with Mr. Dorrance quite yet. "Of course not," she lied. "I'd be happy to show you around when I'm not in the middle of a workday."

The smirk slipped into a smile. "Excellent. How about dinner tonight, and then you can show me around afterward?"

Show him around, or was that code for having sex again? She wasn't totally opposed to the idea of mind-blowing sex with him again, but the whole after part was the thing she wanted to avoid. Maria looked at him for a long moment, words swirling around her head as she tried to pick something to say.

A knock on her door brought her out of her brief reverie. She blinked and looked over to find her grandfather in the doorway.

"I'm sorry. I didn't realize you were busy. I can come back later."

Maria shook her head. "It's okay. It wasn't anything too important," she said with a small smirk aimed at Tomas.

"I know you," Wayne Grayson said, looking at Tomas.

Tomas stood and walked over to her grandfather and extended his hand. "Yes, sir. We met the other night at the charity fundraiser. Tomas Dorrance."

Her grandfather nodded and shook the offered hand. "Ah, yes. I met your father as well. Interesting fellow," Wayne said and released Tomas's hand.

"Indeed he is," Tomas agreed. "I stopped by to invite Maria out to dinner and to take her up on her offer to play tour guide."

Her grandfather looked at Maria, and she shifted a bit under his gaze. "Glad to hear that. She needs to socialize more with people her own age instead of hanging with me and the other old people all the time."

She adored her grandfather but didn't appreciate him trying to arrange her social life. She was far too old for him to arrange playdates. "You know I love spending time with you," Maria said.

"Yes, but you're young and should be out having fun."

"Yes, she should," Tomas agreed.

Maria blinked. Unbelievable. The two of them were ganging up on her. If Gayle were still here, she'd be joining them. Well, she knew a losing battle when she saw one, and right now, she was smack dab in the middle of one.

"I said I'd love to go when it wasn't during the middle of a workday," Maria said carefully, trying to hide her annoyance.

"Why wait? Go now and enjoy the rest of the day," her grandfather said.

Now she was going to have to spend more time with him. Like her father, he knew about her one-night stands, but didn't want to know at the same time. She knew he hoped that she'd meet the right person one day and settle down. Now she was trapped, and she couldn't see a way out of it.

"Splendid idea," Tomas said. He looked at Maria and smirked.

Her hand curled into a fist, and she slid it around behind her back so her grandfather wouldn't see it. She forced a smile for her grandfather's benefit. "Of course, it is. Well, I said it, and I keep my word," she said. "Just let me finish up this one thing, then I'm yours." She flashed a smile at Tomas. Maria looked at her grandfather. "Was there a reason for your visit besides trying to engineer a respectable social life for me?"

Her grandfather laughed. "I was going to invite you to lunch, but you already have plans. If you'll excuse me, I'll go see if I can find another lunch date. Tomas, it was nice seeing you again. Maria, I'll see you later." He left the office, whistling as he did.

"Your grandfather is an interesting man," Tomas commented as he returned to the chair. "He seems to adore you."

"Of course he does," Maria said, not bothering to hide her irritation. "I'm his only grandchild."

"It's nice you have a good relationship with him and got to know him. I barely knew mine. He died when I was very young."

Maria wanted to make a snide comment but held it back. She wasn't a mean person, and he didn't deserve it. "I'm sorry."

"It's okay, but I appreciate the thought. Where would you like to go for lunch?" Tomas asked, looking around the office.

It wasn't a big office in terms of space, but Maria didn't need a large office. Large offices were for men who needed their egos stroked. She knew her worth, and a large office didn't reflect it. The space was large enough for a desk, a chair in front of it, and a small table with two chairs off to the side. However, it did have large windows and a fantastic view of the city. The view mattered the most to Maria.

"Do you always invade someone's privacy and look at their phone to get their number?" She pinned a look on him.

He shifted in his seat. "I'm sorry. I shouldn't have done it."

"You're damn right you shouldn't have. Not to mention show up here without calling. It's borderline stalkerish."

Tomas nodded. "I'm sorry. If you don't want to go to lunch, I understand."

Maria blinked at the apologies. Most men wouldn't have apologized for the invasion of privacy, and most would get defensive about being called out for it.

"Apologies accepted," she said. "Now, what are you in the mood for?" She didn't mean to put more than one meaning behind her words, but she didn't regret it.

"You," he said without hesitation. The deep penetrating gaze he gave her sent a shiver racing down her spine. Maybe having sex with him a second time wasn't necessarily a bad thing. It's not like she was making a long-term commitment or any emotional commitment. It was just sex. He said he was in town for a limited time.

"I was talking about food," she clarified. "There are many different types of restaurants around here that are all excellent." She saved the file she had been staring at for the past half-hour before Gayle walked in. She clicked on shut down and removed the laptop from the docking station.

"Anything you want," he said.

What did she want? More sex? More sex was never a bad thing. It helped her relax and relieved the stress her two jobs brought her. Why not? She got the afternoon off, and there could be worse ways to spend it. She pulled out her phone and opened one of the food delivery apps. "Thai okay?" she asked.

He tilted his head and looked at her. "Delivery or reservations??"

Maria pulled one side of her mouth back in a sly smile. "Delivery."

Tomas smiled. "I'd love some Som Tam if they have it. Otherwise, Pad Thai would be fine."

Maria nodded and tapped in the order. She tucked her phone away when done and stuffed her laptop into her computer bag, then grabbed her purse.

"Ready?" she asked, stepping out from behind the desk.

He stood and smiled at her. "Lead the way."

Tomas laid still for a few moments as his breathing returned to normal. His heart pounded in his chest, and blood thundered in his ears. A thin layer of sweat covered his body, and the adrenaline drained away, leaving exhaustion in its wake. He considered himself in excellent shape, hitting the gym regularly, and he'd admit their latest round had drained the energy out of him.

He put his hands behind his head and laced his fingers. She kept up with him with no problem Maria was in better shape than she looked. He feared he had been forceful with her, but she seemed to handle it and encouraged him. It was refreshing to have a partner physically on even ground with him. It had been some time since he had a woman like her.

He looked over at her lying next to him, but not touching. She had made her thoughts about cuddling well-known the other night. He only needed to be told things once. "You okay?"

She leaned up on an elbow, and her mouth stretched into a smile. "Yes. That was amazing."

"No arguments here," he said. "Maybe we can do this again before I leave New York." It was a risk since she mentioned only having one-night stands, but he was willing to take it. On the other hand, he was in her bed for the second time in a few days. He hoped this would be a regular thing until he left.

"Possibly," she said.

He leaned up on an elbow to face her. He smiled. "It's not a no, and I'll take it."

Maria laughed, and he smiled, savoring the sound of her laughter. "You kept up pretty well," he said. Now that he thought about it, she had kept up rather well. It had been a nice surprise.

"I must confess that I'm a gym rat," she said.

"I've been known to spend some time in the gym myself," he joked.

"Really? I hadn't noticed," she said, then laughed again.

"Why do you live here?" he asked. "I'm surprised you don't have a place on the Upper East Side. I expected you to live there, not in a loft in the Village."

Tomas looked around. The place was spacious for a one-bedroom loft with the bedroom being almost as large as the living room. He particularly liked the exposed brick throughout and the hardwood floors. Although, it was messy with clothes scattered everywhere and empty glasses in various places. He guessed Maria didn't have a cleaning service. The fact surprised him given the state of the apartment and the fact she could afford it.

Maria shrugged. "It's closer to the office, and I don't have people scrutinizing my every action. Here I'm almost anonymous and can come and go as I please. If I stayed at my family's place in the upper East Side, I would have to answer questions where I was going and who I was bringing home. Even the doormen are judgmental."

"It makes sense," he said. "I'm sure your family appreciates your discretion."

"Honestly, they don't care too much about my activities. It's the paparazzi that I'm mostly avoiding."

"Don't they follow you here?" he asked. His family was wealthy, but they didn't have to worry about the press's scrutiny like Maria's family did. He felt a little sorry for her having to hide her actions and whereabouts when she wanted privacy.

She shook her head. "Nope. They don't seem to see me when I'm in normal clothes. They look for fancy clothes and fancy cars. And if you wear the same shirt often, they don't even take pictures."

"How is that even possible?" he asked. "You don't look different except for your clothes."

"See, you'd think that they'd spot me, but they don't. It's like when Christopher Reeve was filming *Superman*. If he went to lunch in the Superman costume, everyone recognized him. If he went out in normal street clothes, no one noticed him. So the whole Clark Kent disguise works. I mean, even Charlie Chaplin lost a Charlie Chaplin look-a-like contest. People expect to see you a certain way, and if they don't, you become almost invisible."

"Interesting," he said.

"It is," she agreed. "New York has a fair share of costumes on all different levels running around, but if no one exposes their secret identities, they don't get recognized."

"So a person could be sleeping with a costume and never know it," he said.

"Exactly." She leaned over and kissed him. "Ready for another round? What are we up to now?"

Tomas shrugged. "Do you know the costumes in New York?" he asked. He was always interested in another round of amazing sex, but after his curiosity was satisfied.

"I know of them, but I don't personally know them." She kissed him again, more demanding this time. It was almost as if she were trying to distract him. It begged the question, what was she trying to distract him from? "We don't exactly run in the same circles."

"Who's the woman in black trimmed with purple and wears the purple mask? Purple eyes too."

Maria blinked and stared at him. "Why do you ask?"

He gave her a small smile. "Just curious."

"That's Balestra. Not sure if she has powers or not, but she's mostly street-level. Not even close to being on the level of the world-saving types."

"How many other enhanced folks are in New York?" he asked.

Maria shrugged. "Half dozen to a dozen, I guess. Never stopped to count them all."

"How many have you seen?"

Maria looked at him with her head tilted. "Why all the interest in the capes? There are better things we could be doing."

Tomas smiled. "In a bit. We have a few heroes in Brazil, but not nearly as many as you have here in New York. I'd love to see a few while I'm here."

"You might," Maria said. "New York has its fair share of crime, but as long as it isn't like a city level destroying kind of thing. The last one like that was bad enough, and we certainly don't need anything big happening."

"What happened?" he asked. He wasn't sure what the last big news story out of New York was that dealt with the powered set. He tried to keep up on hero activity, but sometimes work distracted him from the truly interesting things.

"Some cryokinetic Ice King or something similar to that," Maria waved her hand and continued, "decided to cover a five-block area in a foot of ice. It caused havoc with the morning traffic. He was dealt with, but the ice took a while to remove completely."

"Who took care of that?" he asked.

"Flame took care of the ice, but I don't remember who brought Ice King in." She kissed him again, her tongue invading his mouth and dueling with his. "No more talking," she said after the kiss ended. "Ready for another round? I think we're up to four. Although it could be five."

He hadn't been counting. He remembered the first round before they ate and the second round after their meal. After that, he didn't bother counting. "I don't know. I thought you were counting."

"I thought you were," she teased.

Tomas laughed. "I guess we'll have to start over from the beginning."

"I like the sound of that," Maria said. She rolled and now lay atop him. She was the devil's own temptation, and he didn't mind being damned.

Tomas closed his eyes for a long moment and savored the feel of her body on top of his. Silk seemed rough compared to her skin, and she had curves in all the right places. He removed his hands from behind his head and wrapped his arms around her. He could hold her in his arms forever if she'd let him. He quickly pushed the thought away. Such thoughts were dangerous.

She brushed her lips against his, and he opened his eyes. Her kiss went from soft and tender to fierce and demanding in the blink of an eye.

Her lips ground down on his, and he returned the kiss with equal intensity. His body responded to the sensual stimulus, giving him an erection. The demanding kiss lessened, and she nipped at his lip. The small point of pain excited him more. She moved her mouth from his to his jaw and kissed along his jawline to his ear. Each kiss seared his skin, and he jerked when her lips reached his earlobe. The kiss turned into a playful bite, and electricity coursed through him. He put his hands on her hips and surged up, intending to roll them over, but she resisted.

Through the haze of lust, he was surprised she was strong enough to prevent him from rolling them over.

"No," she muttered against his ear.

"I guess I'm at your mercy then," he said, his voice husky from desire.

Maria purred and moved her mouth from his ear to his neck. Each kiss burned, and he tightened his hold on her hips, trying to pull her onto his hard erection. She resisted his urging and continued kissing him. Her mouth was now at his chest, and she made her way down to his stomach. He removed his hands from her hips and placed them on the sides of her head.

She wrapped her hand around his erection, and he thrust his hips against her hand. She squeezed, and he groaned. This woman drove him mad, and he loved every moment of it. She slowly stroked him, and his body responded to her efforts. Her mouth replaced her hands, and he jerked. The new sensation was almost too much. He put his hands on her head, and she moved her mouth up and down the length of him. He closed his eyes and savored the feel of her efforts.

While her mouth moved on him, she gently caressed his balls, sending new sensations through him. Tomas growled and put his hands under her arms to urge her up to straddle him. She resisted. He wouldn't complain, but he wanted to bring her as much pleasure as she was bringing him. "Maria," he groaned. She stopped and looked up at him, her blue eyes sparkling in the dim light.

"Yes?" she asked.

"You're driving me crazy," he said barely above a whisper. "Get on top of me."

She threw her head back and laughed. "You said you're at my mercy." She didn't wait for him to respond. She put her mouth back on his erection, and he moaned. She chuckled, and the vibrations sent shockwaves through his body. Damn woman. She knew just how to play him.

Her mouth continued to move on him, and he edged closer and closer to coming. She must have sensed it because she stopped and moved her mouth off him and kissed his navel. Frustration seeped in to mix with the lust.

"Damn woman," he growled, and she laughed. She left a searing line of kisses up his stomach to his chest. She moved to the left and licked his nipple. A second later, she nipped at it. Tomas growled again. This woman was going to be the death of him. She laughed and moved her mouth across his chest to his other nipple. She suckled that one while her fingertips pinched the left one.

"Maria!"

"What?" she said against his skin.

"Please. You're driving me crazy."

"What do you want?" she asked, lifting her head to look at him. He didn't buy that innocent look on her face. She knew exactly what she was doing to him, and she relished every second.

"You. Fuck. Me. Now."

She bit her bottom lip as if she were weighing her options. "Maybe."

"Maybe?" he choked out. "Damn you, woman!"

She laughed and dropped hot kisses on his chest. She moved lower and lower, and he inhaled deeply, anticipating her mouth on his erection. Only it didn't come. She continued kissing him but bypassed his groin and continued down his inner thigh. Payback's a bitch, and when he got the opportunity, he was going to tease her worse than she was doing to him.

She kissed his knee and then started back up his inner thigh. She reached his erection, dropped a light kiss on the tip of him, and then moved to his right thigh. He put his hands on her head and buried his fingers in the silky, dark hair. It tickled the back of his hands, and her light kisses tickled his legs. His head reeled, and his breathing came in short, ragged breaths. He had never had a woman torment him as much as she did.

She reached his knee and then started back up. At this point, he didn't know what to expect from her. The weather was more predictable. She covered him with her mouth again, and he let out a heartfelt moan. He closed his eyes and tightened his grip on her hair. She settled into a rhythm, and his body tensed. It started in his toes and traveled up his legs and settled in his groin.

A moment later, he snapped and thrust into her mouth and came. She continued to suck him, swallowing his ejaculate. The breath he had been holding escaped with explosive force, and he released her head. He sank into the bed, spent. She crawled up the length of him and dropped a kiss on his chin. He wrapped his arms around her and held her, despite her opinions about cuddling. He just wanted a few brief moments to relish in the feel of her body pressed against his and the warmth their bodies produced.

She slipped out of his arms and rolled to the side after a few brief moments. A chill raced over him at the sudden loss of heat. If he could, he'd have her next to him the whole night. Maybe one night before he left, he'd get the chance.

Not one to be selfish, he rolled over and pushed himself up to his knees. He moved around to cover her body with his.

"What are you doing?" she asked, looking up and into his eyes. Tomas smiled. "It's your turn."

Maria smiled and surged up to kiss him. The kiss ended, and Tomas slid his left arm under her back. He put his right hand on her left breast and started to play with the pert nipple. Fair was fair, and he wanted to give her as much pleasure as she gave him. There may be a little teasing and tormenting to go with it, but turnabout was fair play. He covered the right nipple with his mouth and sucked the hard nub.

Maria arched back, allowing him to take more of her into his mouth. Her breasts were perfectly sized to fit in his hands. He released her breast and kissed his way across to the other one. He took that one in his mouth and lashed the nipple with his tongue. He teased the other nipple with his thumb and index finger, giving it a slight pinch. She jerked, and inwardly he smiled.

After giving both breasts equal attention, he kissed his way to her navel. He leaned over to test it with his tongue. She flinched, and he held her still with his palm flattened against her lower belly. He tongued her navel again; the shallow penetration satisfying only in that it was another taste of her. She moaned, and he rewarded the sound by edging his fingers down into the curling hair at the V of her thighs.

Her hips pushed against his hands, and he parted the soft folds with two fingers. She gasped, and he smiled against her stomach. He drew his forefinger over the smooth, wet cleft. Her sweet, musky scent rose around him.

"Tomas." His name was a very sexy plea. He drew a finger up

and then down, her body opening under his touch. "Please," she begged.

He moved his mouth down to where his fingers worked her, and he dropped a kiss into the curls between her legs. He didn't stop there. He continued to kiss his way to the left and down her inner thigh while his fingers continued to play with her soft folds. Her hips pushed into his fingers, urging him to put them inside of her. Somehow, he resisted.

Tomas kissed his way back to the mound of dark curls between her legs and slipped his tongue between the soft folds. Maria arched against him as he probed her depths with his tongue. Her fingers slipped into his hair, and he rewarded her by running his tongue over the sensitive nub. Maria gasped, encouraging him. The tip of his tongue moved in small, slow circles around her center. A deep-throated moan escaped her, and Tomas continued the oral attentions.

Maria's fingers curled and grabbed his hand. Tomas focused on the spots that elicited greater responses. Maria tugged his hair, and she gasped, coming undone. Tomas dropped a kiss and then pulled away. He crawled forward to cover her body with his. Her fingers slipped out of his hair, and her arms wound around him.

He looked down at her and smiled. Her eyes met his, and she smiled. He dropped a kiss on her mouth before rolling to the side. He wrapped his arms around her, determined to keep her next to him. He wanted a few more moments of skin on skin. She wouldn't tolerate the closeness or cuddling for long, and he would enjoy every second he could get.

CHAPTER SIX

"I'M SORRY," TOMAS SAID AS HE SLID INTO THE CHAIR AT the table, already ten minutes late to lunch with his sister. "Traffic held me up."

Carolyn raised a brow and leaned forward in her chair. He never could lie convincingly to her and vice versa. "The hotel is a block away."

"I didn't come from the hotel," he explained.

"Obviously. I knocked on your door when it was time to come here," she said, her voice laced with irritation. "Where were you?"

"Not in my room," he answered, not giving her the satisfaction of knowing his activities. "I'm sorry I'm late. I promise I won't be late next time."

Carolyn pressed her lips together. "How's Ms. Grayson?" She smirked.

Tomas knew he couldn't keep secrets from his twin, yet he tried anyway. "She's good."

"So, what's going on with you and her?" Carolyn asked as she picked up a menu. She looked over at him. "Father was wondering where you were this morning. He wanted to talk about business."

Tomas sighed and sat back in his chair. He should have kept

better track of time, but Maria proved to be an excellent distraction. He ended up spending the night at her place, but they didn't get much sleep. They ordered delivery around dinner time and spent about two hours talking over dinner and drinks. Not only did she keep up with him in bed, but she also had quite the capacity to drink alcohol. She continued to surprise him, and he rather liked it.

Tomas looked at his sister, meeting her eyes. "It's just sex."

Was it, though? The more time he spent with her, the more he wanted to be with her. It had been a while since he had felt that way about a woman. He had an active social life and dated, but none of those women fascinated him like Maria did. He wanted to know everything about her.

"It better be," Carolyn warned.

"Since when did you become my mother?" he asked. "Or so interested in my personal life?"

"One, I'm your twin sister. I love you and care about you. Two, it's interfering with the whole purpose of this trip. Father was quite angry this morning when you didn't show."

"I'll deal with father," he said. It wouldn't be pretty, but his father would eventually understand that it involved a gorgeous woman from a very powerful family. He didn't expect his father's reaction to be a negative one. He flashed her a smile. "I love you too, even though you're a pain in my ass."

"I'll be an actual pain in your ass if you have some time for some sparring this afternoon," she said with a grin.

Tomas smiled and nodded. "I'll be there. It's been a while since we've sparred." Tomas and Carolyn had both been taking capoeira lessons since they were around four. They loved it from the beginning and continued it throughout their entire lives. They sparred with each other outside of class and pushed each other to improve. Being twins, they knew each other so well, their sessions ended in stalemates.

"Good. We can't let our skills decline," she said.

"Agreed."

"So, have you learned anything interesting about Ms. Grayson that could be useful?" Carolyn asked right before a waiter appeared at their table. Carolyn gave her order, and Tomas gave his. He went with a 16 oz steak and a large salad. Keeping up with Maria had been an effort, and he had to build up his strength if he was going to spar with his sister later.

"Not much that would be useful," he said after the waiter left. "Nothing you couldn't find out by reading the paper unless you want to know her favorite sexual positions."

Carolyn rolled her eyes. "No, thanks."

Tomas chuckled. "I didn't think so. So did anyone catch your eye?" he asked before taking a sip of water.

"There were one or two," she answered. Tomas blinked in surprise. His sister usually didn't take an interest in anyone unless they served a purpose. He wondered what she was up to.

"Who?"

"One is a Cargill," she said. "The other is a Shea."

"And why the interest?" he asked.

"Possible competition for some business ideas father has."

And there it was. The reason for her interest. He worried about her at times like this. At her age, she should have had a relationship or two, or even had some interest in people. Instead, she remained focused on business and didn't interact with many people. He'd worry less if she saw a guy, or a woman for that matter, just for the sake of seeing someone. He'd even accept meaningless sex. The thought of meaningless sex made him think of Maria, and he smiled.

"Of course," he said.

"What's that supposed to mean?" she asked, her dark eyes narrowing and her voice taking on a dangerous edge.

"I know you're not a people person," he said, trying to derail an argument and her getting mad at him. The last thing he needed was an angry sister to deal with. Prickly, he could deal with.

"You're just figuring that out?" she asked. Light danced in her dark eyes, and a hint of a smile played on her lips.

"Hell, no. Still, it wouldn't hurt you to see someone outside of having ulterior motives or trying to collect information on someone," Tomas suggested.

"You don't know that," she said and picked up her glass of water. The waiter returned with their drinks and placed them on the table in front of them.

"Thank you," Tomas said as Carolyn sipped her water. He picked up his beer and took a sip. One thing he loved about New York was the availability of micro-brews from around the United States. Back home, the selection was limited. The stout had hints of coffee and chocolate. He'd have to remember this label and take some home with him.

He frowned at the thought of going home. He was enjoying New York and the time he spent with a certain New Yorker and didn't want to go home.

"What's wrong?" Carolyn asked.

"Nothing," he said, shaking off the thought. "Just thought about home."

"Why the frown? I can't wait to get home and away from this city."

"What's wrong with this city? It's been great so far."

Carolyn shook her head. "It's too cold, too noisy, Americans are too loud and rude," she said. "Should I go on?"

He held a hand up, stopping her. "No, please don't. I get it. You don't like New York."

"So, do you like her?" Carolyn asked, trying to sound casual and failing. His sister didn't do anything casually. There was a purpose behind every action and every word.

"I do," he admitted. He liked spending time with Maria and not just for the sex. Which was terrific, but there was more to her. She was an interesting person, and he wanted to get to know her better. "I'll probably see her as long as we're here. She's fun and manages to surprise me."

"Don't get too attached and let yourself get hurt," she warned.

"I won't, I promise," he said. "I'm just having some fun. You make it sound like I'm falling head over heels in love with her. I'm not, and I know it's going to end soon."

The waiter arrived with their food. Carolyn went with a salad, which came as no surprise to Tomas. She had gone vegetarian a few years ago and seemed to be liking it. He could never give up steak even if his life depended on it.

"Does she know that?" Carolyn asked, picking up her flatware and giving him a direct look.

"Yes," he said. "Purely physical at her insistence," he said. "So what business did Father want to discuss?" he asked, trying to change the subject from his personal life to something else. He loved his sister, but he didn't need her prying too much into his personal life.

"He mentioned that if this deal with the NYPD went well, he mentioned wanting to expand to other American cities."

Tomas paused in, cutting his steak. "It's a wise decision."

Carolyn nodded as she chewed. "Yes," she said after swallowing her food. "Did you expect anything different?"

"Of course not," he said.

"Do you have plans for this evening?" she asked.

Tomas looked away from his food and at her. "I don't know yet. What about you?"

"Father gave me some work to do."

Tomas wasn't surprised. Their father always had work for the two of them to do, no matter where they were. He didn't believe in his children living a carefree life. They had been involved in the family business since their teens, and their responsibilities only grew as they got older. He just had to make sure he had time for some fun with Maria.

"What are you working on?" he asked her.

"Something," she answered.

Tomas gave her a flat look. "Tell me," he urged. Since when did his twin keep secrets from him? They told each other everything and had since they were young.

"Father wants to play this one close to the vest," she said.

"I'm your twin," he carefully said. "You know I won't tell anyone. Not even God."

"Ask Father if you want to know," she said with a shrug.

"I will." And he would. Carolyn was keeping secrets, and Tomas had to know why. He shook his head. "I can't believe you're keeping a secret from me."

Carolyn sighed. "Not me," she said. "Father. He doesn't want anyone finding out about this."

Tomas pulled back. "Not even me?"

Carolyn shrugged. "I'm doing what he ordered."

"That, I can understand," he said. "Are you going to do any sightseeing while you're here?"

"I don't know," she said between bites.

"Come with me to see the Statue of Liberty," he urged. "We can make a day of it. I'll even go shopping with you." He was not above exploiting his sister's weakness.

Carolyn smiled. "I will go see the statue with you, but if we don't go shopping, I will kick your ass so hard."

Tomas laughed. She'd never let him forget the time he promised to go shopping with her and didn't deliver on that promise. Some of the Carolyn he knew as a child peeked through. She used to tease, laugh, and have fun. That was before their father brought them into the family business. Now she could be as ruthless as he was.

CHAPTER SEVEN

A WEEK LATER, MARIA LOOKED DOWN AT THE BUILDING across the street from her perch on a nearby rooftop. The white van from the other night sat parked outside of the building. With Gayle's help, Maria managed to track the van to this location. So far, no one had entered or left the building. If she had to be honest, she was quite bored sitting here watching the building. The nondescript building housed a few floors of apartments and retail space on the ground floor.

She didn't see any signs of movement or hear anything. Fuck it. She was going in. She walked to the far side of the roof and ran full speed. Maria reached the edge and launched herself into the air, soaring over the street below, landing on the other building's roof. She dropped into a roll, then sprang to her feet. She looked around. Nothing moved, and there wasn't a person in sight. She was sure her landing would have caught the attention of someone inside.

Scowling, she headed for the door. She tried the handle. Locked. She took a deep breath and yanked it open. The door came off the hinges, and she tossed it aside. The sound was surely going to attract the attention. Maria waited for a few minutes, but she didn't hear anyone coming up the stairs.

What was going on? Did they leave by another door and leave the van? Something wasn't right, and she had to find out what exactly was going on. She made her way down the stairs as quietly as she could. She reached a door and opened it up a crack. She peered through the small opening. No one and nothing moved, and silence greeted her. Maria opened the door and slipped through. She closed the door quietly behind her and moved down the hall. Apartment doors lined the hall, but no noise came from any of them. It was well after midnight and most people were asleep by now.

She reached the far end of the hallway and came to another door. She opened it a crack and looked through the opening. She peered into an empty stairwell. Maria opened the door wider and stepped through. She descended the stairs and came to another door at a landing. She opened it and quickly glanced in. Another floor of apartments, just as quiet as the one above it. The floor creaked under her weight, and Maria froze. She heard only the sound of the blood pounding in her ears and her own breathing. Instinct told her to leave, but she pressed on.

She continued down the stairs. Another floor and more silence greeted her. Maria dashed down the stairs and reached a door leading out to the street. It didn't appear they were in any of the apartments. She stepped out onto the sidewalk.

Maria went to the front door of the boarded-up retail space. The doors were locked and had a chain stretched between the two handles. She grabbed the lock and yanked, breaking it and pulling it off the chain. She entered. The front was once a small bodega, but now sat vacant, with rows of empty shelves thanks to gentrification. Light shone through a window of a door in the back of the store.

Maria walked toward the back, taking extra care not to step on anything or make a sound. She reached the door and moved to the side, out of view of the window. Maria glanced through the window, and her blood went cold. Movement caught her eye, and she quickly pulled back. Her stomach churned at the sight of so much blood. She swallowed against the bile rising in her throat.

She held her breath as she heard someone moving on the other side of the door. Maria glanced down at the light pouring through the bottom of the door. Shadows moved, and footsteps echoed. Maria focused on the sounds and readied herself. The door slowly opened, and a dark figure slowly emerged. Maria noticed the bloodstained knife in the figure's hand. This was going to be more difficult than expected.

The shadowy figure was about Maria's height but a little leaner. A woman. No wonder the footsteps were so light. The woman wore a dark gray uniform and a matching mask. Her head was covered, and only her eyes were visible.

Maria grabbed the hand holding the knife and applied pressure to the wrist. The fingers relaxed, and the knife clattered when it hit the floor. The figure spun out of Maria's grasp and jumped, catching Maria on the chin with a kick. Maria took a few steps backward and shifted into a defensive position. She spread her legs shoulder-width apart and slightly bent her knees, lowering her center of gravity. She put her arms up with her hands curled into fists.

The shadowy figure charged, and Maria blocked the incoming punch with her left forearm hitting the woman's and deflecting the blow wide. Maria followed through with her right and a punch to the woman's jaw. Maria put some of her strength behind the punch, and it lifted the woman off the ground, sending her back into the empty shelves. Maria didn't wait for the woman to get up, and she charged toward her.

Her opponent landed on her feet and ducked under Maria's follow-up punch. She delivered one to Maria's stomach and knocked the breath out of her. She doubled over into the hit. She walked right into that one and grew angry with herself. She took two steps backward and regained her footing and her breath.

The other woman rushed toward her, and Maria dropped her shoulder and charged toward the woman. They collided, and Maria's strength gave her the advantage, and she drove her opponent into empty shelves. The woman grunted in pain and brought a strike down on the back of Maria's skull. White-hot pain spiked and raced down her spine.

Maria staggered and stepped backward out of the woman's reach. She shook her head, trying to shake the pain off. Her opponent was powered, about on par with Maria.

Her adversary climbed to her feet and staggered a bit. She dove, and Maria wondered what she was doing before realizing the woman was going for the knife. Maria dove after her and grabbed the woman around the legs as she reached for the blade. Maria pulled, but the gloved hand had a hold of the knife. Maria pulled herself to her knees and used all her strength to swing at her opponent. It worked. Somewhat. The woman slid across the tiled floor and into a wall. Maria climbed to her feet as the other woman did the same.

She charged at Maria, brandishing the knife. Maria took a deep breath and jumped at the last second as the blade whooshed through the air. Her adversary passed under her as Maria tucked and flipped before landing on the floor with both feet. Years of taking gymnastics certainly helped her in this line of work. Maria whipped around in time to deliver a side kick. Her foot connected with the side of the woman's face, and a cry of pain escaped her.

Maria followed the kick with a punch and landed square on the woman's jaw. A sound from the front of the shuttered store grabbed her attention, and Maria spotted another dark figure entering the store. She'd recognize that build and heavy step anywhere.

The woman dashed to the back door and burst through it. Maria thought about chasing after her, but she had to deal with the idiot coming through the front door. She sighed and walked over to stand in his way.

"What the hell are you doing here?" she demanded.

"Me? What the hell are you doing here?" he countered.

"I was trying to stop the person who just slaughtered the drug dealers slash sex traffickers that you let get away the other night," she half-growled.

"If I'm not...what do you mean slaughtered?"

Maria sighed. "There's six of them in the back there. Sliced and diced, and there's blood absolutely everywhere. I caught her right after the fact and was trying to detain her. That's until you decided to come wandering in the front door, allowing her to get away."

He scoffed. "If you were as good as you think you are, you wouldn't have been distracted by me and allowed her to get away."

"Go to hell!" she spat.

He laughed, and it only angered her more. She wanted to punch him but managed to restrain herself.

"This is a total cluster fuck," she said and yanked out the burner phone she used for costumed work. She dialed Rollins and informed him of where she was and what happened. Thankfully, she hadn't set foot in the back room and couldn't be a suspect. Or at least she hoped so. Who knew what the police would say and do once they get here?

He was near the door when she hung up the phone. "Don't go back there," she warned.

He turned and looked at her. "Why not?"

She hurried across the store and stood directly in front of him. He had a few inches on her, and she had to look up. "Because the police are on their way, and the second you enter that room, you become a suspect. There's blood everywhere, and there's probably no avoiding stepping in it or getting it on you."

He remained still for a moment. "You're right."

Maria smirked. "Glad you can admit it."

He scowled. "Only this one time. Want to tell me what happened?"

"Not really, but I don't have anything better to do while I wait for the police. I tracked the van to this location. I came in through the roof and did a sweep of the upstairs. Came down and entered through the front door and heard someone in the back. Went to check it out, and this woman came out carrying a bloodied knife."

"And kicked your ass," he added.

Anger spiked. "No. I was kicking her ass until you interfered."

He laughed a deep laugh. "Right. I only entered, and I wouldn't call that interfering."

"Shut the fuck up," she grumbled.

He laughed harder, and she hated him more.

"You're such an ass," she grumbled under her breath. She walked to the front door and looked out, hoping the police would arrive soon so she wouldn't have to deal with him any longer.

"And you're such a bitch," he said.

She didn't care if he heard her. She didn't care about him or anything he said or did. All that mattered was finding the person responsible for killing the people in the back. They were bad guys, sure, but they didn't deserve to be slaughtered. They should have been arrested and put through the justice system.

"At least we won't have to worry about them any longer," he said, nodding toward the back.

"It'd be better if they were still alive," Maria said. "We'd be able to find out where the drugs and women are coming in."

"True, but there will be other people and other leads." He shrugged. "Fewer pieces of scum on the streets is a good thing."

Maria shook her head. "As bad as they were, no one deserves to be killed. Especially like that."

It was most likely another drug dealer who had them killed, but slicing and dicing wasn't exactly their style. Guns and bullets were the typical instruments used when rival drug dealers went to war. This spoke of something different, and Maria had to find out what.

"It's better they're dead," he said. "They can't harm anyone anymore. Especially the women they were trafficking."

"You can't indiscriminately kill people, no matter what they've done. They should be subjected to the justice system and its laws," she said, knowing her efforts were futile.

He snorted. "The justice system here and in a lot of places is a joke," he said. "It has revolving doors and people like this," he motioned to the back, "end up back on the streets. How many times have you handed over the same people to the police, only to have them back on the streets in little time?"

He had a point, but it still didn't justify what happened to the men in the back.

"What do I call you?"

He tilted his head. "Why do you ask?"

"You don't have to answer," she said. "I can just call you, Asshole," Maria smirked. That seemed more fitting than whatever name he could give her.

"Skanda."

Skanda. Now that was something one didn't hear often. It was a peculiar choice in a codename. "Skanda, the Hindu god who was the son of Shiva, or as in the guardian of Buddhist monasteries?"

"Yes," he answered.

A frustrated sigh came from her. Could he get any more frustrating? "Whatever," she said with a wave of her hand.

"And what do I call you besides Bitch?"

"Balestra," she answered, letting the bitch part slide off her. She wasn't going to give him the satisfaction of getting angry and reacting. Besides, she'd take bitch as a compliment any day in or out of costume.

"I'd say it was a pleasure to meet you, but we both would know I'd be lying," he said. "So, who did this?"

Maria ignored the first part. She wasn't going to let him bait her into a response. She'd rise above his pettiness. She shrugged. "I don't know. They were masked, and only her eyes were visible."

"Her?"

"Her. I can tell the difference between a man and a woman," Maria said. "She was about my size, but a little leaner. She was quick and had martial arts training."

"What style?"

"One I don't know," she admitted.

"What ones do you know?" he asked.

"And give you an advantage? A girl has to have some secrets."

He laughed, and it was the first laugh that didn't make her angry. "Okay, then. Did the police say how long it would take them to get here?"

"Ten minutes from when I called," she said. "Must be a busy night for them."

"Probably," he said. "Until then, I get to enjoy the pleasure of your company."

Maria rolled her eyes. "You don't have to stay. You had nothing to do with this except for letting the woman get away."

"You mean you let the woman get away," he corrected. "I'll stay here until the police are close."

"Gee, thanks," she said, sarcasm dripping from her words. If he would leave, the wait for the police would be quiet, and she could replay the fight with the woman in her mind and possibly find a clue to her identity. At least explaining this one to the police might be a little simpler than the last time. The scene was intact and hadn't been corrupted by either of them.

"You know, we could work together and find the source of drugs and trafficking," he suggested.

Maria blinked and stared at him. "Are you serious?"

He nodded. "I am. I think we'd make a decent team."

They might make a good team, but she highly doubted it. "I'd rather have a lobotomy. I don't work on a team. Never have and never will."

He jerked back a little. Maria bit her lower lip to avoid laughing at him being taken aback over her rejection of his offer. "A lobotomy may increase your intelligence by a few points."

"It's cute when you try to insult me and fail spectacularly." He laughed, and she resisted the urge to hit him. "Don't you have someone else to go annoy?"

"Not really," he said. "She's busy tonight."

"That's what she told you, but like me, probably just enjoys the time when you're not around."

He laughed harder. "I pity any man who has to put up with you."

The sound of police sirens grew louder. "Oh, good. They're here early. Maybe I should tell them you created the corpses the last time we met."

His dark eyes narrowed, and he glared at her. "You wouldn't."

She stared right back at him. "Try me." He growled and glanced out the window. "If you're going to leave, you better do it now. They will question you if you're here when they arrive."

He looked at her and then headed for the door. Maria watched him go and took a moment to appreciate his ass. She wouldn't deny it was a nice ass. Too bad he was a significant pain in her ass and an asshole to boot. She sighed and leaned up against the wall and waited.

CHAPTER EIGHT

Tomas smiled at Gayle as he passed the woman's desk. She gave him a big smile and a thumbs up. He wondered why she gave him a thumbs up, but he could make a good guess why. Apparently, he had a supporter in his corner, although he didn't think it would do him much good. Maria didn't want any type of relationship outside of physical, and apparently sleeping with him a second time had been a big deal. Now he was going to ask her out to dinner, which may be too relationship-like for her tastes. He hoped it wasn't. He enjoyed spending time with her and hadn't seen her in a week. He texted her last night, but she had been busy.

He stopped in the office doorway. Her head was down and reading papers on her desk. He brought a hand up to knock on the door but paused. He took advantage of the brief moment to watch her. It was cute the way she tapped a well-manicured fingertip against the desk in thought. She wore headphones, and he idly wondered what she listened to. He'd bet money it was either rock or pop. She didn't seem the type for other genres of music.

She grabbed a coffee cup without looking and took a long drink. Tomas didn't know her well, but he guessed she ran on an above-average number of cups of coffee a day. He looked at the cup in his hand. Even though she already had coffee, he doubted she would refuse another. She probably approached work with everything she had. Maria was an all-or-nothing type of person. He continued to watch her, and the desire to know more about her grew. He told himself this was temporary, but it didn't stop his curiosity.

He knocked on the door with a knuckle. Maria didn't look up. He knocked again, a little louder this time, and she still didn't look at him. Tomas smiled and walked into the office. He sat down in the chair in front of her desk, smiling when she looked up. Maria removed her headphones.

"Hi," he said, placing the cup of coffee in front of her.

"Um, hi."

"I knocked twice, but you didn't hear me."

Her cheeks turned pink, and Tomas found it cute. "Sorry."

"It's okay," he assured her. "I get the same way when I'm engrossed in work." He leaned back in the chair. "I dropped by to see if you'd be available for dinner tonight."

Maria blinked. "Dinner?"

"Dinner," he said with a smile. "The meal we eat in the evening hours. What do you say? Come to dinner with me tonight."

She remained quiet and just looked at him as she pondered the question. He wanted to go around the desk and kiss her until she agreed. He wanted to kiss her; no reason needed. He didn't think she would tolerate it here in the office. Then again, she didn't seem like the type to care what other people thought. He liked that about her. Well, he liked everything about her, and that was part of the problem. He knew whatever it was they had going on couldn't last, yet he couldn't stay away from her.

"I know what dinner is," she said, giving him one of those smiles he loved so much.

"So what do you say? Me, you, and the restaurant of your choice," he said.

Maria shook her head. "No. I'll go only if you pick the place and surprise me."

Tomas grinned. "Deal. Is there anything I should avoid?" he asked. They didn't exactly spend much time eating together or talking about food. In fact, they didn't do much together outside of sex. He was walking a thin line between trying to keep this casual and wanting to get to know her better. Given the opportunity, he'd make this a regular thing and have it last much longer than his stay in New York.

"Pretentious restaurants," she said.

That was a new one he had never heard before. He expected stuff like seafood, meat, gluten, and the like. How did one figure out if a place was pretentious or not? His forehead furled in thought, and his mouth twisted.

"Something wrong?" she asked.

His mouth straightened. "I'm not sure what classifies a place as pretentious or not."

Maria laughed. "I have faith that you'll figure it out."

That didn't help at all. Though knowing Maria, he should have expected that answer. "I'll try, but you can't blame me if we wind up at a pretentious place."

"I have full faith in your abilities to find a suitable place for dinner," she said. She looked away from him and at a spot over his shoulder. Tomas turned to see her grandfather rolling in the door.

"Tomas, good to see you again."

Tomas stood and offered a hand. "It's good to see you again, Mr. Grayson."

He shook Tomas's hand and smiled. "Please call me Wayne. Mr. Grayson is way too formal."

"Or you can call him Grumpy," Maria teased.

Her grandfather frowned, and Maria laughed. Tomas chuckled, finding it all amusing.

"She has been calling me that since she was in diapers," he explained. He favored Maria with a smile, and Tomas loved how at ease they were with each other.

"It was an accurate description," she said.

"Bratty kid." He smiled at Maria and then looked at Tomas. "What brings you by?"

"I dropped by to invite Maria to dinner."

"Speaking of dinner, Tomas, you'll have to come over for dinner one night."

Tomas looked at Wayne Grayson and blinked a few times. Sure, he was having mind-blowing sex with his granddaughter, but he never expected a dinner invitation. He'd bet money he was the first of Maria's flings to get a dinner invite.

"I'd love to," Tomas said before Maria could object. This wasn't serious, but one simply didn't turn down dinner with Wayne Grayson.

"Great. Maria, let me know which night the two of you can make it."

Maria sat there, staring at her grandfather. She looked at Tomas, and her eyes narrowed. Tomas smiled at her. "I'm free almost every night for dinner."

"Wonderful. Now I better get back to work. I'll see the two of you later." With that, he left the office.

Tomas returned to his seat in the chair. Maria was still staring at him with narrowed eyes. "I didn't plan that," he said in his own defense.

"You could've turned it down," she said.

His mouth dropped open for a moment before he regained his composure. "Turn down a dinner invitation from Wayne Grayson? Are you kidding?"

"No, I'm not kidding."

"Why are you so upset by this?"

"I'm not upset," she rushed to say. "It's just that this isn't supposed to be serious."

"It's not serious," he said. "Your grandfather invited me to dinner, and I accepted."

"Having dinner with the family is *serious*," she said. "Hell, meeting the family signifies serious." Maria rubbed the bridge of her nose. "This is a disaster."

Tomas sighed. He wouldn't go so far as to call it a disaster. Inconvenience maybe, but certainly not more than that. "I promised you this is temporary while I'm in town and no seriousness involved. I can come up with some excuse not to go if it's important to you."

She shook her head. "You don't have to invent an excuse to not go." Is inviting me to dinner tonight all that you wanted? I do have to get back to work."

The shift in her attitude didn't go unnoticed. He'd swear the temperature in the office dropped by a few degrees. He assumed he crossed a line by accepting her grandfather's dinner invitation. "It is," he said with a nod. "I'll pick you up at your place at seven?" he asked, standing.

"Sounds like a plan."

He noticed she used plan instead of date, which it totally was a date whether or not she wanted it to be. He smiled and nodded. "I'll see you later, Ms. Grayson."

Her eyes momentarily narrowed, and he wondered if she thought he was up to something. He was, but he didn't want her to believe he was. "Goodbye Mr. Dorrance."

Tomas chuckled and shoved his hands in his pockets. He whistled as he strode out of the office.

MARIA HAD BEEN PLEASANTLY SURPRISED BY HIS IDEA of dinner. It erased the irritation of him accepting a dinner invitation from her grandfather. He showed up at her door with a bag of Chinese takeout and a six-pack of beer. Who could resist that? It certainly fit the definition of not being pretentious. They sat at the small table in her kitchen, ate Chinese food, drank beer, and talked. It was perfect.

There were long looks and innuendos over dinner. As soon as they were done eating, Tomas pulled her to her feet and kissed her deeply. Her toes curled, and fire raced through her. How did he manage to turn her on with a few looks and a deep kiss? She blamed it on the beer even though she only had one. The kiss ended, and she was breathless. So was he.

He smiled, lifted her off her feet, and tossed her over a shoulder.

Maria laughed as she got an up-close view of his ass. "Ooooh! The caveman routine! I love the caveman routine!"

He laughed and navigated his way through the mess of her apartment to her bedroom. "Somehow, I am not surprised," he said and gave her ass a playful whack. She squealed at the sudden surprise and laughed. This was much better than going out to dinner where they'd have to behave themselves. A small part of her was concerned that he knew her well enough to plan this, but a larger portion of her was quite pleased that he had planned this.

He gave her ass another playful whack, this time groping was added to it, and Maria wasn't going to complain. He was fun, and she was enjoying the time she spent with him. A part of her would be sad when he left, but a much larger piece would be grateful. Attachments weren't a good thing, and she knew she was too attached to him. Past the point of rescue would come before she knew it, and she wanted to nip this in the bud before that happened.

They reached her bedroom, and he stopped near her bed. From her vantage point, she had an excellent view of the floor, and her eyes went wide. Purple stuck out from under the bed, and she prayed he wouldn't notice. She straightened out and slid down the length of his body. She wrapped her arms around his neck and kissed him deeply. While she had him occupied, she maneuvered him around so she could kick the costume under the bed. The kiss continued, and he didn't notice. Or at least she thought he didn't. There would have been uncomfortable questions to answer, and a lot of explaining to do. This was another reason why she didn't get serious with anyone.

A short while later, she lay under him, tired and quite satisfied. She smiled at his body on top of hers and placed a hand on the side of his face. He smiled and turned into her hand, kissing the palm. "You're amazing," he said in a loud whisper.

"You too," she said softly. Talking in a normal volume seemed wrong on a level Maria couldn't put into words. She caressed his cheek with a thumb. Her thumb glided over his skin, and she could tell he shaved before coming over. She had to admit she liked a little stubble on men. It gave them a scruffy look, and she loved scruffy.

He climbed off her and stretched out on the bed with his hands behind his head. Maria sat up, took a moment to appreciate the fine specimen next her, then climbed off the bed. She quickly padded her way to the bathroom, shutting the door behind her.

"What the hell are you doing?" she quietly asked herself in the mirror. "You wanted to curl up next to him, and we can't do that. It's dangerous to get close, you know that."

Her reflection didn't answer.

She put her hands on both sides of the sink and leaned on them. She squeezed her eyes shut and tried to still the dangerous thoughts going through her head. "I can't develop feelings for him," she told herself. "He'll be leaving soon, and all you'll have is heartbreak if you allow yourself to have feelings for him." She shook her head. "It's too dangerous. He'll discover your secret identity and then the shit will hit the fan. You know that."

The words she told herself didn't seem to have any impact. She looked at the door and wanted to go back out there and climb back into bed with Tomas. Not for more sex, but to curl up beside him. It was too dangerous. She'd rather rush headlong into a firefight than cuddle with Tomas.

She sighed and straightened up. Thankfully, her stomach rumbled and held a hollow feeling. Eating would be a good distraction. She took a deep breath, steeled her will, and opened the door.

She forced a smile and grabbed a shirt off the floor. His shirt. She slipped it on and grabbed sweatpants from where the spot where he had taken them off her. "I'm going to reheat some of the leftovers. You want any?" she asked in a normal voice, trying to make the situation more normal and kill the intimate atmosphere.

"Sure," he said, pushing up to a sitting position. He swung his legs over the side of the bed and grabbed his jeans. He didn't bother with underwear and pulled them on. "When should I come over for dinner with your grandfather?"

She had almost forgotten about her grandfather's invitation. She wished it hadn't been extended, and he hadn't accepted. It was such a *serious* thing.

"You don't want me going."

Maria stared at him. A thousand thoughts raced through her mind; most of them were about running far away from him. She couldn't form the words to answer him. She nodded.

"It's okay. I'll come up with some excuse not to go. I can always say my father pulled me away for business related stuff."

"No," she said, the word barely making it past her lips. She inhaled deeply and let it out. The ability to form words came back to her. "It'll be fine. Halloween is in a few days. We always have folks over for dinner and then a party afterward," she explained. "It'll satisfy coming over for dinner." And it won't make them look like a couple or that they were serious.

"In costume?" he asked.

"Of course," she said and walked to the kitchen. "Don't even think about a couple's costume because we are not a couple." *And never going to be,* she silently added.

"I wasn't thinking about it."

"Good," Maria said, almost sagging with relief. She didn't want to have her grandfather notice and then explain to him that she and Tomas would never be a couple. Her parents as well. It would disappoint all of them, and she tried to avoid that whenever possible. She knew her grandfather wanted her to find someone, male or female, and settle down. Just like he wanted her to run the company someday. Only one of those things was going to happen. The other had about the same chance as a snowball in hell.

"Speaking of dinners, my father asked me to invite you out to dinner with him and my sister. Would you like to go? It's okay if you don't want to. They'll understand."

Maria froze. Did she really want to go to dinner with his father and sister? She had no legitimate reason to say no except for the fact that they weren't a couple or dating. Though it'd only be a one-time thing, it didn't sit right with her. At least him meeting her family would be in a group situation.

"Do I have to?"

He eyed her. "Only if you want to."

What she wanted to do was go out and kick some ass on the streets. This whole conversation about dinners with families smacked of relationship things, and she hated it. She wanted distance between them right now.

"Let me think about it."

Tomas nodded. "Take as much time as you need. What costume are you going to wear?"

"I don't know yet," she answered. She had been distracted by him and two jobs that Maria hadn't given much thought to a Halloween costume. If worst came to worst, she could wear her crime-fighting costume with some adjustments, of course. She didn't want it to be too authentic and have people think she was Balestra. Halloween was the one day of the year where she could wear her costume during the day.

He crossed the apartment to join her in the kitchen.

"What about you?"

He shrugged. "I don't know yet. Any suggestions?"

"Maybe a Roman gladiator? Or maybe Napoleon?"

"I think I'm a little too tall for Napoleon," he said, opening the fridge to pull out the leftover Chinese from earlier.

"Napoleon was actually average height for a man of his time," Maria pointed out as she pulled out two plates from a cabinet.

"I know. I was joking."

"Oh," she said. "Any particular period in history that fascinates you? You could pick a person from that period."

"It's a thought," he said. "I'll have to think about it, but I definitely want to go."

"Great." This way, he can fulfill his dinner obligation to her grandfather, but since so many people will be there, she didn't have to worry about her grandfather or her parents giving him so much one-on-one attention. She hadn't brought a person home to dinner in a few years, and she didn't want her family to get any ideas about Tomas.

"The mayor and his wife come every year along with the same crowd you saw at the charity event."

"Who's there doesn't matter too much," he said. "As long as you're there, and we can find some trouble to get into."

Maria forced a smile. "Now you're speaking my language." The part about the trouble. She ignored the part about as long as she was there. That led down roads she didn't want to travel down.

"There isn't much left in terms of leftovers," he said, peering into the opened container.

"You can have it," she said and glanced at the clock on the microwave. It was way too early to go into the office. With him here, she couldn't slip out and do her night job. Anywhere was better than here and talking about families.

"You okay?" he asked.

"Just tired," she lied. "I'm going to go grab a shower. Enjoy the leftovers." She headed for the bathroom and didn't look back.

CHAPTER NINE

MARIA COLLAPSED INTO A CHAIR IN THE CAFETERIA AND yawned. A long night with Tomas combined with an early workday took their toll on Maria. Then again, she defined anything before noon as early. Unfortunately, her grandfather noticed what time she wandered into the office every morning and always commented when she arrived late. Even when he knew of her masked night-time activities. She tried to be in the office between 8:30 and 9 regularly, and she made it for the most part.

She opened her salad as Gayle slid into the seat across from her. Gayle placed her lunchbox on the table. "Tomas keep you up too late last night?" she asked with a smile on her face and a twinkle in her eyes.

"Who says it was Tomas?"

"Then who was it?" Gayle asked.

"Tomas," Maria grumbled.

"I knew it!" Gayle grinned like the Cheshire Cat, and Maria waited for the interrogation. Nosy friends were another reason why she didn't see guys after the first time. She didn't want to answer questions.

"So what if it was him?" Maria stabbed a tomato and some lettuce harder than necessary.

"Because in the past three years, you have never slept with the same man more than twice. How many times has he been over now?"

Maria sighed and dreaded answering the question. "Three or four," she answered quietly.

Gayle's eyes widened. "You have a thing for him!" she accused. The loudness caught the attention of the other employees sitting in the cafeteria. Maria frowned.

"I do not," Maria hissed. "Keep your voice down." She needed a few drinks to go with her lunch, or better yet, a liquid lunch.

"You do, and I'll try," Gayle giggled. "I thought I'd never see the day you got serious about a guy."

Maria sighed and dropped her fork. She leaned over the table toward Gayle. "I am not serious about him. He's leaving New York soon, and once he does, I won't give him another thought."

"Uh, huh," Gayle said.

"He'll be nothing but a memory."

"You keep telling yourself that," Gayle said. "There's nothing wrong with getting serious about him. If his father's company has business here in New York, he's bound to come back. Long-distance relationships can work."

Maria rolled her eyes. Gayle would never give up hope that Maria would fall for someone. Too bad Gayle would end up being wrong about Maria and Tomas. Maria didn't trust anyone enough for a relationship, and she could live without her trust fund. "There's *everything* wrong with getting serious with him."

"No, there's not. You're too chicken to take the risk."

Maria's hands curled into fists. "Excuse me?"

"You heard me," Gayle said forcibly. "You have a thing for him, and you should see where it goes."

"I do *not* have a thing for him, and this isn't going anywhere."

Anger welled up inside of her, and she pounded a fist on the table. Metal creaked under the force and a small indent where she hit marred the surface. The room fell silent, and everyone turned and looked at her. Maria gave them all a hard look, and they turned back to their own business.

"Stop being so damn stubborn. You like Tomas, and I know it. You wouldn't have slept with him more than once. What you want and what happens aren't necessarily the same thing."

Maria sighed heavily and uncurled her fists. Gayle was right about one thing. What Maria wanted and what happened could be two different things, but damned if she let that happen regarding Tomas. This was purely a physical thing and for a limited time. There would be no more seeing Tomas or thinking about him once he returned to Brazil.

"Is he going to your grandfather's Halloween party?"

Maria looked at Gayle and considered lying for a moment, but Gayle was her best friend in the whole world, and Maria wouldn't insult her by lying. But dammit, she didn't want to answer. She knew where it would lead. "Yes. Grandfather invited him to dinner."

"Did he invite Tomas to a general dinner or specifically to the Halloween dinner and party?"

"Dinner in general," Maria answered. "I made it the dinner and Halloween party because with that many people there, Grandfather or my parents can't do any interrogations."

"So you wanted to spare him some direct grand-parental and parental attention then?"

"Yeah."

"You do have a thing for him!" Gayle exclaimed and then laughed.

For a split second, Maria hated Gayle. Only a split second, though. "My asking him to the Halloween dinner and party does not mean I have a thing for him."

Gayle laughed. "Yes, it does. You're trying to spare him some direct attention from your grandfather and your parents. That means you care about him to want to spare him being grilled."

"It means nothing," Maria insisted.

Gayle laughed more, and heads in the cafeteria turned to look at the two women. Maria gave them each another glare, and they quickly decided they had other things to pay attention to.

"I hate you," Maria grumbled.

"No, you don't. You hate that I'm right and that you care for Tomas."

Maria grumbled and picked up her fork. She stabbed some salad and then shoved it into her mouth. She couldn't dig herself deeper if she were busy chewing, and she didn't want to give Gayle any more ammunition.

"So, when is your next date?"

"They're not dates," Maria insisted. "It's just sex. That's it." A pause. "And maybe grabbing some food somewhere."

"Sound like dates to me."

Maria sighed. Gayle was relentless. "How's Charlene?" Maria asked in an attempt to change the subject.

"She's great, but you're not going to change the subject."

"Why not? There's nothing more to say about Tomas. It's not serious, I don't have a thing for him, and it's going to be over soon."

"Oh sweetie, there's so much more, but I'll cut you some slack. Charlene and I are going as the Red Queen and Alice this year. You and Tomas doing a couple's costume?"

"No, because we're not a couple, and we're never going to be one. No matter how hard you try to make it so." No matter what Maria said, Gayle would continue her campaign to make them a couple. She'd be relentless until Tomas left.

"You're so cute when you're disgruntled," Gayle teased.

"And you're a pain in my ass," Maria grumbled.

"But that's why you love me."

Maria couldn't count how many times the two of them had some variation of this conversation. If they didn't have it once in a while, Maria would think there was something wrong. "That I do, but right now, I don't like you much."

"Good thing Charlene knows how far we go back, or she'd be getting jealous."

"Did you two pick a date yet?" Maria asked. "I need to know so I can put it on my calendar."

Gayle shook her head. "Nope. We're still trying to figure out what we want and where to hold it."

"You're going to have it at our house in the Hamptons," Maria said, stabbing her salad with her fork. She wanted to go out and beat up bad guys, but she had five more hours of work.

Gayle shook her head. "We can't."

Maria shot her a stern look. "Why not?"

"I'm not going to take advantage of our friendship."

"Now who's the one being stubborn? You are going to have it at our house in the Hamptons. It will be my wedding gift for the two of you." Of course, Maria would get them an actual gift on top of providing the venue.

"Are you sure?" Gayle asked. "I don't want to impose or be a hassle."

"You're not, and Grandfather adores you. He considers you and Charlene family. He'd be thrilled to throw you a wedding." Maria had to give her grandfather credit. For a man of his generation, he never batted an eye over Gayle and Charlene's relationship. They were always invited to family dinners and occasions. To him, they were a part of the family, no matter that they loved each other romantically.

The broadest smile Maria had ever seen appeared on Gayle's face. "Thank you so much. Charlene will be thrilled."

"Glad you see it my way."

"As if you'd let me have a choice. Now you just have to see things with Tomas my way, and we'll be even."

Maria laughed. "Ain't gonna happen."

Gayle grinned. "You say that now. I think fate has other things in store for you."

Maria waved her hand. "Only fools confuse fate with destiny. Destiny is what happens to you. Fate is what you do despite destiny, and I'm determined to make my own life."

Gayle shook her head. "Oh honey, one day, you're going to be very wrong, and I want to be there to see it."

"You're going to be waiting a very long time."

"Answer me this, then I'll drop it. Why are you so opposed to entering a relationship with Tomas? He seems nice, he's hot for a guy, he's got money, and he seems like he's fun."

"It's not him. It's the idea of a relationship. I'm so not relationship material. He's leaving New York, so I'm going to have fun while he's here." What she couldn't say was that she couldn't trust someone with her heart and her secret identity outside of her family and Gayle. She also didn't want others dictating how she should live her life. Right now, she was happy with the way things were and didn't want something to upend her life or complicate it. She expected Gayle to understand, but maybe her faith in her best friend had been misplaced.

"But what if he stays?" Gayle challenged.

"It's still no," Maria insisted. "I don't want a relationship right now, and I'm not going to change to fit someone's idea of who I should be."

"I don't know what to do with you."

"Going out at night is less risky than getting into a relationship," Maria explained. She'd rather take a hundred punches and kicks than get her heart broken. It was less painful.

Gayle shook her head. "Oh my sweet summer child, you have it backward."

"If you say so."

Gayle grinned. "I do."

Maria glanced at her phone, lying on the table next to her

bowl. "I gotta get back to work. I need to get these reports to the higher-ups." She stood and gathered her belongings and trash.

"Sure, run away when talk gets serious."

"You know me."

Gayle laughed, and Maria walked out of the cafeteria with Gayle's laughter following her.

CHAPTER TEN

FOUR NIGHTS LATER, MARIA WEAVED THE MOTORCYCLE in and out of traffic, pursuing a truck through the streets of New York. She had been patrolling near the docks in Hell's Kitchen and watched four men load up the truck with what she assumed were packages of drugs. She thought about busting them while they were loading but following them was a better idea.

Earlier, she managed to get close enough to the truck to put a tracker in one of the wheel wells and a listening device on one of the doors. She wanted to hear what they were saying and make out of any names they mentioned. So far, their talk had been nothing but what they did during the day. She almost felt sorry for these guys. They seemed to be two of the most boring drug runners she had ever met in the years she had been doing this.

They entered Chelsea, and Maria followed a block behind so she wouldn't be spotted. She could follow closer, but why take the risk? Thinking of taking risks, Gayle's words from their lunchtime conversation played back in her mind. Maria didn't want a relationship, but she did like Tomas, and sometimes long-distance relationships worked. It wasn't like they couldn't afford to travel to see each other. His father had a private jet, as did her family. Plus, there were video calls to think about. No, she had to stop thinking about Tomas right now. Her life depended on her not getting distracted.

She turned the corner and opened the throttle on her bike. It lurched and sped down the street. Thankfully, the late hour meant less traffic on the roads to deal with. Maria loved high speeds on the roads at night. The adrenaline pumped through her veins, and the only way this could get better was having sex after a night of beating bad guys up. Tonight, she'd have to settle for beating up bad guys.

The truck stopped outside one of her favorite dive bars. To say she knew the place well was quite the understatement. Maria spent many nights there putting down glasses of whiskey and flirting with guys. She never took any of those men home. She slept around, but she had standards about whom she slept with.

She pulled over and killed the engine on her bike and listened to the men talking in the cab.

"Did Falcone say someone was going to be here to unload?" one voice asked.

She perked up at the name. Luca Falcone was one of the more prominent organized crime bosses in the city, yet authorities could never seem to acquire hard evidence to finally lock him up in Rikers. One day, he'd be behind bars and the streets would be a better place. At least for a little while until someone took his place. Nature abhorred a vacuum and so did crime.

"Yeah," a second voice answered. "He said that there would be a small crew here to unload the truck quickly."

"Good. You hear what happened to that Columbo crew?"

"Naw. What happened?" the second voice asked.

"All sliced up. Just like those other crews from Bonanno, Genovese, and Gambino families. Ten crews in all, I'm guessin'."

"I haven't heard anyone braggin' about it."

"I heard the boss is workin' with some outside help."

Now that was something new. One of the families sought outside help. While not common, it was definitely worth noting and finding out who was providing assistance.

"Heard it's some foreigners," the one man said.

The other man snorted. They dropped the topic of the outside help and the conversation turned to the subject of the upcoming football game on Sunday.

Apparently, it was back to boring. Six men emerged out of a door in the alley, walked up to the driver's side, and knocked on the window. The doors opened, and both men climbed out.

"Falcone send you?" the driver asked.

"Yeah," the guy answered.

"Good. Now get the truck unloaded. Quickly. I don't want to be noticed by the cops."

"Neither do we," he said and motioned to the other five guys. They walked to the back of the truck, and the driver pushed the door up. Each grabbed a box and carried it down the alley to a side door.

Time to get to work.

Maria climbed off her bike and walked toward the men and the truck. She'd have to incapacitate as many as quickly as she could. Six against one almost made it a fair fight. Even though her boots tapped on the sidewalk as she approached them, they didn't seem to notice her. One remained at the back, handing off boxes to the men that came up to the truck. They disappeared into the building one by one, each carrying a box.

Maria stopped next to the man at the back of the truck, and he turned, offering her a box. She smiled, and his eyes widened in surprise.

"Thanks." She shoved the box into the man's face, and he stumbled into the back of the truck. She delivered a quick right to his head. He collapsed to the ground with the box.

"Get her!" a man shouted, and she spun around to see four coming out of the building.

Maria drew her crossbow, aimed, and fired at one of the charging men. The dart hit him in the neck, and he put a hand up to the spot. A moment later, he fell to the ground. That left two, with another two yet to come out of the door. She dropped the crossbow and charged at the two men. She put her arms out to each side and clotheslined the two men. They were lifted off their feet and fell to the ground.

As soon as they hit the ground, they scrambled off to the side. Maria waited for them to climb to their feet. They both rose with fists swinging, and Maria quickly ducked under them. She delivered a jab to one man in his stomach, and he doubled over in pain. She followed up with an uppercut that sent him flying backward.

The second guy punched the side of Maria's face, and her head whipped to the side. That one hurt. Sure, she was more durable, but she still felt pain.

She shook off the pain and turned her attention to the guy who had just punched her.

"Now that wasn't very nice," she admonished as she grabbed her sticks. She swung. He turned at the last moment, and she ended up hitting him in the shoulder. Maria growled in frustration. The guy swung a fist, and she caught it on the left side of her chest. The breath left her in a fierce gust, and she bit back the pain. Anger spiked, and she lashed out at the guy. She swung, and the stick connected with his face. Blood gushed out of his now broken nose and all over him. He put his hands up to cover his nose, and Maria struck again. She hit his left knee, and it buckled beneath him. She brought the other eskrima stick down on the back of his head where it joined his neck. The man fell to the ground.

A blow landed on the back of her neck, and she staggered a few steps. Guy number one had climbed to his feet and hit her from behind while she was busy with number two. Maria stumbled off to the side and did a quick scan. The last thing she needed or wanted was to get hit from behind again. The remaining two men emerged from the door — time to deal with this asshole now before they reached her.

The stick swooshed through the air and connected with the guy's side, right in the kidney area. He yelled out in pain and stumbled a few steps away from her. Maria went after him, dropping the sticks and intertwined her fingers, bringing her hands down on the back of his neck. He melted to the ground in a heap.

She spun and prepared herself to deal with the other two. They pointed guns at her, planted their feet, and aimed. Maria launched herself into the air as the gunshots rang out in the night. She came down right in front of them and immediately grabbed one man's hand and knocked the gun out of it. She put her weight on her left leg and kicked out to the side with her right. Her foot hit the man's hand, and the gun clattered to the ground.

She turned her attention to the man whose arm she held. She pulled back her free arm and launched a punch at him. The other man slammed into her from behind and tackled her to the ground. She landed with him on top of her.

"You didn't even buy me dinner," she told him and put her hands between them on his chest. She heaved him, and he went flying and crashed into the side of the building. She had less than a second to regroup before a foot came stomping down toward her face. She rolled, and the boot landed, catching her ponytail. Her head yanked back. Maria scrunched her eyes against the pain. The foot lifted, and she scrambled out of the way before he could stomp on her face.

She sprang to her feet and charged toward him. She circled his waist with her arms and tackled him to the ground. He tried to fight her off, but with Maria being stronger, he had no choice but to go along with her. Maria released him and drove a fist to his head. Blood and perhaps a tooth went flying, and Maria threw another punch. He went still, and she sighed in relief. She allowed herself a few seconds to catch her breath.

A shot rang out, and the bullet whizzed past her head. She forgot about the truck's second guy and the remaining man from the six that came out. "Fuck!" she cried out and went into a forward roll. When she was out of the roll, she sprang to her feet, leaping at the two men standing at the mouth of the alley.

She put her arms out and crashed into them, taking the two of them to the ground. One grabbed her arm while she dropped an elbow on the face of the other one in a move usually seen in entertainment wrestling. That guy went still as a punch from the other one landed on the side of her face.

"Sonovabitch," she growled and pulled her arm back to deliver a punch. The man ducked at the last second and gut-punched her. She doubled over in pain. The bastard was going to pay for that. She straightened and headbutted him. Her forehead connected with the guy's nose. The crack of a breaking nose was unmistakable, and blood spurted out. Maria took a deep breath and headbutted him again. His eyes rolled back into his head, and he fell over.

She slowly climbed to her feet and looked around at the eight of them lying on the ground. She pulled out her burner cell and dialed Rollins. She gave her location and the status of the situation. He told her it would be fifteen minutes.

Apparently, it was another busy night in the city. Maria disconnected the call and tucked the cell away. Her body ached from the blows they managed to land. Tomorrow she'd be sporting some bruises. Enhanced durability meant that things that would incapacitate an average person would only bruise her. She should have been knocked out, but genetics kept her on her feet.

The world exploded in a burst of white-hot pain as something collided with the back of her head. A shadow detached from the darkness, and a foot or fist connected with Maria's jaw. She took a few steps backward and tried to shake the pain off. She managed to get a glimpse of the woman from the other night before another blow landed on her throat. She took a few more steps away from the dark figure and coughed. Breathing took effort, and she rubbed the spot on her throat while she brought her other hand up for defense.

The woman came at her again, and Maria was ready this time. She ducked the fist coming at her, and her hand shot out to connect with the woman's stomach. There was a grunt of pain, and she took a step backward. The pain in her throat died down, and breathing became more comfortable. She didn't have time to ponder the woman's connection to all of this.

Maria slipped back into a defensive stance and waited for the woman to make her next move. She moved to the left, and Maria moved with her. The last thing Maria needed was the woman to land blows on her unprotected sides. She stared at the cold, dark eyes, the only part of the woman exposed. The next attack came much quicker than Maria expected.

The blows were aimed for Maria's head, and Maria put her arms up, pressed together. The punch hit her forearms, and pain shot through them, but more importantly, the blow missed her head. Maria dropped low and sent a punch to the woman's stomach. This time, she put more strength behind the punch. She usually pulled punches since she didn't want to seriously hurt someone, or worse, kill them. She ran with angels, not demons.

The blow landed, and the woman went flying back and into the wall of the building. Maria didn't rush toward her but stayed where she stood. The dark figure slid down the wall and landed on her feet. She stood still against the wall, and Maria wondered if she had enough. Apparently not as she charged toward Maria.

A flash of light came too late for Maria to avoid the knife. The blade slid across Maria's stomach and cut through some of her costume and bit into flesh. Thankfully, it had been a shallow cut and barely broke the skin. Maria threw a right and caught the woman on the side of her face. Her head whipped around, and her body followed. Maria kicked her in the ass and sent her straight toward the wall. Her speed didn't slow, and for a moment, Maria thought she would hit the wall face first, but Maria watched her run two steps up the wall and then do a flip. She landed on her feet and then spun around. The knife flew straight toward Maria.

Maria leaned backward and watched the knife aimed at her head fly over her. She'd be dead if she hadn't moved. Anger bubbled up, and Maria growled. Now she charged toward her opponent, and the two women collided, grappling with each other. Maria's extra weight gave her the advantage, and she lifted the woman off her feet and flung her to the side. She sailed through the air and then slid along the sidewalk to a stop. She looked up at Maria, and Maria would have been dead if looks could kill.

"Is that all you got?" she half-growled to the other woman.

Silence answered her.

The woman scrambled to her feet and charged toward Maria, who patiently waited and stepped aside at the last moment. Her fist shot out and connected with the woman's shoulder. Maria heard a pop and knew her opponent now possessed a dislocated shoulder. She grabbed it with her other hand and glared at Maria.

"Kick her ass!" a male voice shouted, and Maria turned in the direction the shout came from. A group of people, probably from the bar, gathered and were watching the fight.

An audience was the last thing Maria needed. *Where in the hell were the cops?* She turned to face her opponent, only her opponent was gone. Disappeared like the shadow she seemed to be. *Dammit!*

Maria shook her head. Apparently, tonight wasn't her night. She looked around the alley for any trace of the woman. She looked up at the rooftops and saw a familiar figure looking down at her. What was he doing here?

She tore her eyes away from him and looked at the unconscious men. One or two of the bystanders tried to approach her, but she gave a look that made them remember they needed to be elsewhere. Maria grabbed one of the unconscious men not knocked out by a dart and slapped him gently on the face to wake him up.

"C'mon now. Wake up."

The man's eyes fluttered open. He looked at her, and his eyes widened.

"Good. Now that I have your attention, I want to know who Falcone is working with. Start talking."

The man shook his head.

"Who is Falcone working with?" she growled.

"I don't know," he said. "Some foreigners. We were hired to be here to move stuff. That's all I know."

"Dammit!" She pulled his hands behind his back and fastened restraints on his wrists.

It took the police, and Dorrance's company, some time to get there. Not surprisingly, Tomas's father was with the officer in charge. Their eyes met, and Maria narrowed her eyes and glared at him. He stared right back at her, and Maria didn't flinch. No way in hell she'd give him the pleasure of intimidating her. He looked away when one of his men walked up to him and started speaking.

Maria shook her head. She would know who Falcone was working with. She did not tolerate drug dealers and human traffickers.

Rollins caught her attention, and she walked up to him. He asked for her the details of what happened here, and she told him the events of her evening from start to finish. Including the fact Falcone was working with outside help.

"Is that all?" he asked.

Maria nodded. "Yes."

"Do you have any idea who the woman was?"

Maria shook her head. "I wish," she said. "I believe she's the same one who slaughtered the men in the empty store the other night."

"Why do you think that?" Rollins asked.

"Because she was wearing the same costume," Maria answered. "None of this is making sense. She slaughtered those other men, but tonight it seemed like she was trying to stop me from bagging these guys." Did that mean she was working for whomever was helping Falcone and was trying to protect the shipment?

"I'll make a note for the NYPD to keep an eye out for her. We have enough strange things going on all over the city."

"Strange? How so?" Maria asked. Her interest was piqued.

He looked around and then spoke in a low voice. "We had a few scenes like the one in the empty store," he said.

"More?" Maria asked.

Rollins nodded. "Drug dealers and traffickers slaughtered."

"In the same way? And how many?"

He looked around again to make sure they weren't being overheard. "Yeah, in the same way. Bodies and blood everywhere." He shrugged. "Four or five different crime scenes tonight alone. All pushing Boost."

It added a whole new angle, and Maria wondered how exactly it fit in. Was it the same woman performing all the killings? The critical question was, why? Granted, drug dealers and traffickers were never wanted anywhere, but who was making it a point to kill them all?

"I'll look into it and see what I can find," Maria told him.

He nodded. "You better get going before they want to question you more."

Maria gave Rollins a smile. "Thanks. Take care of yourself."

"You too," he said before she leaped up to the roof of the three-storied building.

She landed not far from where Skanda was standing.

"So what's the situation?" he asked.

She eyed him. Did he have a role to play in all of this? If so, what was it? Was he helping the woman? Maria didn't believe that. At least right now. He had been just as shocked as she had been when he first saw the bodies, and he didn't try to help the mysterious woman tonight. It was either a genuine reaction, or he was one hell of an actor. Right now, she went with the former.

"I busted up a drug deal," she told him. "That same woman from the other night showed up. I managed to dislocate her shoulder before she disappeared."

He nodded. "You seemed to have everything in hand."

"You were expecting different?" she asked.

"No."

"Uh huh," she said and rolled her eyes. Why did he always show up when he wasn't wanted? "Don't you have somewhere else to be? Go save a kitten from a tree or something."

He laughed, and she curled a hand into a fist. She managed to not hit him. She took a deep breath and uncurled her fist. All she wanted was to go home and fall into bed.

"You're quite testy tonight," he commented.

"I've been dealing with annoying people all night and still am." Maria turned her attention to the scene in the alley below. She watched Dorrance talk to a few of his men and the police officers. He must have felt the weight of her stare as he looked up a few times. Maria didn't try to hide. She wanted him to see her and know that she was watching. He climbed into a car, and the car sped away.

"What are you looking for?" he asked, standing next to her, and looking down at the scene below them.

"Answers to too many questions," she replied. "There have been brutal killings of drug dealers and traffickers all over the city. Usually, they shoot each other, but they've all been sliced and diced. Something strange is going on."

"Good," he said. "They're dead, and it doesn't matter how."

"You're an idiot," she half-growled. Maria shook her head. She was not going to get into that argument with him. It was time to go home. She walked over to the other side of the building and put her foot up on the ledge. "I do not have the time or the crayons to explain this to you."

"Where are you going?" he called after her.

"Home and away from you." Maria stepped up onto the ledge and then walked off.

She landed on the ground, not far from her bike. She glanced up at the roof to see him watching her. She turned around, walked to her bike, and climbed on. She started the engine and pulled out in a squeal of tires.

A short while later, she pulled her bike into the parking space she rented in a garage a few blocks away from her apartment. She killed the engine, her anger still running hot. She pulled out her personal cell and called Gayle.

"Hello?" Gayle's tired voice drifted through the phone.

"I need a huge favor," Maria said as she climbed off the bike.

"Do you realize what time it is?" Gayle asked, more awake and highly annoyed judging by the tone of her voice.

"I do, but this is an emergency." It wasn't the first time Maria called Gayle in the middle of the night, waking her up, and it certainly wouldn't be the last.

"Everything with you is an emergency," her best friend grumbled.

"It's a real emergency. Can you dig up any information on Luca Falcone and see if he's working with any foreign organizations?" Silence. "Gayle?"

"I'm still here. Why? What's going on?"

Maria sighed. She should have expected push back from Gayle. "I can't say right now, but I need that information. Will you get it for me?" More silence.

"Fine, I'll get on it in the morning."

"First thing."

"First thing," Gayle confirmed. "Anything else?"

"Tell Charlene hello for me," Maria said.

"I will in the morning," Gayle grumbled and disconnected the call.

Maria chuckled and thanked the heavens for her best friend. No one else would tolerate Maria.

She left the parking garage and walked over to the nearby building. She looked around for a moment and then leaped to a third-floor fire escape. She paused for a long moment and then jumped across the alley to the neighboring roof and toward home.

CHAPTER ELEVEN

AFTER A ROUGH NIGHT LAST NIGHT IN COSTUME, MARIA needed to kick back and relax. Badly. That called for whiskey and karaoke; two of her favorite things in the world after sex and monster trucks. She went out with the only two people she knew who tolerated karaoke. It wasn't everyone's cup of tea, but Gayle and Charlene liked it well enough to go with Maria. Of course, after a few rounds of drinks, they loved it as much as a sober Maria, but not nearly as much as a drunk Maria.

They met at Maria's favorite karaoke bar, *Maru*, and Maria bought the first three rounds. She put in for her turn after the first round and waited patiently to be called.

"All drinks are on me tonight," Maria told the two women. "Consider this an engagement gift."

"Thank you," they said in unison with smiles.

"My pleasure," Maria grinned. "We haven't done this in a while."

"You've been busy or too busy getting busy with a certain Brazilian," Gayle teased.

Charlene laughed. "So tell me about tall, dark, and Brazilian," she prompted.

"I don't know what Gayle told you, but this is nothing more than a fling while he's in town on business," Maria explained. "He's in town with his family, and they have business with the NYPD. We've been having mind-blowing sex on most nights."

Charlene's eyes went wide. "You've slept with him more than one time? It must be serious."

Maria sighed. "It's not. It's just sex and yes, more than once with the same guy."

"Uh, huh," Charlene said. "Sure, it is."

Gayle grinned. "That's what I keep saying."

"And you're both wrong," Maria told them.

They both laughed, and Maria glared at them before downing the rest of her drink. She signaled to the waitress for another round. There wasn't enough alcohol in New York to deal with the two women across from her.

Paul, the extremely gay and awesome karaoke guy, called Charlene's name, and the woman jumped out of her chair and ran up to the stage. The music started, and Maria recognized it as one of Charlene's favorites to sing. "Man, I Feel Like a Woman" by Shania Twain. It was a karaoke classic, and Maria had sung it quite a few times in the past. Even a few times with Charlene.

"Did you find anything on Falcone and who he may be working with?" Maria asked once the song was in full swing.

Gayle took a long drink of her margarita and then nodded. "I did."

"And that was…" Maria prompted.

Gayle shook her head. "Not here. I'll swing by your place tomorrow morning and tell you."

Maria pinned a look on her. "Are you seriously going to make me wait until tomorrow morning?"

"Hell, yes! We're going to have a good time tonight, and you can focus on work tomorrow," Gayle told her.

"Fine," Maria grumbled and may have pouted a little.

"You're cute when you pout," Gayle said. "But you're still not getting it from me until tomorrow morning."

"I said fine."

"Drink more," Gayle ordered. "You'll be happier."

Maria laughed and saluted. "Yes, ma'am." She looked at her empty glass. "Unfortunately, I am out of alcohol right now."

"You know, I love this place, but the service can be slow."

"Yes," Maria agreed. "But it does have the best selection of songs for karaoke."

"That it does," Gayle said as the waitress arrived with another round of drinks.

Maria, Gayle, and Charlene came here frequently enough to know the staff, and the staff knew what they drank. All they had to do was signal they needed another round, and it was brought to them. It saved everyone effort and time. Maria also tipped very well.

"Thank you," Maria said as she accepted her drink. "Can you bring another round? This one will be gone in no time." Maria grinned at the waitress, and she smiled.

"Of course," she said and left.

"It'll take her ten minutes to come back," Gayle commented as the woman left.

"Yeah, that's why I ordered it now," Maria said.

"Good thinking," Gayle said.

They turned to watch Charlene finish the song and cheered loudly when she was done. Charlene returned to the table, kissed Gayle deeply, then sat down. Maria raised her glass in a salute and then drank some of the whiskey.

Paul called Maria's name, and she sprang to her feet. She bounded up to the stage and waited for the music to start. Every time she did karaoke, her first song of the night was Bonnie Tyler's "Holding Out for a Hero."

Maria got into the song and belted it out as always. Holding back never crossed her mind. Like everything she did, she gave it her all. The tiredness and soreness from last night washed away under the effects of the alcohol and the music. They were Maria's go-to cures for anything wrong. The song finished, and Maria bowed to the audience.

She skipped over to the table and fell into her chair.

"Now, there's a surprise that you sang that song," Charlene teased.

"Have to keep the traditions," Maria grinned.

"Of course," Gayle said. "I should be up after this guy."

Maria turned to look at the guy now singing. Bon Jovi's "Living on a Prayer" was a karaoke favorite of a million white guys, this one being no exception. Maria didn't judge. There was no judging in karaoke like there was no crying in superheroing or baseball. Sure, some people murdered songs, and some sounded like a dying cat, but if everyone had fun, Maria didn't care.

"So when am I going to meet Tomas?" Charlene asked.

Maria shrugged. "Never. Is that good for you?" Maria teased. "We don't exactly go out in public."

"Too busy getting busy," Gayle teased.

Maria shrugged. Going out in public with him meant the paparazzi, and she didn't need their picture plastered on a front page. She looked at Charlene. "Probably at the Halloween party." She pulled her phone out and checked for new texts. None. She placed it on the table. "I'll be right back." She stood and headed for the bathroom.

As usual, there was a line. There was always a line. It was a constant in bars all over the city, all over the country. Deciding not to wait, Maria walked into the men's room, nodded to the men at the urinals, and slipped into a stall. She did her business and left the stall. She washed her hands and headed back to the table, sliding into her seat. Gayle and Charlene were both grinning at her, and Maria eyed them. They both looked like a cat who caught a pigeon.

"What's going on?" she asked.

"Nothing at all," Gayle said. "We were just talking about Tomas."

Maria's eyes narrowed. "What about him?"

"Nothing," Charlene said.

"Uh-huh. You two are up to something, and I'm afraid to ask." Maria would have pressed them for an answer, but Paul called her name, and she left for the stage.

This song was "I Will Survive" by Gloria Gaynor, another go-to karaoke song for her. She had a list of about ten that she picked from regularly, and a few more she sang when the mood struck her. She left the stage after she was done and headed for the bar. It'd be easier and quicker to get their drinks instead of waiting for the waitress.

The place was crowded as usual on a Saturday night, but Maria always managed to get a table. She arrived here when the bar opened at five and started drinking hours before the karaoke started.

She returned to the table and set the glasses down. She fell into her chair. All the alcohol was catching up to her. Even with her abilities, the room started to spin a little. Maybe she should slow down and give her liver a chance to metabolize the alcohol. Who was she kidding? She never slowed down. At least until she could barely stand on her own.

The three women didn't talk as they watched the next few people go up and sing. Maria's name was called again, and there were cheers as she made her way to the stage. Movement in the front of the house caught her attention, and she saw Tomas enter. So that's what Charlie and Gayle were up to. They had used her phone to contact Tomas while she used the bathroom. Devious. That's what she got for leaving her phone where the two women had access to it.

A KARAOKE BAR WASN'T PRECISELY WHAT TOMAS expected, but for some reason, it seemed fitting. Maria was a mercurial woman and possessed tastes and interests the people of her social status didn't have. Or they did and didn't admit it. Maria held no such qualms about revealing what she liked. The text saying to meet him here came as a pleasant surprise. He gave his father and sister an excuse, which he knew they didn't believe and left the hotel to come over. He only hoped Carolyn didn't decide to pry and follow him here.

He stepped through the door and into the crowded bar. His eyes were instantly drawn to the stage where Maria was singing. His heart rate quickened, and the temperature in the room went up a few degrees. She finished the song, and their eyes met. He cheered the loudest of anyone in the bar, and she looked at him. Pink colored her cheeks. Was she flushed from singing or embarrassment? It had to be singing. Maria didn't seem the type to get embarrassed.

He smiled, and so did she. He missed that smile in the past few days. Her face softened, and she seemed almost glad to see him. She looked away, and he did a quick scan of the room. He spotted Gayle and another woman at a table, and he made his way toward them. Maria approached the table from the stage.

"Hi," she said with a broad smile.

"Hi."

"I'm not surprised to see you here," she said, giving Gayle and the other woman a stern look. The two women grinned.

Tomas noticed the exchange and Maria's phone lying on the table. He pieced together what must have happened. One of the women, if not both, was the one who texted him to meet Maria here. He fell for it, but he wasn't sorry. He had been hoping to do something out in public with her.

"Well, you did text and say to meet you here," he said, playing along with the game the two women seated at the table were playing.

"I didn't text you, but I'm glad you're here," she said.

"I almost believe that you meant what you said," he teased.

She grabbed his shirt and pulled him to her, capturing his lips in a deep kiss. Next to her, the two women cheered. The kiss caught him off guard, but he wasn't going to let the opportunity to pass. He wrapped his arms around her and crushed her against his body. He deepened the kiss and let it go on longer than what was appropriate in public.

"I believe you," he said.

"Tomas, you've met Gayle. This is Charlene," Maria said, gesturing to the other woman. "Charlene, this is Tomas Dorrance."

"Nice to finally meet you," Charlene said with a grin and offered a hand.

"Nice to meet you," Tomas said and took the offered hand, giving it a shake.

He didn't have to ask how Charlene fit into their group. He could clearly see that she and Gayle were a couple. They wore matching diamond and sapphire rings and sat close to each other. They made a cute couple, and he wished them all the best.

"Please, sit," Maria said and offered him the empty chair next to her. She fell into her own and signaled for the waitress.

He took the offered chair and looked at the drinks on the table. Margaritas for Gayle and Charlene. Whiskey for Maria. Not surprising in the least. "So, karaoke?" he asked Maria.

Maria grinned. "Yup. One of my favorite things in the world right after Monster Truck rallies."

"And sex," Gayle added.

"He's well aware of that one," Maria said.

Tomas chuckled. "Yes."

Charlene and Gayle laughed, and Maria shook her head. They amused Tomas to no end.

"Do you sing?" Maria asked him, hoping he'd say yes.

"Yes, but not very well," he answered.

"Good. You're going to sing with me," Maria said and sprang to her feet. His eyes followed her as she expertly navigated the crowd to reach the man running the karaoke. From there, she made her way over to the bar. She returned to the table with drinks in her hand a few minutes later.

"Thank you," he said, accepting the offered drink. He loved the way her eyes sparkled. He didn't even care that it was because of the alcohol and not because of him.

"You're welcome." She lifted her glass in a salute and took a drink. He echoed her motions and took a sip.

"So Tomas, how long are you going to be in New York?" Charlene asked.

"Not long," he answered. He glanced at Maria. He'd stay longer if she asked, but he knew she would never ask. She insisted this was a temporary thing, and he believed her. "Another week or two at most."

Maria frowned for an instant, then quickly straightened her face. She looked away from him. Tomas somehow restrained himself from smiling when Maria frowned. Maybe she was changing her mind toward whatever it was they had. He wouldn't complain in the least bit.

"Maria," Tomas said and touched her arm.

She practically jumped. "What?"

"They called your name," he said, nodding toward the stage.

"Oh! C'mon then," she said, springing to her feet. She grabbed his hand and tugged. He stood, and she pulled him along with her. They stepped up onto the stage.

"What are we singing?" he asked.

"Johnny and June's 'Jackson,'" she answered as the music started.

"Thankfully, I know that one," he said.

They sang the song, each of them singing their respective parts. Gayle and Charlene yelled the loudest when they finished, and Maria's face was bright red. He pulled her in and gave her a deep kiss. The kiss ended, and they left the stage. Her face was redder than it had been before the kiss.

"You two are great together," Gayle announced when they reached the table. Maria laughed as she took her chair.

"I think so," Tomas said as he sat in his chair. He reached out and took Maria's hand, giving it an affectionate squeeze. She didn't pull away, and it pleased him. "What do you think?" he asked Maria.

"Not bad," she said and pulled her hand out of his.

Tomas wanted to laugh but didn't. Little by little, he tore down the walls around her. He wondered how long it would take him to get past them. All walls crumbled at some point, and he was willing to put in the time and energy.

"Up for another?" Maria asked him.

Tomas nodded. "Sure. Just make it something I have a good chance at knowing," he said.

"I'll try," she said with an impish smile. She stood and went over to the man running the show. Somehow, Tomas knew it wouldn't be a song he knew, and she'd pick it just to trip him up.

"So, what's up with you and Maria?" Gayle asked.

Tomas shrugged and eyed the redhead. "What has she told you?"

"That it's just sex, and it ends when you leave," Gayle answered. "Is all that correct?"

Tomas knew the two were good friends, Maria frequently mentioned Gayle, and he knew the woman was looking out for Maria. "More or less," he said.

"What's more?" Charlene asked with a smirk.

Tomas gave her a half-smile. "Well, I'd like it to be more," he admitted. "If given a chance." Which would not come, based on Maria being quite adamant that this wasn't a serious thing.

"Good to know," Gayle said.

"If Maria wants it, of course," he said. "I wouldn't put any undue pressure on her. No one should."

Gayle put her hands up. "I wouldn't dream of it. I only want what's best for her."

"I believe you," he said.

Maria returned to the table and looked at him and at the two women. "What's going on? What are you telling him?" she asked Gayle.

"We were just chatting," she answered. "About you, but all good things. I swear."

"We were discussing your love of Monster Trucks and karaoke," Tomas said. A little lie wouldn't hurt. He didn't want Maria thinking that he and her best friends were ganging up on her. Tomas would always take Maria's side in any friendly arguments between her and the two women.

Maria looked at Gayle and then at Tomas. He offered her a smile. "I don't believe anyone sitting at this table, but I'll let it slide for now."

Gayle laughed and signaled the waitress for another round of drinks.

"What song did you pick?" Tomas asked.

"You'll see." Light danced in her eyes, and Tomas had come to learn that was her mischievous look. Whatever she picked, it would be a challenge for him. As long as it wasn't something by a boy band. That was all he asked.

"You're in for it," Gayle warned.

"Yeah, I kind of figured." He drank some of his whiskey, knowing he'd need the liquid courage.

"But right now it's my turn," Charlene said, rising from her chair. The trio at the table watched her weave her way to the stage. Charlene smiled at them and started her song.

They whooped and hollered when the song was over, and Charlene's cheeks turned a shade of deep red. Tomas turned and watched Maria. He enjoyed seeing Maria out with her friends; it was refreshing to see a different side of her. She was at ease, and smiles and laughs came easy. He had seen work Maria, sexy Maria, and now easygoing Maria. He wondered how many more sides she had to her. Whatever the number, he wanted to see them all.

She looked at him, and their eyes met. Her lush lips parted as if she were about to say something, then closed. Memories of what she could do with that mouth came to mind, and his temperature rose.

Her mouth stretched into a smile, and he smiled in return. Her blue eyes sparkled, and a light shade of pink touched her cheeks. Her black hair was pulled back into a ponytail at the nape of her neck, but a few strands flew in every direction. Right now, she looked more beautiful to him than she did the night of the charity party when he first met her. She didn't need all the trappings of high society to stand out. If he had to admit it, she looked more comfortable here than she did at that fancy party. She looked away first, and he turned his attention back to the stage. He didn't want her to creep her out by staring.

"We're up," Maria said, jumping to her feet and grabbing his hand. Tomas barely had his feet under him when she pulled him toward the stage. He still didn't know what they were going to sing.

They reached the stage, and he looked at the monitor. Well, at least he knew this one. The song started, and he sang his parts. She sang hers. Before long, they were looking at each other, their eyes locked, and not the monitors. He knew the song well enough. He didn't need to see the lyrics. All he saw was Maria and her shining eyes. The crowded bar and all the people in it faded away, and just the two of them existed.

In what seemed like the blink of an eye, the song was over, and the presence of the other people came rushing back as they cheered. Tomas returned the mic to the stand and offered a hand to Maria. She set down her mic and placed her hand in his. It was warmer than his, and he closed his hand around it, soaking up the warmth.

He led her to the table and pulled out her chair for her. She gave him a quick kiss and sat down, Tomas sat in his chair, his hand still holding hers. She didn't pull hers away, and he placed their hands on the table. He looked over and noticed Gayle looking at their hands. She looked up and directly at him, winking. Gayle turned her attention to Maria. He smiled and turned his attention to the people at the table.

The night moved quickly under the influence of a good time. Maria and Tomas did another duet, and Tomas even did two on his own. Gayle and Charlene did a duet as well as individual songs. Maria did a few more solos. Before they knew it, last call came, and they had a last round. Maria slapped her credit card on the table, and Tomas snatched it up and replaced it with his. The look she gave him could have melted steel, but he smiled and handed the card to the waitress. He offered her card to her, and she grabbed it out of his hand and tucked it in a back pocket.

Tomas stood and stretched a little. The two women stood and slipped on coats while Tomas grabbed Maria's off the back of her chair and held it up for her. She eyed him for a long moment and slipped her arms in. He settled it on her shoulders, then pulled his own on.

"I had a good time tonight. Thank you, ladies," he said with a nod to them.

"You're welcome!" Gayle beamed. "We did too! You should come out with us again."

"Definitely," Charlene added.

"I'd like that," he said.

"I'm sure we can do it again before Tomas leaves," Maria said.

He nodded and tried to push thoughts of leaving New York to the back of his mind. He found it interesting how Maria kept bringing the subject up at every opportunity. "Anytime you want." He waited for Maria, Gayle, and Charlene to go, and he followed them to the door.

The refreshing cold night air woke him a little and helped clear his head from the alcohol. He slipped an arm around Maria's waist, and surprisingly, she leaned into him, not pulling away like he thought she would. Gayle noticed and gave him a small, knowing smile.

"Goodnight," Charlene said, her arm around Gayle's waist. Gayle had her arm around Charlene's waist.

"Goodnight," Tomas and Maria said at the same time.

Gayle flagged down a cab, and the two women climbed in. They watched it pull away, taillights blending in with the rest of the traffic.

"Goodnight," Maria said, slipping out of his arm and turning toward him. "I had fun, and I'm glad you came."

He wasn't going to say goodnight. Not quite yet. "I had fun too, and I'm glad I came. Even though it wasn't you who texted and sent the invite."

Maria sighed. "Yeah. I should've known better than to leave my phone where those two can get to it."

"I have no complaints that they did it."

A slow smile stretched her mouth. "I don't either."

Tomas leaned in and gave her a soft kiss. He didn't want the evening to end, but he knew it had to. Or did it? The kiss ended, and he dropped a kiss on her forehead. "Come back to my hotel with me," he urged.

She looked up at him. He could see her weighing her options. "Okay," she said.

Tomas smiled, and this time, the kiss was fierce and demanding. He pulled her back against his side and hailed a cab.

CHAPTER TWELVE

MARIA LOOKED AT HER WATCH AND FROWNED. ROLLINS was late. As usual. He requested the meeting, and she would oblige, but he could at least have the decency to be on time. She had things to do tonight and, more importantly, someone to do. Tomas invited her over to his hotel again tonight, and she eagerly accepted. Rollins wanting to talk hadn't been on her evening plans, but if he had any information on the import and distribution of Boost, she wanted to hear it.

She looked at her watch again. Another minute passed, and her annoyance grew with each passing minute. She could be getting friendly with a hot Brazilian instead of standing on a rooftop in costume. She'd be sure to let Rollins be on the receiving end of her annoyance. Footsteps behind her caught her attention, and she spun around.

"It's about time," she grumbled.

"I'm only eight minutes late," Rollins said.

"Eight minutes and no message saying you were going to be late," she chided.

"I'm sorry. I'll text next time."

"Thank you," she said. "Now, what do you have for me?"

"Straight down to business, as usual. How about a change of pace and ask me how I'm doing or how my night's going?"

"Normally, I would entertain your sense of humor, but I have things to do tonight." She smiled at the thought of a naked Tomas, and she wanted this to be over as soon as possible. She usually enjoyed Rollins's sense of humor, surprised that a cop had one, but not tonight. Especially since he arrived eight minutes late.

"Sorry to keep you from whatever you need to do, but we found a few more dead drug dealers," he said.

"Where and when?"

"Various locations around the city, all in the past few days."

""Similar to the others?"

Rollins nodded. "Yeah. All slaughtered and blood everywhere."

A string of profanities fell from her mouth in English and in a few other languages. Why swear in one language when multiple would do? "Any leads?"

Rollins shook his head. "No. Do you have any?"

"No, unfortunately," she said. "No leads or ideas outside of Falcone, or the Lucchese family in general, trying to consolidate control over the sale and distribution of drugs in the city, particularly Boost. I haven't seen any signs of the woman either." Of course, she hadn't been on patrol last night, and tonight would be an early night.

"We've noticed an increase in the usage of Boost," he said. "Thankfully, the powered set isn't too interested in it. Yet. Though it's a matter of time."

Maria nodded. "That's the only saving grace. If the powered set gets their hands on it, things are going to get worse."

"You don't need to tell me," Rollins said.

"You get anything out of the goons about who Falcone's working with?"

"No. Not a word. What about your friend? Do you think he's involved?"

For a second, she thought he meant Tomas since he was the

dominant thought going through her brain at the moment, but then realized he meant Skanda. "He's not involved. He seems focused on stopping the drugs and the human trafficking."

"Are you sure?"

"Yes. I found that scene before he even arrived, and the person responsible was still there. I'm sure he can change out of costume quickly, but he can't change from a woman into a man that quickly." She couldn't rule out the possibility Skanda was a shapeshifter, but she doubted he was.

"What's his name?" Rollins asked. "Why didn't you tell me about him?"

"I had my reasons," she replied. Despite her personal feelings about Skanda, she wouldn't throw him under the bus unless vital. It wasn't right now. "He goes by Skanda."

"Do you know where he's from?"

Maria shook her head. "No. And before you ask, I don't know his real identity. We don't go pulling our masks off for each other. It's not show and tell."

"I wasn't going to ask."

Maria chuckled. "Yes, you were."

"You don't know me as well as you think," he said.

"I know you well enough."

There were roughly 36,000 cops in New York City she could work with, but she liked Rollins. She liked his no-nonsense approach to the job and possessed an open mind.

He laughed. "You only think you do. Got anything else for me?"

"Not really. Do you have anything else for me?" she asked.

"No."

"You could've texted me this information," she said, irritation lacing her words.

"And miss seeing your beautiful face?" He smiled and the dimples in his cheeks stood out. Maria thought him cute in a big brother kind of way.

"Are you developing a crush?" she asked.

"No."

"Liar," she accused. "Oh, Detective, you couldn't handle me on a good day."

"I wouldn't mind finding out," he said.

Rollins was sweet, and he was easy on the eyes, but so not Maria's type. A costume dating a cop would never in a work out. Not to mention, he was a good man. Good men weren't her type. Her type was Bad-For-Her men, and she attracted them without any problems. She wondered how Tomas would be bad for her. They always were in the end.

"Go find a nice office assistant or a barista. I know a few I could set you up with."

Rollins laughed. "They'd never compare to you."

"I'm not the type you bring home to meet the family over dinner. But you're cute. I'll give you that."

Rollins grinned. "It's a start."

Maria shook her head. "Anything else?"

"No. Thanks, Balestra."

"You're welcome. Text me when you learn anything new."

He nodded. "I will. You do the same."

"I will. Take care of yourself, Detective."

"You too."

Maria flashed him a smile and ran to the edge of the roof and leaped off.

"Showoff!" he yelled, and she laughed.

Maria dropped down to the street and climbed on her bike as Rollins's words chased circles in her mind. Falcone appeared to be killing off the other major players in the New York drug trade. To her, it made complete sense. If the Lucchese family was vying for control, killing off rivals would be the best and probably most straightforward way to gain power. The strange part is that the others had no idea Falcone and Lucchese were behind this. If they did, there would be much more violence between the families.

It begged the question of who was this third party who could take out the others in a relatively short time. She slipped on her helmet and started her bike. The tires squealed against the pavement as she pulled out.

CHAPTER THIRTEEN

MARIA OPENED THE DOOR TO THE RESTAURANT AND held it for Tomas. She smirked as he walked through the door. It had become a sort of a game to see who reached the door first and held it open for the other. Most of the time, he won, but Maria wasn't above cheating like tonight. She walked ahead while he was paying the cab fare.

She followed in after him, and they reached the maître d' stand. Tomas gave his name and asked if his father had arrived. The man said yes and offered to lead them to the table. BLT Steak was one of Maria's favorites, and the maître d' recognized her. She smiled and followed him with Tomas bringing up the rear.

The table he led them to was toward the back and sectioned away from the rest of the dining area. Interesting that they had to be placed away from the other patrons. Maria's grandfather did the same thing on occasion, but most of the time, they sat at whatever table they were shown.

Tomas's father and sister were seated at a table. Devon Cargill sat with them. Cargill was the last person she expected to see here and the last person she wanted to see.

"Hello," Tomas's father said, rising from his chair. "It's good to see you again, my dear." He pulled a chair out next to him for Maria.

"Hello, Maria," Cargill said, also rising from his chair.

"It's nice to see you again," she said to the elder Dorrance. Antonio kissed her cheek, and she kissed his cheek. She took the offered chair. "Devon. Ms. Dorrance," Maria said with a nod to each of them.

"Ms. Grayson," Carolyn said, returning the nod.

Tomas's father was in a suit, probably Armani judging by the look, and Carolyn wore a black dress with a small black jacket. Tomas was in a suit with a purple tie. She didn't comment about it, but she found it amusing that it was the same color as the purple in her costume. She would have never guessed him the type to wear a purple tie.

"No need for such formalities," Tomas said, taking the chair in between Maria's and his sister's.

"Tomas is correct. There is no need for formalities. This is a casual dinner," his father said. "I didn't realize you knew Devon."

"Maria and I have known each other for quite some time."

"Since kindergarten I believe," she said. She flashed him a smile, and he twitched. Daddy posted bail as Maria expected, and there had been very little media coverage of the arrest and allegations. It had to be daddy's influence again. Whoever did the makeup to cover the bruises on his face did an amazing job.

She promised herself she'd be on her best behavior tonight and make sure her brain to mouth filters were working. Cargill sitting with them wouldn't make it easier. She didn't know how easily offended Tomas's family could be, and she didn't want to find out. Tonight was for Tomas's benefit and even a little for her grandfather's. He tried to connect with influential, powerful people, and Maria didn't want to ruin his chances of making connections with Tomas's family.

She even dressed a little conservatively, for her, tonight. She wore a simple sapphire blue dress that reached mid-thigh, a sensible pair of matching shoes, and simple jewelry. She didn't even have much cleavage showing.

"How are you finding your stay in New York?" Maria asked. "I hope it's going well for you."

"It's been enlightening," his father replied.

Maria knew a diplomatic answer when she heard one. She wondered what he had to be diplomatic about. "In what way?"

"I've been going out with the police when they respond to calls, and I ran across some costumed individuals," he said.

"Oh?" Maria asked. "Did you run into any problems?"

"They have no place interfering in police business," Antonio said. His distaste for costumed individuals was clear in his voice. She wondered what his reaction would be if he discovered she was one of those costumed individuals he ran across at crime scenes. Most likely, Tomas would be forbidden from seeing her.

"I've heard Balestra has been busting quite a few drug dealers lately." Devon twitched again, and it amused Maria to no end. She would make tonight as uncomfortable as she could for him. "Are they really interfering when they're the ones apprehending criminals busting up in progress crimes?" Maria asked. An answer didn't come right away. A waiter arrived, introduced himself, and asked for their beverage orders. Maria had been tempted to order a whiskey, but then she remembered she had to be on her best behavior. Not to mention, she usually reserved whiskey for dive bars, karaoke, and drowning her problems. Wine would be her drink of choice tonight.

"If I may order the wine?" Antonio asked.

"Of course," Maria replied with a nod.

"Father is a wine snob," Tomas said, leaning over and whispering in her ear while his father ordered. The warm breath brushing over her ear sent a shiver down her spine, and she smiled. Memories of his mouth on her body rose to the surface, and a flush of heat washed through her.

Her eyes met Cargill's, and his eyes narrowed. Maria wanted to laugh. Cargill had been after her for some time now, and she'd never give him the time of day. The only thing she wanted was to see the man behind bars. Hopefully, the current charges would stick and there would be some time served.

"It's okay," she assured him.

Wine order in, the waiter handed them each a menu. The next few minutes passed quietly as the four of them focused on the menus. Maria was going to play it safe with filet mignon. She loved a wide variety of foods, but steak was her second favorite. She'd pick a good burger over anything else. Unfortunately, burgers were way beneath places like this, so steak it was.

"You haven't answered Maria's question, Father," Carolyn said, giving Maria a direct look. Maria met the look without flinching or blinking.

"Perhaps we should find something else to discuss," Tomas suggested.

"That may be best," his father said. "Tomas has mentioned that you have visited our country a few times. How did you find it?"

Maria wanted to hear the answer to her question, but she could let it go. No sense in ruffling feathers that didn't need ruffling. "Vibrant. Exciting. Even a little exotic. I particularly loved the food. I wish I had more time to explore, but work comes first."

Tomas smiled. "That accurately describes my country."

"Have you visited Brazil?" Antonio asked Cargill.

"A few times," he replied. "For Carnival."

"Did you attend university?" Antonio asked Maria.

"I have my MBA from NYU," she said. "My mother instilled a love of learning in me. She's a high school teacher."

"What subject?" Tomas asked.

"English and literature," Maria answered. "Apparently, she wanted to name me Desdemona, but my father wouldn't have it. So, Maria, it is."

"What does your father do?" his father asked.

"He works for the family business. He's been in London for the past few weeks. He's expected home soon."

"Hopefully, I'll get to meet him before I leave," Tomas said. "I'd love to meet your mother as well."

Maria turned and looked at Tomas. Him meeting her parents. She hadn't thought about it before, but she didn't object too strongly to the idea anymore. She knew her parents would like Tomas. She didn't want them thinking that Maria and Tomas were a couple or serious. Which they would. She knew her parents.

"You will," she said. "They'll be at the Halloween party."

"What is this?" his father asked.

"My grandfather holds a Halloween party every year," Maria said. "Basically, the group at the charity event will be there. You and Carolyn are more than welcome to join us. It's always a great time."

"I can confirm that," Cargill said.

His father lifted a brow and looked straight at Maria. She didn't flinch under the intense gaze. "Are Halloween costumes required?" he asked.

"Required, no. Encouraged, yes."

"I see," he said. Maria would bet money the elder Dorrance wouldn't wear a costume.

"Are you going to go?" Tomas asked.

"Perhaps," his father said.

Tomas looked at his sister. "And you?"

"Probably not," she answered, lifting her glass of wine to her lips.

"Halloween parties aren't everyone's cup of tea," Maria said. Maria studied Carolyn. When the woman brought the wineglass up to her lips, obscuring the lower half of her face and leaving her eyes clear, a slight chill ran down Maria's spine.

Could she be the woman who had slaughtered drug dealers around the city and fought Maria? It wasn't out of the realm of possibility, but it begged the question to what end? Why would

Tomas's sister be slaughtering drug dealers, and how did his father fit in? Was Tomas involved? Skanda happened to show up at the most inopportune times. But on the other hand, he never did anything to stop Maria from busting up the drug deals. No. It was crazy to go down that path of thinking. Tomas wasn't Skanda. Not in a million years, and Carolyn certainly wasn't slaughtering drug dealers.

"Certainly not mine," Carolyn said.

"Tomas said you were going to show him around New York. What sights have you seen?" his father asked.

"Maria has taken me to some great restaurants," Tomas said.

"Is that all?" Carolyn asked.

Maria could hear the disapproval in her voice and didn't give a shit what Carolyn thought. Answering Carolyn with the truth that Maria and Tomas had spent most of their time together screwing like bunnies lingered on the tip of her tongue.

"I've been busy and had very little time to do some sightseeing." Tomas countered.

Getting busy would be more like it, and Maria smirked a little. She didn't mind not doing tourist stuff with Tomas. What they did was much more fun.

"Excuse me a moment," she said and stood. Maria headed to the restroom. Thankfully, it was empty, and she had some relative privacy. She put her hands on both sides of the sink and bowed her head. Her mind raced with possibilities.

Maria grabbed a paper towel and wet it, then pressed it to her neck. The coolness sent a shiver across her skin, but it helped her relax and bring her heart rate back down to normal. She just had to get through this dinner. Hopefully, it would be the only one with Tomas's family. She took a deep breath.

The door opened, and she looked in the mirror. Carolyn.

"Are you okay?" she asked.

"Yes," Maria answered and forced a smile. "I'm fine. Just need a moment. It's been a long day for me."

Carolyn nodded. "I understand. May I ask, what's going on between you and Tomas?"

There it was—the real reason for her checking on Maria. Maria chalked it up to sisterly concern for her brother.

"Nothing serious, if that's what you're concerned about. We're enjoying each other's company." Maria sized the other woman up. She was the right height and build to be the costumed woman, but Maria didn't want to accept it. It could possibly mean that Tomas was involved, and she didn't believe that for a moment.

"I was just curious," she said. "I've never seen my brother so taken with someone before."

Maria blinked. Certainly, she didn't hear that right. "Oh. We're seeing each other while he's here. When he leaves for Brazil, it's over."

Carolyn nodded. "I'm glad he's happy while he's here."

Maria blinked again, totally not expecting that sentiment from Carolyn. "I'm happy he's happy." She was. She enjoyed the time spent with Tomas, but couldn't be allowed to turn into something serious.

"If I may ask, is there something going on with you and Devon?" Maria asked.

The other woman eyed her for a moment, her dark eyes narrowing a bit. She shook her head. "No."

"I see."

Carolyn tilted her head. "Why do you ask?"

"He has a fondness for drugging and raping women," Maria said. Anger rose inside of her, and Maria pushed it down. "He was arrested for it once, but his father got him cleared of the charges. Balestra stopped him from raping another one. Twice now. She gave him a good beating each time. He's out on bail now for it, but I'm sure his father will get him cleared on the charges. Again."

Carolyn's eyes widened for a moment as Maria's words registered. "Really?"

"Yeah," Maria said. "Just be careful around him and avoid situations where you're alone with him."

"Thanks for the warning. I'll make sure to never drink anything he offers and avoid being alone with him."

Maria nodded. "Good. Women need to look out for each other."

"We do."

"I'm going to head back to the table," Maria said. Carolyn gave her the briefest of smiles, and Maria left the restroom.

Tomas stood and pulled her chair out for her when she returned. She smiled her thanks and took the offered chair. He pushed it in as she sat. He sat in his chair and put a hand on her thigh.

"Everything okay?"

"Yes, thanks," she said. "Just had to use the facilities." She forced a smile and then glanced over at Carolyn taking her chair. The woman looked at her, and for a long moment, the two women eyed each other. Maria smiled and then looked away. She looked at Devon and narrowed her eyes. Even though she didn't know Carolyn well, Maria didn't want anything to happen to her. She wanted to see Devon behind bars where he should be. She'd mention it to Tomas later, so Carolyn would have another person looking out for her around Cargill.

Maria planned to reward herself for getting through this dinner with a bottle of her favorite whiskey and her current boy toy. She placed a hand on Tomas's and gave it an affectionate squeeze. She looked at Tomas, and their eyes met. She smiled and focused on the after-dinner activities.

CHAPTER FOURTEEN

MARIA ROLLED TO TOMAS'S SIDE AND THEN STRETCHED out next to him. She put her head on his chest and draped a leg over his. He pulled back and looked at her for a moment before putting his arm around her. He held her against his body. Maria smiled and kissed his chest. She sighed contently, and he placed his other arm over her hip, his hand on her back. He caressed her back, his hand making small, slow circles. She shuddered as a shiver raced along her spine.

This wasn't a wrong way to end an evening that included dinner with his family. She blocked out the thoughts that plagued her during dinner. Such thoughts could wait until tomorrow.

"Cold?" he asked, breaking the shroud of silence.

"No," she answered. She soaked up the heat he generated. His tender touch comforted her, and she didn't reject it. She pressed her ear to his chest and listened to the strong thudding of his heart. Time slowed, and she could only hear his heartbeat and their breathing. Maybe this is what people meant by a perfect moment. It was just the two of them, and her mind was impossibly still, not racing or overthinking the situation.

She could stay in this moment forever. More importantly, she wanted to stay in this moment.

"Are you okay?" he asked in a soft voice.

"I'm good," she answered. The adrenaline from the sex drained out of her, and exhaustion flooded in behind it. She yawned and knew she should get up and use the bathroom, but she was reluctant to leave the warmth of his embrace. "Perfect even."

"Is that so?" he asked.

"It is," she said. She lifted her head and dropped a kiss on his mouth. "There's no place I'd rather be right now." She placed her head back on his chest.

He squeezed her against his body with his arm. Maria closed her eyes and smiled. Nothing beat the feeling of the safety and the warmth he provided. Maybe there was something to this cuddling thing. Danger lurked, but she shoved the thought to the back of her mind. She knew whatever this was with Tomas wouldn't last. She'd enjoy it while she could.

He kissed the top of her head, and she smiled in response. His hand rested on her ass, and occasionally he squeezed it. "Are you sure you're okay?"

Maria lifted her head and looked at him. "Yes, I'm sure." She tilted her head. "Why do you ask?"

"We're doing what could only be called cuddling, and you seem to be okay with it," he said. "According to you, you don't do this."

"I can move if you want me to," she said.

Tomas responded by holding her closer to his body. He put his other arm around her and gave her a deep kiss.

Maria laughed when the kiss ended. "I'll take that as a no."

"As you should," he said. "I thought that cuddling wasn't in your vocabulary."

"It wasn't, but I reserve the right to expand my vocabulary." She smiled.

"Have you added any other words to your vocabulary?" he asked.

"Nope," she answered. She prayed that he wouldn't bring up other words she didn't dare to say. She wasn't sure where she currently stood on those issues, and she didn't want to declare it. She liked him, she didn't doubt that fact, but she didn't know where things were going, if they were going anywhere. She had already broken a few of her steadfast rules.

"I guess one is progress," he said. "I'll take it because I'll admit that I like lying here with you pressed up against me."

"I like it too," she carefully said. She could admit it now, but the problem was she wanted more of it. He was a drug she couldn't get enough of. Each time they said goodbye, she looked forward to when she could get her next fix. No one had ever affected her like he did.

"Yeah? What else do you like?"

"You," she answered.

"What do you like about me?" he asked.

"All the very naughty things you do to me." She grinned and gave him a quick kiss.

"You mean like this?" he asked and tickled her side. Maria squealed and squirmed against the tickling. He continued to tickle her, and she laughed.

"No," she laughed. "Stop!"

The tickling turned into caresses, and Maria stopped squirming. The caresses quickly turned into groping, and his hands cupped her ass and gave it a firm squeeze. He moved them from her ass to her chest. His hands covered her breasts, and his thumbs rubbed her nipples. It sent a shiver through her, and she rolled on top of him.

"I'm sorry," he said as Maria dropped a kiss on the tip of his chin.

"For what?" she asked.

"For my sister's behavior at dinner."

Maria lifted her face and looked at him. This was so not the time to bring up family members, especially with the suspicions she had about them. She shook her head. "There's nothing to be sorry for."

"Still, I know she was raised to have better manners. She seemed to give you the cold shoulder."

"It's not a big deal. Now, let's not talk about family members when we're in bed and naked." She dropped a kiss on his mouth. "In fact, we never mention family members when we're naked together."

He smiled. "Deal. Let's talk about what we can do while naked."

Maria gave him a deep kiss. "I'm more of a showing kind of girl instead of a talking kind of girl."

"I like the way you think," he said.

"Somehow, I am not surprised," she grinned. "Before we start another round, did you pick out your costume for the party yet?"

"No," he answered. "I admit I'm having a difficult time deciding. You?"

"Oh yes," she said. "I know what I'm wearing."

"Do I get a hint?" he asked. "Or a special preview?"

"Nope."

"Why not?" he asked.

"Because it's a surprise," she answered.

"Okay. I guess I'll have to wait for the party to see it." He rolled the two of them, putting Maria on her back with him on top. He climbed off her and the bed.

She leaned up on her elbows. "Where are you going? Thought we were going another round."

He leaned over and kissed her. "Bathroom. I'll be right back."

"Oh," she said after the kiss. She watched him walk out of the bedroom, admiring his perfect ass as he walked. Perfect body more like it, and lucky her got to play with it regularly.

Maria stared at the ceiling. The thought of playing with him regularly didn't scare her as much as it would have in the past. The sex was great, of course, but she also liked talking to him. He shared a similar sense of humor, and they made each other laugh. Secretly, she wished he would stay in New York longer. She didn't have to try to find a playmate for the night, and she had someone she could take with her to company and family functions.

Maria blinked. What was she doing? She knew she was getting attached to him, and that meant heartbreak at some point. Things always ended badly, and she should save herself the heartache and not see him any longer, but dammit, she was having fun. There were even brief moments where she considered asking him to stay in New York longer. She could even envision a future with him in it.

Maria yawned and closed her eyes for a moment.

TOMAS EXITED THE BATHROOM AND PADDED HIS WAY back to the bedroom. He tripped over a shoe and swore. He reached the bedroom door and stopped in the doorway.

She snored softly as she lay stretched out across the bed. Tomas hadn't been in the bathroom that long. At least he didn't think he had been. She must have been exhausted and fell asleep the first moment she got comfortable. He shrugged and continued into the room. He grabbed a blanket that had been tossed over the foot of the bed and draped it over her. He grabbed his pants and slipped them on. He may as well get something done while he wasn't tired.

He picked items off the bedroom floor. He tossed clothes into a nearby hamper and placed the shoes on the rack in the closet. He shook his head and continued to pick up items off the floor, including some empty water bottles. He adored her, but she was a slob. He cleaned up as best as possible and moved into the living room, carrying the laundry hamper with him.

Somehow, the living room remained mostly clutter free. Clothes and shoes littered the floor, but not nearly as much as the bedroom. Clothes went in the hamper, and he put the shoes in the closet by the front door. Tomas discovered a washer and dryer in the hallway closet and started a load. He didn't know if the discarded clothes were clean or not, but it wouldn't take long to do a load or two.

Once the living room was somewhat in order, he moved to the kitchen and tackled the pile of dishes in the sink. He wondered if Maria's lack of cleaning sprang from being too busy to do it, or if it was pure laziness. Maria didn't seem like the type to be lazy. It then begged the question of what she did in the evenings that she was too busy to clean? She never mentioned what she did in the evenings they didn't spend together.

She was a mystery he wanted to uncover if given a chance. Too bad he was heading home to Brazil soon He had thought about staying in New York longer, but she hadn't given him any indication she would like him to stay. She kept mentioning that whatever this was between them would be over when he left, telling him that she wanted him to go. He didn't want to go. He wanted to stay here with her. All she had to do was to say the word, and he'd tell his father he would stay and run operations here in New York.

He shook his head. There wasn't a chance she would ask him to stay. He could hope all he wanted, but the invitation wouldn't come. He would enjoy whatever time he had left with her. It wasn't all about the sex either. They shared a similar sense of humor and enjoyed most of the same things. They even had similar backgrounds.

Tomas finished the dishes and tossed the clothes in the dryer when the washer finished. With the apartment mostly clean, he returned to the bedroom to find her lying on her stomach with her legs and arms outstretched, taking up most of the queen-sized bed. Tomas didn't even bother to try to slide in next to her. He returned to the living room and stretched out on the couch. He closed his eyes and drifted off to sleep.

Something, or someone, nudged his thigh. He opened his eyes to find Maria standing over him and holding two cups of coffee. He smiled and pushed himself to a sitting position.

"Morning," he said.

"Mmmmhmmm." She offered him a cup of coffee, which he gladly accepted. He took a tentative sip. Hot, strong, and black. Perfect. He paused for a moment. He didn't recall ever telling her how he liked his coffee. They got coffee together a few times, but he had always ordered for himself, which meant that she had noticed and made a note of it.

Tomas moved over on the couch, making a space for her to sit. Maria smiled at him and sat next to him. He glanced over for a moment and then refocused his attention on the cup of coffee in his hands. Tomas wrapped his hands around the mug and sipped the dark, steaming liquid. He glanced over again. Her attention was focused on the coffee, and, at that, he knew she was like him. Nothing before coffee. Not even speech.

He gave her the time she needed to wake up. The caffeine slowly made its way through his system, and he became more awake and more aware. He looked over at her and smiled when he noticed she was wearing his shirt. Her dark hair flew in all directions, and no makeup adorned her face. She remained beautiful.

"Morning," he said again.

"It's morning," she mumbled.

"Thanks," he said and held his cup up.

"You're welcome. I'm not verbal without coffee."

He smiled. "I figured as much."

She paused and then looked around. "You cleaned."

"Yes," he said with a nod. "I wasn't tired last night after you fell asleep, and I tripped over a shoe on the way back to the bedroom."

"Sorry," she said quietly.

"It's okay. So I cleaned up a bit."

"Thank you." She took a sip of her coffee and closed her eyes. "I'm a slob. I admit it," she said, opening her eyes. She looked over at him.

"It's okay. I didn't want to break anything, namely me, so I cleaned up a bit. Plus have some dishes for breakfast. That's all."

"Can I hire you regularly?" she asked, drawing her mouth up into a half-smile.

His breath stayed in his chest for a long moment before he could breathe again. "Only if you pay in sexual favors," he teased.

"As if I would pay in any other way," she said with a wag of her eyebrows.

Tomas laughed and leaned over to kiss her. "Sounds like a good deal to me."

"So what are your plans for the day?" she asked.

He shrugged. "Not sure. I should see what my father has for me to do today. You?" he asked before taking a drink. She made good coffee.

"Heading into the office," she answered. "I have a ton of papers on my desk that I need to go through."

"Sounds like fun. Only not."

Maria chuckled and nodded. "Yeah."

"Hungry? I can make breakfast," he offered.

"Yes, but you can't make breakfast. I'm even worse at buying groceries than I am at cleaning. But if you want to get dressed, we can head to the diner."

"Sounds like a plan," he said. He stood and offered Maria a hand. She looked up at him and then placed her hand in his. She stood, and he let her go first to the bedroom. He followed with a smile on his face.

CHAPTER FIFTEEN

Tomas adjusted his mask and entered the ballroom. He hadn't seen Maria since dinner ended twenty minutes ago and assumed she was somewhere putting on her costume. She hadn't given him any hints to what she was going to wear, and he was eager to see it. He eventually settled on wearing a Zorro costume. It was a safe route and one that wouldn't cause any controversies.

Superheroes seemed to be the dominant theme for costumes. There were even a few fictional heroes, like Superman and Batman, thrown into the mix. He had even spotted a few villains. He hoped they were just costumes and not the actual villains. None of the heroes in this room would stand up to one of them.

He grabbed a glass of champagne from a passing waiter and sipped it while looking around for Maria. A flash of purple caught his eye, but it disappeared among the other partygoers before he could see who wore it. He weaved his way around people and reached the spot where he had seen it. He scanned around the room and found Maria. She wore a purple, white, and black costume with a purple mask. He sipped his champagne, hoping it would take away the sudden dryness in his mouth.

She smiled when their eyes met, and she walked toward him. Her costume barely covered her. The top was purple and white, ending just below her breasts. Her midriff was exposed, and a pair of small shorts covered her front and barely covered her ass. Two purple suspenders were fastened to the bottom and went up over her shoulders. She wore a purple half cape that ended at her lower back, and her boots were black with purple trim, coming up to her knees. Her thighs were bare. She wore a purple mask that flared out to the sides a little and rose to points above her head. She even held a small crossbow in her left hand. Her makeup consisted of purple lipstick and purple eyeshadow.

"There you are," she said when she reached him. Her eyes reminded him of a bright summer sky. Light danced in them, and he recognized Maria's mischievous look.

He pulled her in for a kiss. "You look great," he said. "Even if I don't recognize who you're supposed to be."

Maria smiled. "Huntress from DC comics. She's always been one of my favorite heroes."

"Ah. That's why I didn't recognize your costume. I'm only familiar with the names like Batman, Superman, and Wonder Woman."

"I used to read comics with my dad when I was little. He got me into the whole superhero thing."

Tomas smiled, and envy welled up inside of him. The earliest memories he had with his father were his father teaching him the family business. Tomas and Carolyn spent their whole lives so far being groomed to run the family business. His mother was the one who tried to give the twins a normal childhood by giving them toys and taking to them to things like the circus and amusement parks.

"You'll have to tell me about them sometime," he said and hooked her arm with his.

"I would like that. My father has a collection of comics beyond counting," she said. "Speaking of my father, I'd like you to introduce you to my parents."

Tomas nodded, albeit a little surprised. "I'd like that." He had seen them at dinner, of course, but the table had been very long, and he had been seated away from them. Strangely enough, Maria had been seated next to him, far away from her parents. He wondered if it had been intentional or accidental. Though knowing Maria, it had been intentional, so they wouldn't have the chance to ask her about him.

"Then come with me," she said, taking his hand.

They weaved in and out of the crowd of people in the room. Dinner had been in a large formal dining room and the party part in the ballroom. Wayne Grayson sure knew how to entertain. There had to be at least fifty people in attendance. All of whom had been at the dinner. The amount of wealth represented was obscene.

Maria led him toward one side of the room where Wayne Grayson held court with a small group of people around him. Including Tomas's father. Out of costume, of course. Antonio Dorrance wouldn't be caught dead with a Halloween costume on. He was one of a handful without a costume. Even Maria's grandfather had a costume on. Caesar seemed an appropriate costume for one of the richest men in New York.

A tall man with dark hair peppered with gray stood next to Wayne Grayson. Tomas could see the family resemblance in the nose and chin. That had to be Maria's father, who was also in a costume. Marc Antony, Tomas guessed. He didn't see anyone near them that could be Maria's mother.

Maria and Tomas approached the small group, and her father and grandfather both smiled when they saw her. Tomas looked around at the people in the small group. Most were from the wealthiest families in New York. Tomas's family certainly didn't lack wealth, but they were nowhere near the families' levels represented here.

"Sorry to interrupt whatever business stuff you all are talking about," Maria said with a smile to the small group of men and women. "You all know this is a party, right?" Most of them chuckled, including her father and grandfather. Tomas's father, of course, didn't chuckle. "Can I steal you away for a moment?" she asked the man Tomas had correctly identified as her father.

"Of course, sweetheart," he said. "If you'll excuse us?" he said to the small group. Maria, Tomas, and her father took a few steps away from the group gathered around her grandfather.

She took a deep breath, and Tomas knew how difficult this was for her. He appreciated the effort she was making. He knew she never intended for him to ever meet her parents, but here they were. In all honestly, he expected her to find some excuse to not introduce him to them. "Dad, this is Tomas Dorrance. Tomas, this is my father, Rikard Grayson."

"A pleasure to meet you, Mr. Grayson," Tomas said, extending a hand.

"A pleasure to meet you, Tomas." He accepted the hand and shook it. "Please call me Rick. I've heard absolutely nothing about you." He gave Maria a pointed look, and she looked away. A response Tomas expected from Maria.

"Maria and I just started seeing each other," Tomas said carefully. Her father released his hand. "I haven't heard anything about you either."

Her father chuckled and turned to look at Maria. "How long have you been seeing each other?"

"I wasn't counting," she said with an impish smile.

"A little while now. Not too long," Tomas answered. He didn't want Maria thinking he was taking her father's side against her. He took her hand in his and gave it a squeeze.

"I see." Her father looked directly at Tomas with blue eyes, a lighter shade than Maria's. Tomas didn't flinch under that scrutinizing gaze. He survived more intense looks from his father; he could survive them from hers.

"It's nothing serious. I'm showing Tomas around New York. Tomas is from Brazil and is in town with his family while they have business here," Maria explained.

"Oh? What kind of business does your family do?"

"Private security," Tomas answered.

Her father nodded. "Yes, now I remember my father mentioning a private security firm working with the NYPD. Is that you?"

"Yes, that's my family's company," Tomas said.

Her father smiled. "Excellent. How long will you be in New York?"

"I'm not sure," he replied. "I believe my father just purchased a penthouse in the city." Maria gave him a look. He hadn't planned on telling her because he didn't want her to think that he lied when he said he was in the city for a limited time. He gave her a smile. "I just found out." The flat look she gave him led him to believe that she didn't believe him.

"Great," he said with a smile. "Hopefully, I'll see more of you."

"Tomas is busy helping his father run a company," Maria pointed out. "You know how that is."

Her father nodded. "Indeed I do, but I hope Tomas can take time and visit me when you do. If she visits me. I expected to see more of my daughter since I returned home, but this is the first I'm seeing her."

"We'll see," Maria said.

Her father laughed. "We all know that's Maria speak for no."

Tomas made a mental note. He'd take any insights into Maria he could get. He wanted to know everything he could about her. If his father buying a residence meant he'd be in New York longer or often, he wanted to see her as much as possible. Maybe turn this into something more if she was willing.

He envied the easygoing relationship father and daughter seemed to have. Smiles came easy for them, and love laced their words to each other. It was easy for Tomas to hear. He wished he had a relationship with his father as Maria had with hers.

"I've been busy, and you have a phone. If you wanted to see me, you could have texted or called," Maria groused.

"Have you introduced Tomas to your mother yet?" her father asked. Tomas now knew where Maria got her subject changing skills from.

Maria shook her head. "Going to do that next."

Her father smiled. "Good. Tomas, it was nice to meet you. Now, if you'll excuse me?"

Tomas nodded, and he and Maria watched her father return to the small circle around her grandfather. She turned and faced him.

"Why didn't you tell me your father bought a residence here?" Her blue eyes flashed, and Tomas couldn't tell if it was anger or annoyance. He'd bet on anger.

"I just found out today," he said in his defense. "I was going to tell you when we had a quiet moment alone." Her eyes narrowed for a moment and then returned to normal. He took one of her hands and brought it up to kiss her knuckles. "I swear."

She smiled when he kissed her knuckles. "Okay," she said. "Does this mean you'll be in New York longer?"

"I honestly don't know," he answered. "Depends on what my father wants me to do. Rikard is an unusual name."

"My grandfather's best friend was named Rikard. He died saving my grandfather's life so my dad was named Rikard to honor him."

"That is a nice way to honor a fallen friend." He gave her a light kiss. "Now, you can introduce me to your mother."

"Sure," she said, hooking her arm around his.

Maria steered him toward the other side of the room to where a small group of women stood. Tomas immediately spotted Maria's mother. The woman stood an inch or two shorter than her daughter, but she possessed the same mane of black hair, only hers was streaked with gray. She wore a

Cleopatra costume, and Tomas realized she must have coordinated with Maria's father. The two women shared the same blue eyes, and hers were locked on Tomas and Maria as they approached. A smile stretched her mouth as Maria and Tomas drew near.

"Hello, sweetheart," her mother said her smile widening.

"Hi Mom," Maria said, returning the smile. "Mom, I'd like to introduce you to Tomas Dorrance. Tomas, this is my mother, Helen Martinelli."

"A pleasure, Tomas," she said, holding out a hand.

Tomas smiled. "The pleasure is mine, Ms. Martinelli," he said, taking the hand and placing a kiss on the knuckles.

"Please, call me Helen," she said and withdrew her hand. "Maria has told me almost nothing about you," she said with a smile.

"For good reason," Maria said with an impish grin. "I didn't want Tomas to run away in fright."

"Don't be a brat" her mother chided. "Where is your family from, Tomas?"

"Brazil. We're in New York for business," he replied.

"How long will you be in New York? We have to have dinner before you return home," she said.

"I'm not sure," he said and smiled. "But I would like that." He didn't miss the look Maria shot toward him. Guess she didn't count on both of her parents inviting Tomas over. He'd make it up to her later if he had to.

"Excellent," her mother said. "Maybe Maria's father will join us."

"I'm sure he'll be busy," Maria added and smiled at her mother. Tomas almost laughed. She clearly did not want both of her parents at dinner with him. Divide and conquer seemed more her style.

"We'll see," her mother said.

Maria sighed, and Tomas smiled. Only a little. He didn't want to make Maria angry. Not when the night was going well so far. He didn't want to sabotage it.

"That means you'll make sure he's there," Maria grumbled. Her phone beeped, and she pulled it out and looked at it. Tomas wondered where she had kept it in the skin-tight, skimpy costume. Maybe later he'd search her to see what else she was hiding. She looked at it and frowned.

Her mother laughed and patted Maria's shoulder. "Of course, I will."

"It's okay if he isn't," Tomas said. He picked his battles, and this is one time he could side with Maria. He loved the easy, laid-back relationships she had with her parents. Her mother reminded him of his own and how much he missed her right now.

"See? Tomas is okay if Father isn't there," Maria said, tucking her phone away.

"If your father can make it, I promise we won't interrogate Tomas, okay?"

Maria grinned. "Only if you give me your word."

Her mother laughed. "I give you my word."

"Good," Maria beamed. "Now Tomas and I are going to go mingle."

Maria's mother nodded. "It was nice to meet you, Tomas."

"It was a pleasure to meet you," he said with a nod. Maria hooked his arm with hers and steered him away from her mother and toward the bar. She ordered a vodka martini, and he ordered a glass of bourbon. Once they had their drinks in hand, she led him to a small spot away from the main crowd.

"So tell me why you don't want me to have dinner with both of your parents?" he asked.

"They'll interrogate you and ask a million and one questions about us," she said.

"Is that so bad?" he asked.

"Yes," she said. "There is no us, and I don't want to explain to them that we're using each other for sex while you're in the city."

"You don't believe in telling them the truth?" he asked.

"I do."

"But?" he prompted. There was always a but.

"I don't want them to think we're serious or something," she said.

"Of course," he said. "Because we're not serious."

Maria smiled. "Exactly."

He looked around the room, suddenly wanting to be somewhere else alone with her. He didn't need to be at a party rubbing elbows with New York elites. He needed to be with her, with no one else around. Preferably naked.

"Everything okay?" he asked.

"Yes, why do you ask?"

"When you looked at your phone, you frowned."

"Work," Maria said with a wave of her hand. "Nothing important."

"How about we call it a night and head somewhere else for the after-party before my father decides he wants to talk to us?" he asked.

She smiled brightly, and mischief twinkled in her eyes. "That's the best offer I've had all night."

"You've had other offers?"

Her smile grew, and his heart beat faster in response. "Of course, I have."

He went along with her and scowled. "Who else made offers? Point them out so I can beat them up."

Maria laughed, throwing her head back with it. "You're cute. Let's go."

"Lead the way," he said. "Where you go, I follow." He wanted to get somewhere as fast as possible and get all their clothes off. In all honesty, he just wanted to be alone with her. Clothes on or off. It didn't matter much.

She tucked her arm around his waist and turned him toward the doors to the ballroom.

CHAPTER SIXTEEN

Balestra jumped off the roof and plunged toward the ground. She landed and let the momentum carry her into a crouch. She put her hand on the ground to stabilize her body and regain her balance. She straightened and looked around to see if the men in the alley had seen or heard her. They hadn't.

Maria took a deep breath and walked toward the parked van. This time, it was black. What was it with bad guys and vans? Did they get discounts on them or something? Sure, they could carry a lot, but so could an SUV or a truck. Vans were so cliche, and she would have thought they would have realized it.

Rollins texted her last night and informed her about another scene of slaughtered drug dealers. The killings were escalating, and Maria felt guilty for taking last night off. She had been taking quite a few nights off patrolling because of Tomas. Tonight she was making up for it. Playing with Tomas could wait for another night.

There were four men altogether. It almost wasn't fair. Maria did keep an eye out for unexpected visitors, specifically the costumed woman, who could be Tomas's family. Maria had yet to verify her suspicions. Eyes over a wine glass triggering a sense of familiarity didn't prove anything. Maria had to catch her in the act without getting herself killed.

There was also Skanda, who kept showing up at the crimes she was trying to stop. Unlike the woman, he helped defeat the bad guys. It was all a mess, and she didn't want to think about it. She could mull it all over later after kicking bad guy ass.

"Evening," she said with a smile as she approached the van. "What have we got going on here? A drug delivery, perhaps?"

They all stopped and looked at her. Maria forced a smile. Maybe a surprise attack would have been better. They drew weapons and took aim. Maria dove to the side, landing at the front of the van as the shots rang out.

She crouched and slowly side walked to the edge of the van. She peeked around the corner just in time to see a woman reach the front of the van. The woman took aim, and Maria lunged for the woman. Maria wrapped her arms around the woman's waist and tackled her as a shot blasted out of the pistol. The shot had been toward the sky, and Maria hoped no one was on the fire escapes lining the alley. They crashed to the ground, Maria landing on top of her.

Maria scrambled up to her knees and delivered a fist to the woman's face. The woman moved her head, and Maria's fist went into the pavement, leaving a small dent. The woman reached down and, a second later, slashed at Maria with a knife. Maria yelled out as the blade bit into her upper arm. Her costume was good at blocking bullets, but not so good at blocking knives. Maria growled and slammed her fist into the woman's face. The woman's eyes closed, and she went still.

The blow crashed into the back of Maria's head and white spots danced in front of her eyes. She rolled to the side just in time to avoid another blow. She rolled again and sprang to her feet, landing ready to face the man who had come up behind her.

He fired, and thankfully, her costume absorbed it. Though it still hurt like hell, and she stumbled back a few steps. Another shot rang out, and Maria waited for the bullet to hit her, but it didn't. The man who had fired at her crumpled to the ground. Maria frantically looked around and saw a dark shadow on the roof above the alley. Him. She couldn't be too upset about his unexpected presence, but he didn't have to kill the man. He probably just saved her life. A lucky headshot, and she'd be a goner.

Maria didn't waste time. She pulled out her crossbow and aimed it at one of the figures. She fired, and the dart hit the target. A few moments later, the man fell to the ground. She turned to face the other to find Skanda, now on the ground, aiming a gun at the last remaining man.

"No!" she yelled, but the pistol went off, and the man fell to the ground.

He turned and looked at her. "Is that all of them?" he asked.

"I think so," she said, wincing against the pain in her chest. Breathing hurt. She'd be sporting a bruise for a while. Her costume stopped bullets, but they hurt and left her bruised.

"You okay?" he asked.

"More or less," she hissed.

"You get hit?" he asked and approached her.

"Why the hell do you care?" she half-growled.

"Even though you are a pain in the ass, you are effective," he said.

"Me a pain in the ass?" Her mouth dropped open. "Look who's talking. This was my scene until you came in uninvited."

"It looked like you needed the help." He smirked, and she wanted to wipe it off his face.

"I surely didn't need your help," she said. "You better leave before the cops arrive."

"Are you okay?" he asked.

"I'll be sporting a bruise and took a knife in the arm," she said, wondering why she bothered to answer him. She looked at the back of her arm. It wasn't bleeding too bad and would be healed in an hour or so.

"Come with me, and I'll stitch up your arm."

Maria laughed. "I have a person that will take care of it if it's needed. Cops will be here soon," she warned. "Unless you want to go to jail for shooting two of those guys, you should leave."

"They deserved to be put down," he said.

Maria shook her head. "No. No matter what they did, they didn't deserve to be killed. You are not judge, jury, and executioner."

"Says who?" he challenged.

"The law!" Maria threw her hands up and walked away from him, heading toward the woman lying on the ground. Maria put restraints on her wrists and started searching the woman's pockets.

"That's more than a scratch," he said.

"Go to hell!" she called back. Sirens blared in the distance, and they would be here soon. "Don't you have somewhere to be?" Nothing. She found nothing in the woman's pockets. Maria wanted to find something connecting these drugs to the elder Dorrance.

"I want to make sure you're okay," he said.

She left the woman and walked to the rear of the van. The sirens grew louder. "Why?" she asked as she opened the rear doors.

There were bricks of drugs stacked in the back, along with stacks of money. Boost. Maria would bet money on it. She had to track down the people helping Falcone flood the city with this poison and murdering people. She swore and slammed the doors shut.

"Meet me on the roof after you deal with the police," he said. He ran down the alley and jumped, grabbing the ladder to a fire escape. Maria watched him climb the fire escape, admiring his ass.

Once he was out of view, Maria started searching the bodies of the other three. They turned up very little. Although one did have a slip of paper with a phone number on it. Maria shoved it in a pocket just as police cruisers pulled up at the end of the alley. Black SUVs pulled up alongside the cruisers. She recognized the logo for Dorrance's security company.

Maria explained what happened to Rollins with the senior Dorrance looking on disapprovingly. She attributed the bullet wounds to them shooting each other while trying to shoot her. It did happen in certain situations, just not this one. She hated lying to Rollins. Why was she covering for Skanda? This is the second time now. Anger coursed through her.

She looked up at the roof and glared, hoping he felt the weight of it.

Once she finished with the police, she leaped up to one of the higher fire escapes. She leaped again and landed on the roof where he was waiting.

"Impressive," he commented.

Maria would have smiled and basked in the compliment, but she was too pissed to do it. "Don't you ever do that again!"

"Do what?" he asked.

"Kill people," she said, getting in his face. "I had to lie to the police because of you! Again!"

"I didn't ask you to lie to them," he pointed out.

"If I didn't, they would have brought me in to question me about you," she said and poked his chest. "Do you want to go to jail?"

"So you lied to cover your own," he looked around her, "beautiful ass."

Maria rolled her eyes and somehow kept from wiping that smile off his face. She wanted to hit him in the worst way. It was a familiar feeling whenever she was around him. One day she may just do it, and it would feel good.

"I'm not going to do it next time," she said. "I don't care if I have to answer a million questions from the police."

"Go ahead."

Maria's eyes narrowed. Was this a challenge? She wasn't bluffing. "I'll do it."

He smirked. "Go ahead. Let's see if you have the guts."

"I do."

He laughed, and she took a swing at him with her right. He caught her hand at the wrist just inches from his face. Granted, he only managed it because she didn't put any of her strength behind the punch. Maria narrowed her eyes and glared up at him. He stared down at her, and time seemed to stop.

"Don't try that again," he warned.

"Or what? You'll spank me?" Her chin went up, almost daring him to do it.

One side of his mouth pulled back into a half-smile. "Something like that."

Maria scoffed. "You'd be lucky to get to spank me."

"Damn straight." He released her wrist.

His dark eyes gleamed and took on a predatory cast. Maria's mouth went dry, and her stomach hollowed out. Blood raced, and her heart pounded in her chest. What the hell was wrong with her? He leaned over, and his mouth hovered an inch away from hers.

"No more killing," she said barely above a whisper.

"I'll think about it," he replied.

His breath was warm, and he radiated heat. Maria wanted to submerge herself in it and soak it up. A shiver raced down her spine.

"No killing," she repeated, her mouth almost brushing against his.

"Deal. No killing," he whispered.

Maria brushed her lips across his. "There. The deal is now sealed."

He smiled. "Okay, then."

Maria didn't move. Her aches and pains faded away. He was all she could focus on, and a little voice inside of her head warned her to get away from him. He was so wrong for her and exactly Maria's type. She possessed a long, sordid history of finding the wrong Mr. Right, and he didn't need to be added to the list.

He pulled away, and Maria breathed a sigh of relief. "Let me see your arm," he said.

Maria blinked in surprise. "Why?"

He sighed. Maria could hear the exasperation in the sigh. "Because you're hurt," he said.

"It's fine. What are you going to do? Kiss my boo-boo?" She showed him her arm anyway. "It's already healing." The blood flow had stopped. A few hours and she'd be as good as new.

He grinned and grabbed her arm at the elbow. He kissed her arm above her wound, and Maria blinked, then laughed. He laughed with her but didn't release her arm.

She eyed his hand holding her arm and then looked up at him. "You can let go now."

A mischievous gleam appeared in his eyes. "What if I don't?"

"Then I'd have to kick your ass," she said matter-of-factly.

"You think you stand a chance?" he asked.

"I do," she replied.

"It's cute when you think you can do something you can't."

Irritation spiked. "Oh, shut up." She did the only thing she could to shut him up. She kissed him. Hard. He was still for a second and then kissed her back. His mouth ground down on hers. He parted her lips with his tongue, and it entered her mouth.

Maria moaned into his mouth, and he pushed her back against the roof access point wall. God, she loved a forceful man. Too bad he was the wrong man. She pushed him away and took a deep breath. No. She wouldn't do this, even though part of her wanted to. One, she didn't like him much and two, not while she was seeing Tomas. What she wouldn't give to get a peek under his mask, but if she asked, he'd want a look under hers, and that wasn't going to happen.

"Something wrong?" he asked.

She shook her head. "No. Everything's fine." She reminded herself she didn't like him. She didn't like herself much right now.

"You don't look like everything's fine."

"I'm tired and sore." She looked at him and the smile that appeared on his face. "Don't flatter yourself. I took a bullet and got cut. The only place where there will be anything more is in your dreams." Maria checked her mask to make sure it was on securely.

"Uh-huh," he said with a smirk.

Maria sighed. "No killing!"

He laughed as he walked to the edge and jumped off.

She pulled the slip of paper out of her pocket and looked at it for a long moment. Maria pulled out her burner phone and dialed the number. She looked over the ledge at the police and Dorrance's men. A man standing next to Dorrance pulled out a cell phone and pressed a button. The call on her cell connected.

"What's the status?" a male voice asked. "He wants an update."

Maria disconnected the line and stared down at Dorrance. *What the hell was going on?* Her stomach twisted up and a hollow feeling formed in her chest. Her mind refused to acknowledge the implications of Dorrance's man answering that call. Tomas's father couldn't be involved. Could he?

CHAPTER SEVENTEEN

MARIA YAWNED, AND THE WORDS ON HER COMPUTER screen seemed to blend together. Today would have been a perfect day to stay in bed, but her day job wouldn't allow it. She didn't want to have to tell her grandfather why she wasn't in the office. He wouldn't be angry with her, but Maria hated disappointing him. That was always worse.

"Tomas keep you awake too late last night?" Gayle asked from the doorway.

Maria looked up, and of course, Gayle was grinning like the Cheshire Cat. Maria sighed. "No, but I wish that were the case."

Gayle sauntered into the office and plopped down in a chair in front of Maria's desk. "Dish. Now."

"I was in costume last night," Maria said.

"Ah. So what happened?"

"Who says something happened?" Maria closed her laptop. She knew this would take a while, and it was close to lunchtime. Might as well go to lunch and eat while they talked.

"Because you look like something the cat dragged in. You don't normally look like this after a night of patrol."

Maria sighed. Sometimes it was fantastic having a friend who knew you well. Now was not one of those times. "I ran into Skanda again."

Gayle's eyes widened, and she leaned forward in the chair, resting her arms on Maria's desk. "Start at the top."

"I was busting a drug thing and took a knife to the arm. Then I took a bullet to the chest and have a nice bruise to show for it. I had the situation under control, and he showed up." Just talking about it made her angry.

"You're so cute when you're disgruntled," Gayle said with a grin.

"Go to hell," Maria grumbled.

"So then what happened?" Gayle asked. To Maria, the woman looked like she should be eating popcorn. Maria was glad her life was entertainment for her friend.

"He killed a few of them," Maria said.

"Oh, boy. So what did the cops do?"

"Yeah. Nothing," Maria said. "They don't know it was him."

"Why not? Why didn't you tell them?"

"I don't know why I didn't tell them," Maria said. And she still didn't know why. She thought about it as she drifted off to sleep but hadn't been able to find an answer. "But he made a deal to not do it going forward."

"Do you think he'll keep the deal?" Gayle asked.

Maria shrugged. "I hope he does."

Gayle peered at her, and Maria tried to keep her face from betraying her, but it was futile. Gayle knew her too well. "And what else happened?"

And there it was. Dammit. One day, Maria would be able to not have her face give her away. Maybe. "We made out."

Gayle's eyes went wide, and her mouth fell open. "What?"

Maria sighed and glanced out the door. A few people were looking in the direction of her office. "You heard me."

"Why? What about Tomas?"

Maria rubbed the bridge of her nose and ignored the first

twinges of a forming headache. "I don't know why," Maria said. " I don't know about Tomas. We never talked about being exclusive. Not once. It was just making out."

"Are you going to tell him?" Gayle asked.

"I don't know," Maria answered honestly. "He's leaving soon, so what does it matter that I made out with someone else?"

"Oh my sweet summer child," Gayle sighed. "You should be honest with him."

"You watch too much *Game of Thrones*," Maria chided. Gayle named her cat after a character in the show and had some memorabilia on her desk. Maria didn't understand getting so involved in a show. Then again, Maria really didn't have time to watch television. She didn't even have a television in her apartment.

"There's no such thing," Gayle defended. "I think you should tell Tomas."

"I don't know," Maria said. "Why ruin what little time we have left together?" While it wasn't serious, she did enjoy spending time with him. She didn't want to sabotage what little time she had left with him. And they never mentioned being exclusive. That was too much like having a relationship with him.

"You don't know that it will ruin it," Gayle pointed out.

"It will ruin it," Maria insisted.

"Why'd you make out with that guy?"

"I wasn't thinking," Maria said.

"Obviously," Gayle said flatly. "I got more information on Tomas's father for you."

Maria pinned a look on her. "'And you're just now mentioning it?"

Gayle laughed. "Your life is too amusing to bring anything up before we talk about it."

"I'm so glad my life amuses you." Maria pressed her lips together in a thin line. Her life had been simple; now, it was a mess. All thanks to getting emotionally attached to Tomas. Dammit. Why did she let herself do it? She knew better.

"I really want you and Tomas to work out," Gayle said, turning serious. "You two are good together."

"And I probably just messed things up," Maria said with a sigh. Maria held out her hand. "Information now."

"Demanding as always," Gayle said, handing over the file she held.

Maria snatched the manila envelope out of Gayle's hands and opened it. She leaned back in her chair and started skimming the papers inside.

"It's not much," Gayle admitted. "There are some shady things, but nothing concrete of actual wrongdoing. Why did you have me look at him?"

Maria leaned forward and whispered, "I saw something I don't want to be true."

"Like what?"

"I found a phone number on one of the goons and when I called it, Dorrance's man answered.""

"You mean…"

Maria grimaced. "Yes. I think he's involved in the recent drug activity." Telling Tomas about his father's criminal activities would be a more massive bomb than telling him about her making out with another guy. Maria didn't want to tell him either thing, but she knew she'd have to tell him about his father. Only after she had enough cold, hard proof. That would definitely be one way to end whatever this was between them.

"Looks like telling Tomas about the make-out session will be easier," Gayle said, echoing Maria's thoughts.

"That's what I was thinking. I don't want to tell him either thing."

"Don't blame you there," Gayle said. "But maybe you won't find enough proof that his father is a criminal."

"I can hope," Maria said. "But you know me. I don't want to believe Tomas's father is involved in all of this."

"Yeah, I do. You're part bloodhound."

Maria managed a small smile. "Yeah. Maybe a vacation is called for? I could disappear for a while." Spending a week or two on a beach somewhere sounded good. She could work on a tan, get drunk, and get out of the colder temperatures of New York.

Gayle laughed. "No, you won't. Your sense of justice is too strong, and you love kicking bad-guy butt."

"Guilty," Maria confessed.

"You ready for lunch?" Gayle asked. "I'm starving."

"You just don't want to work," Maria accused.

Gayle grinned. "Guilty. Let's go." She stood, as did Maria. Maria knew a losing battle when she saw one. She may even make it a liquid lunch today; drinking sounded good. Drinking a lot sounded even better.

"Where are we going?" Maria asked, walking out from behind her desk. "Wherever we go, they better have alcohol."

Gayle hooked her arm with Maria's. "Liquid lunch today?"

"Damn straight. There is not enough alcohol in the world right now," Maria said.

"I hear you. We started working on wedding plans. There's nothing worse in the world."

Maria pinned a look on her. "Really?"

"How about you plan a wedding with Charlene, and I'll tell Tomas you made out with another guy and his dad could be a criminal?" Gayle suggested.

Maria blinked and then laughed. "Deal!"

CHAPTER EIGHTEEN

MARIA GLANCED DOWN AT HER WATCH. THREE AM. SHE should have been in bed since she had to work in the morning, but bad guys did most of their evil deeds late at night. How inconsiderate of them not to take other people's schedules into consideration. Very rude. She yawned and wished she had coffee.

She looked over at Skanda. She wasn't sure why he wanted to be in on it, but she wasn't going to complain. Much. They were across the street from a warehouse, and two vans pulled up a few minutes ago. Both wore black. How original. Six people climbed out and entered the warehouse.

"It looks like they're all here," he said.

"Give it another minute. There's always someone running late, and I'd like to get them all. Besides, it's always a good practice to not have someone come up behind you."

"I can't argue with that."

"I wasn't asking your opinion on it," Maria said. Things had never been good between them since they met, but now it was weird. Weird was actually good. There would be no repeats of the other night. Maria was still mulling over the guilt she carried for making out with him. Thankfully, between her and Tomas, they had been too busy to see each other in the past week.

"I don't care," he said.

She couldn't wait for this whole mess, whatever was going on, to be over, and they could each go their own way. It was a partnership made in hell. Yet something nagged at the back of her mind, and Maria couldn't put her finger on it.

A car pulled up, and two people climbed out. They entered the warehouse, and the street went quiet again.

"See? Always someone running late."

"I'll give you that one," he said.

She'd take the win. And would remind Skanda of it later. "Looks like everyone is here. Time to get this party started." She grinned.

"Do you think I could get a lift down to the ground?" he asked.

Maria sighed. "Fine. Next time, if there is a next time, you find your own way down."

He chuckled and wrapped his arms around her waist. Maria ignored the heat he put off and the light smell of his cologne. Of course, someone she didn't like shared the same taste in cologne as Tomas. She wrapped an arm around his waist. She reminded herself she was working and had no time for play. That could come later with Tomas.

"Hold on," she said and jumped. The two of them fell to the ground, landing on their feet. She looked at him. "You can let go now." He smirked and released his hold on her. Maria grumbled under her breath. "How do you want to do this?"

"You go in the front, and I'll circle around to the back?"

"Sounds good," she said. It would put some distance between them, and Maria could use the break from his presence. "I'll give you three minutes."

He nodded and disappeared into the night.

Maria decided to check out the two vans and the car while waiting for him to get in place. She opened the back doors of one of the vans and found it empty. She moved to the other van, and like the first, it was empty. Guess it was her night to be disappointed. The car didn't produce anything either.

Maria glanced at her watch. It was time to go in. She opened the door and hoped it didn't squeak, giving her away. Thankfully, it opened without a sound, and she slipped in.

Darkness filled the interior. There was just enough light filtering in from the high windows to see crates and boxes stacked around the room. Where were the eight people who entered? They hadn't come out, and she would have heard the commotion if they had exited and ran into Skanda. Something weird was going on. Maria hated weird.

She carefully maneuvered around the boxes and crates, looking for any signs of movement. She carried her dart pistols, ready to use them. She looked up. Even the office tucked into the back corner was dark. She could make out the outline of the stairs leading up to it, and nothing moved.

She stopped and listened. Silence echoed in the large space.

"Skanda!" she called out in a loud whisper.

"Over here," he answered. She turned and looked to find him coming out from behind a stack of crates.

"Find anyone?" she asked.

He shook his head. "No. Not one person."

"This is all wrong," Maria said. The lights flared to life, and Maria held her hand up against the sudden bright light. Maria spun around, looking all around her. The eight men they had witnessed going inside, plus an additional four that must have already been inside, surrounded them. All twelve of them had guns drawn and aimed at the two of them.

Maria put her back to Skanda's. "Now what?" she asked in a low voice.

"Make our last stand?" he asked.

"I'm not dying here, like this, with you," she said.

"You make it sound like you don't like my company."

"I don't," she replied.

"You did the other night," he said as the men surrounding them closed in.

"I'm trying to forget that," she countered. She had been trying to forget what had happened, but it wasn't easy. A part of her didn't want to ignore it. Another part of her nagged her with guilt.

"You wound me," he said.

The men closing in around them were about five feet away. Not close enough yet to engage in hand-to-hand combat. They held the upper hand at a distance with the guns.

"Ready to do this?" she asked so only he could hear her.

"Ready when you are," he replied.

"No killing," she reminded him. "Three." They were four feet away.

"Two," he said. Three feet away.

"One," she said and rushed the man directly in front of her. She lowered a shoulder and collided with the man. He grunted, and Maria wrapped an arm around him. She planted her feet and whipped the guy around, using him as a shield. Gunfire shattered the silence, and bullets flew in all directions.

The guy she used as a shield took a bullet and went limp in her arms. She didn't release him. She held him there and grabbed his gun from his hand before it fell to the floor. She aimed and fired at the one who had shot at her. She hit him in the leg, and the man screamed in pain. He dropped to the floor, holding his leg.

A bullet whizzed past her head, and she dropped the man she had been holding up. She aimed and fired, hitting the man in his arm. The gun fell from his hand, and he clutched his arm where he had been shot. She drew her crossbow and took aim, the tranq dart hitting the man in the chest. A moment later, he went down. Three down.

She glanced over to check on Skanda. He was fighting two, and she believed he could handle it. She hoped he could handle it. A noise came from behind her, and she moved on instinct. She spun and delivered a kick to the side of the man's head. He stumbled back a few steps, and Maria followed. She punched him in the face, and he folded, collapsing on the floor.

She glanced at Skanda. His two were down, and he faced two different men. Half down. Six more to go. A bullet slammed into one of her legs, and she winced against the pain. She growled and charged the man who had fired. His eyes went wide when he saw her coming at him and turned to run, despite holding a gun. Maria would never understand criminals. She caught up to him and tackled him to the floor. One quick punch, and he went still.

Maria climbed to her feet and looked over at Skanda. He was dealing with a new opponent, and another approached him from behind, wielding a crowbar.

"Behind you!" Maria yelled, too late. The man swung the crowbar and smashed it into Skanda's side. Maria felt that hit. The man brought the crowbar back and struck Skanda again in the same place. Someone was going to have some broken ribs. She had let her attention stray and paid for it when a bullet slammed into her chest. Right near the spot that was sore from a shot a few days ago. Dammit! That's what she deserved for being sloppy and letting her attention wander. She growled and brought up her crossbow and fired at the man.

The dart hit him in the neck, and he staggered a bit before falling to the floor. She charged toward Skanda. The man with the crowbar hit him again as another fired and shot him in the chest. She didn't worry about the shot. His costume would protect him from that, or she hoped. It didn't help much when it came to blunt force.

Maria lunged for the man with the crowbar and tackled him to the ground. The crowbar fell from his hands, and Maria grabbed it as it fell to the floor. She whacked the man on the arm, putting a little more of her strength behind it than she usually would. The man screamed. Maria brought the crowbar up again, and the man scrambled to get away. She let him get a few paces away and then hurled the crowbar at his legs. It struck him, and he fell to the floor.

She turned just in time to avoid being pistol-whipped. She kicked at the man, hitting him in the chest with her foot. He went flying backward and crashed against some stacked crates. She did a quick check on Skanda. He favored his injured side but managed to get the man he had been dealing with down. Only three men remained standing.

They fired at Maria, and she dove. She rolled when she hit the floor and sprang to her feet right in front of one of the men. She sent an uppercut to his chin, and the hit lifted the man off his feet and sent him backward. He landed on his back a few feet away and was still.

Maria turned to find her next opponent. Skanda shot one man in the leg, and the man went down. Amazing. He didn't kill him. Maria took the small miracle. The last remaining man realized his chances weren't good and made a break for the door.

"Go!" Skanda yelled, clutching his side.

Maria ran and managed to catch the man as he opened the door. She slammed the door shut and grabbed the man by the front of his shirt. She pulled a fist back, ready to strike, and he put his hands up in surrender.

"Please don't hurt me!" he begged.

Maria sighed. "Fine," she growled. She pulled a zip tie out of a pocket and released the man. "Hands behind your back." The man put his hands behind his back and turned around. Maria fastened the zip tie and pushed him back toward the middle of the warehouse.

Skanda stood, clutching his side, and it looked like he was struggling to breathe. He probably had broken ribs and maybe even a punctured lung. Dammit. Maria grabbed her burner phone and sent a message to the police. It shouldn't take them long to get here.

She looked back at Skanda. What was she going to do about

him? He shouldn't be here when the police arrived, yet Maria couldn't just leave the scene. Dammit, dammit, dammit. She looked at the bound bad guy. He was the only one that was a threat of leaving before the police arrived.

Maria shot him with a dart. The man looked at her in surprise and then fell to the floor.

"C'mon," she said to Skanda, walking over to him. She put an arm around him, her shoulder under his, and steered him toward the door.

"What are you doing?" he wheezed.

"Don't talk," she said. "I think you may have a punctured lung. Save your breath. I'm going to get you out of here before the police arrive."

He shook his head.

"You don't have a choice in the matter," she said. "Either you let me help you, or I'll knock you out. Either way, I'm getting you out of here."

He glared at her for a long moment and nodded.

"Glad you saw reason," she said as they neared the door. "I know a person who is discreet and will patch you up." He nodded. At least he was smart enough to try not to talk. "I only have a bike. Do you think you'll be able to hold on?"

He nodded. Maria helped him down the street to where she had parked her bike. She helped him on, then climbed on in front of him. His arms wrapped around her, and he leaned on her.

"Don't pass out, or we'll crash," she warned as she started the bike. "It's not far."

"I won't," he wheezed.

Maria prayed and pulled out. She took it slowly to not jostle him too much, but as fast as she dared to get him medical attention. Eventually, she pulled up to a 24-hour clinic. She parked the bike and then helped him off.

"Not too much farther," Maria told him as she helped him

through the door. A woman in scrubs rushed up to them as soon as they entered. Maria knew her well.

"Find Dr. Connor," Maria ordered. "Most likely broken ribs and probably a punctured lung."

The woman nodded. "Put him in room two."

Maria nodded and helped Skanda down the short hallway and opened the second door on the right. She held the door for him and closed it once he was through.

He went over to the bed and lifted a leg to climb up but stopped and put his leg down. Maria sighed and walked over to him. "This is probably going to hurt," she said as she scooped him up in her arms. He groaned loudly as Maria gently placed him on the bed. "Sorry."

He clawed at his mask. "Can't...breathe..." He tore his mask off, and time froze. The mask fell to the floor, and Maria stared at Skanda's face.

The breath froze in her chest, and her muscles refused to push it out. Her world had suddenly been turned upside down, and she didn't know which way was up.

Tomas.

Skanda was Tomas. Tomas was Skanda.

Her brain refused to believe what her eyes were seeing. She wanted to reach out and touch him to verify this was all real and not some elaborate trick. How could it be Tomas? No. This was some sort of hallucination or elaborate trick or something. It couldn't be him. It just couldn't.

But it was.

Her brain raced with the new information. How could she not see it? How did she miss the little clues? There were always clues. As Skanda, he didn't speak with an accent, and even the tone of his voice was different. Skanda even moved differently than Tomas.

Except when they had made out. Maria remembered a sense of familiarity with Skanda, and now she knew why. The only good thing out of all of this was that she hadn't technically cheated on Tomas. That little lingering bit of guilt she had carried around with her faded away.

A thought crept into her mind. He had made out with Balestra, not knowing it was really Maria. Did he feel any guilt about cheating on her, even though they never mentioned being exclusive?

He coughed and put his hand up to cover his mouth. He pulled his hand away, and it was covered in blood.

The sight of blood covering his hand brought Maria out of her state of shock and forced her into action. She grabbed some paper towels from a dispenser near the small sink in the corner of the room and handed them to him. He smiled his thanks.

"I'm going to go see what's keeping the doc."

He looked at her and nodded.

"I'll be right back," she said, forcing down her feelings. She could deal with them, and this revelation later. Much later. And with a copious amount of alcohol. Right now, he was all that mattered. She yanked open the door to find Dr. Connor reaching for the handle. Maria held open the door for her.

"Somehow, I'm not surprised to see you here," Dr. Connor said to Maria.

"I'm not your patient tonight. He is," Maria said and nodded toward Tomas.

"I see."

"He took a few crowbar shots to the side," Maria said. "Broken ribs and a punctured lung."

"How about you let me examine him and make a diagnosis?"

"Just trying to help," Maria said.

Connor shook her head and went over to Tomas's side. She put her hands on Tomas's side and pressed. Tomas groaned. She pushed around a little more. "You need to go to the hospital. I can put a tube in to help you breathe, but you need to go."

"No hospital," Tomas wheezed.

"If you're concerned about your identity, we'll remove your costume and put you in clothes before we have you transported. Will that work?"

Tomas nodded.

"Good," Dr. Connor said and grabbed a plastic mask hanging next to the bed. She placed the strap around his head and settled the mask on his face. She adjusted a dial and the flow of oxygen.

Dr. Connor turned toward Maria. "You're gonna help me remove his costume,"

"Sure," she said and was already in motion to the other side of the bed.

"Do you want something for the pain before we do this? It's going to hurt when we move you."

Tomas shook his head.

Dr. Connor sighed. "I knew you were going to refuse," she grumbled. She looked at Maria and nodded.

It took some time, but they managed to get Tomas's costume off without jostling him too much. He was left in his boxer briefs when they were done with him. Maria was too concerned to appreciate his semi-nakedness. Dr. Connor put a hospital gown over him.

"I'm going to go arrange for an ambulance to come get him."

Maria nodded. Tomas nodded.

"I'll be right back." Dr. Connor left the room,

Maria turned to Tomas after the door closed. "Do you need me to contact anyone for you and have them meet you at the hospital?"

Tomas shook his head.

"Are you sure?" Maria asked. If their positions reversed, she'd want a family member there. Tomas had two in the city, and one of them should be there.

He opened his mouth to speak but started coughing instead. He pressed the wad of paper towels to his mouth. Maria hurried to his side and put her hand on his back, lifting him forward a little. The coughing stopped, and the paper towels were stained red.

"Please let me call someone," she urged.

He glared at her and shook his head.

"Stop being so damned stubborn," she half-growled. She walked over to the chair where Dr. Connor had discarded Tomas's costume. She searched for pockets and found one. She shoved a hand inside and came out with a phone, not his personal phone, but a burner like the one she carried. She returned to the bedside and shoved the phone at him.

"Dial the number of someone to meet you there," she ordered. "I'll tell them where to meet you."

He looked at the phone and then at her. He glared at her, his dark eyes looking deep into her soul. Maria stared back at him. She wouldn't be the one to back down. She considered going with him, but she couldn't in costume. Maria had been seen with Tomas in public, and someone could assume she was Maria. Going with him wasn't an option.

"Fine. If you don't want a family member meeting you, is there someone else?"

He nodded and held his hand out. Maria handed him the phone, and he dialed a number. He offered the phone back to her.

Her personal phone vibrated in her pocket, and she thanked all the gods out there she had it on silent mode. Only an idiot went on patrol with their phone not silenced. Her ringing phone would have given away her identity. Sure, she considered removing her mask and revealing her identity to him, but she resisted. He was injured and shouldn't be speaking. If he knew her real identity, there would be talking. Maybe yelling. No, she'd tell him after he was healed. Maybe.

She put the phone to her ear and left a message for herself. It was surreal, but she managed to get through it. She disconnected the line and handed the phone back to him. He nodded.

"You're welcome," she said. "Hopefully, they'll get the message soon and be able to meet you there."

"Do I get to see your face?" he wheezed.

"This isn't show and tell. Maybe one day."

"That's not fair."

Maria managed a small laugh. "Life's not fair, and I certainly don't play fair."

It wasn't fair, but Maria didn't know how he'd react. The thing she feared the most was someone revealing her identity to the media. She'd never be able to be Balestra again.

Maria walked over to the door and peeked out. Two EMTs entered the front door and rolled a stretcher between them.

"EMTs are here," she told him. "That's my cue to leave."

He nodded.

Maria looked at him and then slipped out of the room. She hurried down the hall away from the EMTs. Now to rush home, change, and go meet Tomas at the hospital. Only her life could be like this.

CHAPTER NINETEEN

Tomas winced as he bent at the waist to help Maria pull his jeans up. He'd been in the hospital for the past four days. It hadn't been all bad, though. His father and sister visited, but Maria spent the most time with him. She had been the one to meet him here after the ambulance brought him in and waited until he was out of surgery. Maria was the lucky one who got to help him get dressed and drive him home.

"Stop that," she chided. "You're not supposed to bend over. You'll pull your stitches out."

"You're such a bully," he grumbled and straightened out.

She looked up at him, and he smiled, seeing those blue eyes. "I know. Now cooperate, or you'll see how much of a bully I can be."

"Yes, ma'am."

Her eyes narrowed, and she resumed pulling up his pants. She got them on his hips, and he batted her hands away. She glared at him, but it had no effect on him.

"I am fully capable of buttoning and zippering my pants," he told her.

She grabbed the shirt from the chair. She stepped behind him and held up the shirt for him. "Be careful. Don't lift your arms too high. You'll pull your stitches."

Tomas sighed and lifted his arms a little, but it was enough for Maria to slip each arm into the shirt. She pulled it up and set it on his shoulders. She moved around to the front and started buttoning it up. Tomas didn't even try to stop her. Her forehead creased, and it pleased him that she cared enough to worry, but he couldn't help to think about the other night and how he had made out with Balestra.

Maria and he never mentioned anything about being exclusive. Hell, they both insisted many times about how they weren't a couple. Was it actually cheating if they weren't a couple? It didn't matter. Guilt twisted his stomach a bit each time he looked at Maria. He knew he'd have to tell her about Balestra at some point.

"Doc said I'll be fine," he said, trying to reassure her.

"I know," she said. "You still haven't said how you managed to break your ribs and puncture a lung."

"Stupid accident," he said, looking away from her. He knew he should tell her the truth, but she wouldn't understand why he put on a costume and went out to fight drug dealers and whatnot. She liked the costume set, he knew that, but given his injuries, he figured she'd have some strong objections to him doing it. They were due for a serious talk soon.

"So, you've said. Without details."

He shrugged and regretted it. The problem with ribs was that every little movement of your chest, including breathing, hurt. He had been prescribed painkillers, but he opted not to take them. He didn't want a fuzzy head. Thinking clearly was a little more important than not hurting.

He gave her a quick kiss. "Can we stop somewhere for real food?" he asked, trying to change the subject. Her eyes narrowed for a moment, then returned to normal. "All I've eaten for the past four days has been hospital food. I need good food."

Maria sighed. "Yes. If you promise not to overdo it. If you pull your stitches, I'll kick your butt."

Tomas smiled and kissed her. Thankfully, kissing could be done without bending or moving too much. Maria shook her head when the kiss ended and grabbed his coat. She moved around him and held it up.

He lifted his arms ever so slightly, and she slipped the coat on his arms. She settled it on his shoulders and then slipped around to the front and zipped it up."

"I feel like a kid who can't do anything for himself again," Tomas commented dryly.

"I don't care how it makes you feel. You're going to take it easy until you're healed."

"Total bully," he said, flashing her a grin.

Maria smiled. The door to the room opened, and an orderly wheeled in a wheelchair. The woman smiled and looked at Tomas.

Tomas shook his head. "I don't need a wheelchair. I can walk just fine."

"Hospital regulations," she said.

"You heard the woman," Maria said and motioned toward the chair.

Tomas sighed, and his ribs protested the movement. Knowing he was outgunned, he sat in the chair and smiled up at Maria. Maria smiled in return and waited for the orderly to go first. The smile didn't quite reach her eyes. Was she that worried about him? Or was it something else?

They wheeled him down to the main entrance, and Maria went ahead to open the waiting car door. They were using her grandfather's car and driver again. Hopefully, she had cleared it with him and hadn't left him stranded somewhere. The orderly wheeled him to the car, and he rose from the chair.

"Thank you," he said to her and carefully climbed into the car. There wasn't a part of his chest that didn't hurt. He leaned back in the seat, grateful to not have to move. Maria climbed in next to him and gave the driver the address of his father's penthouse.

He glanced over at Maria, and she was looking out the window. Was she mad that he wouldn't tell her exactly what happened to him? He hoped not. He liked her, and he wanted to spend as much time with her as he could. These injuries may delay him returning home, which necessarily wasn't a bad thing in his book.

"You okay?" he asked.

She turned and looked at him. "Yeah. Fine. I'm having food delivered to your father's penthouse for you."

"You're quiet. I don't think you've ever been this quiet."

She shrugged. "Just thinking."

"About?" he prompted.

"Too many things," she answered.

"Care to share them with me?" he asked.

She looked away. "Not really."

So it was going to be like that. Whatever it was, it had to be serious. Maria never hesitated to tell him what was on her mind. Even when he hadn't asked for it. He'd chalk her mood up to worrying about him. At least he hoped it was that.

"These injuries may delay me going home," he said. He waited for a reaction. None came. "Maria?"

"What?" she asked, turning back to look at him.

"I said these injuries may delay me going home," he repeated.

"Oh. That's nice."

That's nice? That was her reaction? He expected something more. Either positive or negative. Instead, he got indifference. What was going on? Was this all because he wouldn't tell her the details of how he got injured? He doubted that was it. He hoped that wasn't it.

The hospital wasn't too far from his father's penthouse, and the car made it there in a relatively short time, even with New York traffic. Maria climbed out of the car ahead of him and walked around to the other side. She held out a hand to him. He accepted it with a smile, placing his hand in hers and giving it a squeeze. She smiled, but Tomas could tell it was forced.

He climbed out, his bandaged ribs protesting the movement with pain. Maybe taking some of the painkillers wasn't such a bad idea. He could take them, fall into the bed, and not move. Though it'd be even better if she stayed with him and stretched out beside him. He didn't think that was going to happen by the way she was acting.

"Thanks," he said.

"Of course," she said, releasing his hand once he was out of the car. "Will you be okay getting up to the penthouse?"

Tomas blinked and looked at her. "You're not going to walk me up?"

Maria shook her head. "I have to get back to the office. There's a pile of paperwork with my name on it."

"Oh," he said, trying and failing to not sound disappointed. He couldn't be too disappointed. His father had meetings that he couldn't get out of, or so he said, to come and get him from the hospital. He had no idea what Carolyn was doing.

"I'll stop by and check on you later. Okay?"

Tomas nodded. "Sure. I'd like that."

She gave him a quick kiss and climbed back into the car. He watched it pull out and disappear in traffic.

CHAPTER TWENTY

MARIA ENTERED THE SPACIOUS PENTHOUSE THROUGH the rooftop door and prayed she had disabled the security system correctly; breaking into Antonio Dorrance's new penthouse would be challenging to explain to the police. If the police would be the ones to respond. She'd bet money that it would be Dorrance's personal security force instead. Thankfully, she knew Dorrance, Tomas, and his sister were out having dinner and hadn't changed their plans. She had been invited to dinner, but used work as an excuse as to why she couldn't go. It just happened to be her night job and not her day job.

She turned on her night vision glasses and looked around. The penthouse was about the same size as the one her grandfather had here in the city. Dorrance seemed the type to want the biggest and best. Apparently, it was a thing with wealthy men. She had no ambition or desire to have the biggest and best of anything. She suspected it had something to do with having a penis.

The penthouse was scarcely furnished, and Maria couldn't tell if it was intentional or just a lack of opportunity. Dorrance had recently purchased it and maybe didn't have time to furnish it or didn't care enough to get more than the basics. Either way, it made her job more manageable. She didn't have to worry about running into things and have many things to go through.

She crossed the living room and made her way to the stairs leading up. She prayed he had a home office, or this whole endeavor would be for nothing. She ran lightly up the stairs to the second floor. A hallway stretched out ahead and led to a pair of double doors. The master suite. She'd bet money on it. Which meant that one of the four doors that lined the hall was the office. One was also Tomas's room.

Her chest tightened at the thought of him, and her stomach hollowed out. The emptiness where her heart was located became more pronounced, and she pushed the feeling down. She turned it into anger and used it to fuel her steps down the hall.

She opened the first door on her left and peered inside. The spartan room echoed the emptiness of the penthouse in general. A bed, a lamp, and a dresser filled the room. The bed was neatly made with a discarded sweater at the foot, and Maria guessed this was Carolyn's room. The room reflected the coldness of its inhabitant. Maria closed the door and opened the one on the right.

Tomas's presence overwhelmed her. His cologne lingered in the air, and Maria closed her eyes and buried her feelings. She took a deep breath and opened her eyes. A few discarded items of clothing lay on the floor, and his bed was unmade. Like his sister's room across the hall, it contained a bed, dresser, and a small lamp. Maria entered and grabbed a discarded shirt from the chair. She held it up to her nose and inhaled the scent of him. She lowered the shirt and shook her head. Focus! She tossed the shirt back on the chair.

She left his room and headed for the door next to Tomas's. This, too, was furnished like the other two. Guest room. Had to be. Which meant the last remaining door had to be the office. She hoped it was the office. She turned the knob and pushed open the door. Maria frowned. A bathroom. Which meant the office was probably in the master. Of course. Dorrance was the type to keep business stuff close. She closed the door and turned toward the master.

Once inside, she spotted a large desk off to the right and next to the floor to ceiling windows. She walked over and sat down. His laptop sat in the middle of the desk and was turned on. Maria removed a thumb drive from a pocket and inserted it. The screen flared to life, and the computer unlocked. The IT folks at Grayson Enterprises concocted an electronic skeleton key to use on employee laptops when needed, and it worked like a charm.

Maria didn't waste time hunting for what she needed. She copied the whole hard drive to the thumb drive. While the files copied over, she pulled on a drawer to find it locked. Not a problem. She pulled a set of lock picking tools out of a pocket and set to work. In under a minute, she had the drawer unlocked and rifled through the papers.

Her mind told her Tomas was involved in his father's activities, but her heart refused to listen. Tomas was a good man and couldn't be involved despite the evidence in front of her eyes. She grabbed her phone and took a picture of each of the pages. Once she finished, she returned them to the drawer and tidied up, so it didn't look like someone had gone through the contents.

The other five drawers turned up little in terms of information regarding any criminal activities, but it did offer up business and personal information. Maria closed the last drawer and looked at the copy progress. Fifty percent and going. She expected it to take some time, and in the back of her mind, a little voice told her they could arrive home any minute.

A photo to the left of the laptop caught her eye, and she picked it up. The Dorrance family smiled happily for the camera, even the elder Dorrance, on what looked to be a yacht. Tomas and Carolyn looked to be about ten in the photo. Tomas's mother was there, and she could see the resemblance to Tomas and Carolyn. Mother and daughter possessed the same long, dark hair and shape of their nose. Tomas favored his father more.

She replaced the photo and checked the progress of the copy; it read sixty percent. She said a silent prayer for it to move quicker. Patience was not Maria's strong suit.

She pulled out an electronic bug from a pocket in her bag and fastened it to the underside of the desk. Bug sweepers wouldn't find it if they scanned the office since it was a passive transmitter. It uploaded audio twice a day only if there were no ambient sounds in the room. The men in research at Grayson Enterprises more than earned their salaries, and the military contracts were a godsend.

Maria glanced at the computer and the copy progress. Seventy-five percent and rising. She tapped her foot against the carpet. This was taking way too long. She stood and walked over to the dresser. One by one, she opened the drawers and looked inside. She didn't disturb anything in each of them. She just wanted to get a sense of who Antonio Dorrance was.

Once she finished the dresser, she moved to the nightstands next to the bed. Nothing. Maria didn't expect much. They had traveled to New York on business, and the penthouse purchase was new. They didn't have time to make their impression on the space. The computer dinged, and Maria crossed the room. She verified that one hundred percent had copied, and she removed the thumb drive. She locked the computer and pushed the chair back in.

She exited the master bedroom and walked down the hall, not giving Tomas's room another glance or thought. She froze at the top of the stairs when voices drifted up from below. Tomas's voice tugged at her heartstrings, and she quickly pushed the feeling down. She didn't want to see him, and more importantly, she didn't want any of them to see her. She couldn't even begin to talk her way out of this one.

Maria ducked into the guest room and quietly closed the door. She pressed her back against it and listened. Minutes ticked by, and silence roared in her ears. Her heart pounded against her chest, and she pushed down the panic forming. Time seemed to slow as she stood there, listening for the sound of voices. She couldn't leave until they were all in their rooms for the night. Goodness knew how long it would take for them to do that. She had been in worse spots before; she just couldn't think of any at the moment.

Footsteps on the wooden floors in the hallway grew louder, and Maria's heart jumped into her throat. Logically, she knew that they had no reason to enter the guest room. Or so she hoped. She held her breath as the heavy steps of an adult male reached the door. Maria sent a silent prayer that the door wouldn't open.

The steps continued past the door, and a moment later, the door of the master bedroom opened and then closed. Maria breathed a heavy sigh of relief. One down. Two more to go. Those two would be the ones that would possibly make her sit here for a few hours. Maria stood there listening for signs of Tomas and Carolyn going into their rooms, but only silence answered her.

She glanced at her watch. It was only nine pm. Good thing she didn't have any plans tonight besides breaking in here. Otherwise, it'd be difficult to explain why she was late. Her phone vibrated against her ass, and she pulled out her cell. It was a text from Tomas saying hello and seeing if she wanted to go to dinner tomorrow night.

Did she want to go out with him tomorrow? Her first instinct was to say yes, but then she remembered the mask being pulled off his face. The scene shifted, and she saw the man standing next to Dorrance answer the phone. Then she saw the butchered drug dealers. She couldn't continue to see Tomas. Not until she knew the extent of his involvement. If any.

She replied, saying she'd have to play it by ear. She did have a lot of Grayson Enterprises work to catch up on and could use it as an excuse to decline a date. She hated lying, but it was the only thing she could do. She wouldn't be in this situation if she had refused to see him after the night they met. She should have declined the dinner invitation that day he showed up at the office. There were a lot of should-haves when it came to Tomas.

She glanced at her watch. 9:05 pm. Five whole minutes. The longest five minutes of her life. She had hoped to be on her way home, but no, she was stuck in a guest room waiting for the inhabitants of the penthouse to go to bed. Unfortunately, one of them was a night owl and stayed up rather late. The other she could only guess.

Footsteps approached, and she pressed her ear to the door. They were lighter footsteps, and Maria assumed Carolyn was going to her room. Her assumption was correct when the door in the next room opened and then closed. Music drifted through the wall. Two down. One more to go.

Maria stood and listened for the sound of Tomas's footsteps over Carolyn's music. Tomas's sister had horrible taste in music. Maria would have never pegged Carolyn to listen to bubble gum pop and boy bands. Not only did Maria have to sit and wait for Tomas to go to bed, but now she had to be tortured by music that should be outlawed. It didn't even make for good karaoke songs.

The music continued and time slowly trickled by. The only way this could get worse was if she had to pee. Thankfully, she never drank anything before going out on patrol. Finding a bathroom could prove difficult, not to mention getting in and out of her costume wasn't exactly the simplest thing on the planet.

Time moved at a crawl. Maria slowed her breathing and cleared her mind, using meditation techniques she had learned over the years. Her racing mind stilled, and a sense of calm enveloped her. The turbulent emotions, usually swirling around, slowed, and her mind focused on the task at hand.

She took a deep breath and inched the door open, praying that the hinges wouldn't squeak. Luck was with her, but luck could be fickle. She wasn't going to press it. Maria slipped out of the guest room and tiptoed down the hall. She paused at the top of the stairs. Tomas's snores came from down below, and Maria slowly and carefully descended the stairs.

Halfway down, the snores stopped, and Maria froze in place. Blood thundered in her ears, and her heart raced in her chest. Panic threatened to consume her, but Maria shoved it down. She couldn't afford to panic and alert Tomas to her presence. Drinking later would take care of her nerves, turbulent thoughts, and thoughts of Tomas.

The snoring resumed, and Maria allowed herself a breath of relief. She inhaled and continued down the stairs. She reached the bottom and slowly walked across the living room toward the door leading out to the rooftop terrace. Her steps were slow and measured, trying to keep the noise to a minimum.

Halfway across the room, she glanced over at Tomas. Her stomach twisted into a knot and the hollowness inside of her became more pronounced. She wanted nothing more than to walk over and brush back the lock of hair hanging down in front of his face. She wanted to wake him with a deep kiss and feel his hands all over her body.

She clenched a fist and pushed down all the feelings she had for him. She resumed walking. She reached the door and risked another glance back at him. Her heart ached, and she wished he wasn't involved in his father's schemes. But he probably was involved, and she couldn't be with him any more than she could give up her costumed life. Regret filled her, and she slipped out the door and into the night.

CHAPTER TWENTY-ONE

Tomas navigated his way through the cubicle farm toward Maria's office with her father walking next to him. No texts or calls from her in the past week. He called her, and each call went to voicemail. All his texts went unanswered. Something was going on, and he was going to find out what exactly it was. He thought they had an agreement to see each other until he left New York, but now he wasn't sure and didn't understand where her silence came from. He thought they were fine.

Unanswered calls and unreturned texts meant an in-person visit. Tomas arrived at the Grayson offices in mid-town in the morning. He had a meeting with her father and grandfather and figured he would swing by her office when they were done. He managed to get a contract with Grayson Corp for a security review, and he planned to take Maria out to lunch. Two birds with one visit.

He nodded to Gayle as he passed her cubicle, and she gave him a smile and he nodded to her. Okay. Her best friend wasn't giving him a death glare. Always a good sign. If Maria was mad, he assumed her best friend would share that anger, and Tomas wouldn't be getting smiles from the woman.

The two men stopped in the open doorway of Maria's office. Maria, on the phone, looked over and smiled when she saw her father. Her eyes met Tomas, and the smile faded. She didn't glare, which meant she wasn't angry, but the smile faded. What did that mean?

She hung up the phone, and the two men entered the office.

"To what do I owe this pleasure?" she asked.

"Tomas and I had a meeting this morning, and I thought I would escort him down here," her father said.

"I couldn't refuse," Tomas said with a grin. Mr. Grayson offered before Tomas could even ask. He took that as a sign of approval from the man.

"A meeting about what?" Maria asked with a tilted head.

"We're talking about Tomas's family's company doing some security contracting."

Maria's eyes narrowed, and she looked directly at Tomas. "Why?" she asked and turned her attention back to her father.

"Because we could always use an outside opinion on our security measures," her father explained. "Now, if you'll both excuse me, I have a lunch meeting with my father."

"Of course," they said in unison.

Tomas waited for Maria's father to leave the office before he spoke. "Is everything okay?" he asked. He didn't wait for her to offer a chair. He crossed the office and sat in one of the chairs in front of her desk, her gaze following him.

"Yes, why do you ask?"

"I've called and texted but didn't receive any responses," he said. "It made me believe you were trying to avoid me." He leaned back in the chair. "If you are avoiding me, I'd like to know why."

She looked away for a moment and then back at him. "I've been busy."

"Too busy to text or call?" he challenged. Despite the somewhat harsh question, she didn't back down or flinch.

"Yes, and I'm sorry. I should've responded," Maria said. "Work has been hectic the past week." Her stance softened, and Tomas didn't doubt her sincerity.

Tomas nodded. "It's okay. For a while there, I thought you were ghosting me."

"I wasn't ghosting you. How are your ribs?"

Tomas touched his left side. "Healing," he replied. "Still sore, though." He wanted to be honest with her and tell her they were about healed, but he couldn't. If he told her the truth, he'd have to come up with some explanation as to why he was healing faster than average. He had already lied to her about how he injured them. She was the last person he wanted to discover his nighttime activities outside of the bedroom. Just how did one explain putting on a costume and beating up bad guys?

"Have you been taking it easy?" she asked.

"Trying to," he answered. "It's rather boring."

She smiled, and his day seemed much better. "I bet. I'm not good at handling boring either. I go stir crazy when I'm sick and can't do anything."

Tomas smiled. "I figured you were the type to handle boring as well as I do."

"Birds of a feather and all that," she said with a small wave of her hand. "So, what will your company be doing for Grayson?"

"It's not my company," he clarified, "but we'll be analyzing your physical and digital security and making recommendations."

Maria nodded. "Makes sense."

"It should keep me in New York longer," he added.

Their eyes met, and he noticed she didn't smile. He thought that would have been good news to her, but seeing her reaction made him think otherwise. He knew she wasn't the relationship type, at least to hear her say it, and maybe she viewed him staying longer as something more akin to a relationship. He hoped not. He looked forward to each time he saw her and loved spending time with her. Not just because of the sex. Maria approached life with the energy he had never seen before, and she possessed a sharp mind. His interest in her went beyond the physical.

"Not that I'm expecting anything more or serious," he said. "We can keep what we're doing or something else."

Maria stared at him. He wanted to know what was going through her mind. He'd give anything to be a telepath right now. Instead, he got higher durability, more strength, and quicker healing. In terms of powered people, he was on the low end, and he didn't mind. "It's up to you," he added. "You call the shots."

Maria blinked and then nodded.

"If you're not busy tonight, I'd love to take you out to dinner."

"Dinner?"

"Yes, dinner," he said with a smile. "You know that meal that's eaten in the evenings?"

A small smile appeared on her face at his lame attempt. Sure he used it before, but if it got her to smile, he'd say it a million times. "Sure. What time?"

"Seven work for you?" he asked.

"It should," she said. "If I get held up here, I'll let you know."

As soon as she said those words, he knew she wouldn't be going to dinner with him. Everything changed in a second. All he could do was nod. A hollow feeling developed in his chest, and his stomach twisted. "I was going to invite you to lunch, but I can see you're busy." Tomas stood. "I'll see you tonight." He flashed her a forced smile. She returned it with a small smile of her own.

"See you tonight," she said.

Tomas took a long look at her, realizing that this could be the last time he saw her. He turned and headed for the door, smiling ruefully as he stepped through the doorway. He didn't regret anything when it came to her; he just hoped he saw more of her after today.

CHAPTER TWENTY-TWO

"I THOUGHT YOU WERE GOING TO GO TO DINNER WITH Tomas tonight," Maria's father said as he appeared in the doorway to her room. Maria looked up from her phone.

She pushed herself up to a sitting position on the bed. She decided to have dinner with her grandfather and father instead of Tomas. Once dinner finished, she retreated to her room in her grandfather's penthouse. She thought about going back to her apartment, but tonight she needed the safety, security, and feeling of home. Her heart ached, and she needed some comfort.

"I was, but I changed my mind. It's been a while since I've had dinner with you and grandfather." Dinner with her father and grandfather was preferable to dinner with Tomas at the moment. She couldn't spend time with him knowing that he could be involved with his father's possible criminal activities. Her stomach twisted at the idea of Tomas being involved, and she banished the thought as quickly as it had popped into her mind. It had been a while since she spent some time with her two favorite men on the planet. The only two men in the world who wouldn't break her heart.

"Did something happen?"

Concern laced his words, and Maria looked at her father. She sighed, and she knew she had to tell him. He had worn a costume and had beaten up bad guys; if anyone would understand, he would. She patted the side of the bed.

He entered the room and sat down in the designated spot. Maria took a deep breath and told him of meeting Tomas, running into Skanda during nightly patrols, the drug dealers, the massacres of local drug dealers, and overhearing mention of foreigners helping Falcone. She also told him of the suspicions she had about Dorrance's possible involvement with Falcone. Maria also mentioned breaking into the Dorrance penthouse and copying senior Dorrance's laptop hard drive. She even told him about Tomas being Skanda.

Maria stopped talking and looked at her father.

"You've had quite a bit happen in a short time," her father said, shattering the silence that had grown.

Maria nodded. "Yeah, I guess."

"What are you going to do?"

Maria shrugged. "Go through the information first," she answered. Facts came before action. She had to know everything she could possibly learn before deciding what action to take.

"And then?" her father prompted.

"No idea," she said. "I suppose bring Dorrance down when I have enough evidence."

"You will need rock-solid evidence to bring down someone like Dorrance," he said.

"I know," Maria agreed. Dorrance wasn't Grayson level rich, but they had considerable assets and the power to go along with that wealth. The evidence would have to be rock-solid, or all of this would be for naught. He was the biggest fish she had ever gone after.

"Unless, of course, you can catch him in the act, but Dorrance doesn't seem like the type to personally get his hands dirty."

"He's not," Maria said. "He shows up with the cops after I do the hard work. Probably to see how much damage I've done to his business."

Her father nodded. "That makes sense. Do you think Tomas is involved?"

"I want to believe that he isn't, but it's very likely he is," Maria answered. "I'm almost positive his sister is."

"Maybe he isn't involved. As Skanda, he assisted you in breaking up some drug shipments," her father pointed out.

Now that she thought about it, Skanda had helped her break up the shipments. He could have stopped her if he had been working for his father. Or he was keeping an eye on her and whatever was lost in those shipments were acceptable losses. "True. He's either not involved, or he's an outstanding actor and good at throwing off any suspicion," Maria pointed out. "Either way, I'll never see him again."

"Never say never," her father warned.

"I know."

"What are you going to do?" her father asked.

That was the million-dollar question. "Take down whoever is involved," Maria said, her heart breaking as she said it.

"Even if it's Tomas?" her father asked.

Maria nodded. She wanted to verbally respond, but the words stuck in her throat.

Her father put an arm around her, and Maria leaned against him, her head on her shoulder. "I'm sorry, honey. I know you had feelings for him."

"I did," she admitted. She'd never lie to her father, even if it meant admitting she held feelings for Tomas. "You have no reason to be sorry. This is a mess of my own making."

"Would you like some help?"

Maria removed her head from his shoulder and looked at him. "Did you just say what I thought you said?"

He smiled. "I did. I'm not too old to put on a costume and help you. Neither is your mother."

The gesture meant a lot. "Thanks, but it's my mess, I'll take care of it."

"That's my girl," he said and kissed her temple. Maria closed her eyes and smiled. "I'm here if you need help, and I know your mother would help too."

"I know," she said. "Thanks, Dad."

"You're welcome," he said. "I assume you're staying the night."

Maria nodded. "Yeah. I don't feel up to going on patrol tonight." It was only part of the reason she wanted to stay here tonight. The other part was Tomas wouldn't show up here. Right?

Her father hugged her against his side. "Understandable. Did you talk to your mother about this?"

"Not yet," Maria answered.

"I see. Maybe tomorrow night the three of us can have dinner and talk?"

"That sounds great," she said. Her parents never got married, but they remained close. They both said they were best friends, and Maria never doubted them for a moment.

"Great. I'll go call her and set it up. Sleep well."

"You too," she said.

He rose from the bed, leaned over, and placed a kiss on the top of her head. "Good night."

The gesture reminded her of the nights in her childhood when her father tucked her in at night. Maria smiled. The love and comfort he offered were exactly what she needed at the moment.

"Good night," she said before her father closed the door.

Maria sank deeper into the pillows and closed her eyes.

CHAPTER TWENTY-THREE

"THAT WAS AMAZING," HE SAID AS HE ROLLED OFF Maria and fell beside her. He put his hands behind his head, and a grin stretched his mouth. Maria moved away from him and pushed herself to a sitting position, her back to him. She draped her legs off the edge of the bed. Maybe she should have spent another night at her grandfather's.

"I'll be ready for round two in a few moments."

"Shut up," Maria growled. The buzz from her insane self-medication of alcohol dwindled, and emptiness threatened to consume her. Alcohol and sex had proved to be temporary remedies at best. She couldn't remember how many shots of tequila she had put down, and the sex was less than mind-blowing. Disappointing didn't even begin to describe it, and it sure wasn't memorable. Then again, the first man after Tomas was bound to be a disappointment.

"Hey, something wrong?" he asked and put his hand on her naked back.

She pulled away from his touch, and his hand slipped from her back. The fake concern almost made her laugh. She wasn't anything to him just as he meant nothing to her outside of a lay. If he was hoping for a second round, he was about to join her in the land of disappointment. "Get out."

"C'mon, babe," he urged. "We're having a great time."

Maria whipped around and glared at him. Anger welled up, and somehow, she resisted the urge to grab him and throw him out the window. "Get. Out. Now."

His blue eyes widened, and his mouth dropped open for a second. He scrambled off the bed. He bent over and picked up a discarded article of clothing, and her anger grew. She didn't want to hear him or see him. She wanted him gone and sent to the deep recesses of her mind. Just as she had done with Tomas.

"You don't need to be such a bitch," he said.

"Get out," she growled. Each word he said grated like sandpaper and assaulted her dignity. Regrets after meaningless sex were a novel feeling, and she found she didn't like it.

"I'm going as soon as I get dressed," he said, sliding a leg into his pants.

"Get out!" she yelled.

He jumped and ran out of the bedroom with one leg in his pants and carrying his shirt. A few minutes later, the apartment door slammed shut, and Maria slumped over. It wasn't...she couldn't even remember his name. She tried alcohol and sex, and she still had one more option left to her. If this didn't help banish thoughts of Tomas to the deep recesses of her mind, nothing would.

Maria stood and walked to the closet. She opened the door and grabbed her costume. She gave it a hard yank, and it ripped off the hanger. Maria eased the heavy material up her legs and over her hips. As the costume came on, she put Maria Grayson aside, and Balestra took control. Now she could focus on the anger and rage bubbling inside of her and let it engulf and burn away the emptiness.

She sat on the edge of the bed and slipped her feet into her boots. The supple black leather enveloped her legs like a second skin up to her mid-thigh. She curled her toes and smiled. She stood and walked to the bathroom, her boots tapping on the hardwood floor. She opened the medicine chest and pulled out the small container holding her contacts. Maria loved the violet contacts and wished she could wear them outside of her night work.

With her costume on and contacts in, it was time to go out and kick some bad guy ass. Maria grabbed her mask and exited her apartment via a window, jumping down to the ground. She landed on her feet and walked the few blocks to the garage that housed her bike. Straddling the bike, she started the engine, and the tires squealed as she pulled out of the garage.

THE PUNCH HIT HER SIDE, RIGHT IN THE KIDNEY AREA, and her breath left her in a whoosh of air. Pain exploded and radiated through her torso. A string of curses fell from her lips as she stumbled a few steps backward. There would be a bruise tomorrow to remember that hit along with a few others like her jaw and shoulder.

The asshole hitting her was powered or on Boost. Her costume absorbed non-powered punches, and they were nothing more than taps, but his punches hit like punches. Maria took a deep breath and bit back the pain. Payment for this fight would come in the form of soreness later.

Another punch came and hit her in the face. Her head whipped back from the force of the blow. White spots danced in front of her eyes, and pain rattled around her skull. Maria shook her head as she stepped away from the guy. How could she let herself be so sloppy?

Anger flared and the dam holding back all her emotions broke. A wildfire of anger blazed inside of her; rage at the thought of Tomas working with his father. The drugs his father poured into the city. This creep and his buddies trying to shake down a store owner for money. The wild torrent of emotions swirled inside of her and swept her under. The pain faded away under the flood, and energy flowed in.

A primal scream erupted from her, and she charged toward the man. She threw a full-powered right and then a left. The man went flying backward and into the wall of a nearby building. Bricks and mortar gave way, creating an impression. He grunted and extracted himself from the masonry. He growled and charged at Maria.

Their bodies collided and lifted Maria off her feet. She slammed into the opposite wall, the breath escaping from her chest and pain registering in the dim recesses of her mind. She pushed off against the wall and pushed the man backward. She threw quick punches and followed up with a kick to his head. He staggered under the blows, but he didn't go down.

He yelled and countered with punches. A right to her jaw and her head whipped back. A left connected with her stomach, and she doubled over, a knee going to the ground. Maria sucked in a deep breath and threw her right fist straight out. Her punch hit him right in the groin, and he doubled over. Extra durable or not, all guys were vulnerable in that spot.

Maria wiped the blood flowing out of a split lip with the back of her gloved hand and climbed to her feet. She charged toward him and unleashed a flurry of punches. He took the blows and hit back with a series of his own. Each impact increased her anger, and she hit back, each punch stronger than the previous. He growled and withstood her blows. He charged and grabbed her. He heaved, throwing her into a wall, and he followed her.

Her back screamed with white-hot pain as she slammed into the wall. Her eyes watered, and her head swam. She lashed out wildly with her fists. One. Two. Three punches in quick succession to his head caused him to back off. Maria pushed off the wall and stood straight. She wobbled slightly but remained standing. She shook her head, clearing her thoughts. Enough. She knew she couldn't go toe to toe with this guy, whoever he was. He was stronger and more durable, and her body was almost ready to give up.

They stared at each other for a long moment before he charged toward her. Maria reached down to her belt and pulled out a tranquilizer dart. Normally, she fired them from a crossbow, but she didn't have time to reload. The preloaded ones took down this guy's buddy.

He wrapped his arms around Maria, and her ribs protested with pain. She bit back the pain and stabbed the dart into the man's neck. He grunted and squeezed her harder. Maria struggled to draw breath, and white spots appeared in her vision from the pain. His arms tightened, and Maria ceased breathing. The world spun, and any moment now, she'd be swept under and lose consciousness.

He dropped his arms, and Maria fell. Her legs buckled, and she fell to the ground. She drew in a deep breath and instantly regretted it; her ribs were cracked or broken. Just what she needed. At least one wasn't punctured. A small miracle, and she'd take it. She looked over, and the man stumbled backward. He put a hand up and leaned against the wall, trying to shake off the effects of the tranquilizer. He put a hand to his neck and yanked the dart out. It fell to the ground, and Maria hoped he'd follow suit.

This sonuvabitch better go down. Maria didn't know what she would do if he didn't. She couldn't take any more beatings tonight. The only thing she wanted to do was go home, take a long, hot shower, then fall into her bed. Though if she had to admit it, the shower was optional. She wanted to lie down and not move for the rest of her life.

The man took two steps toward her and then crashed to the ground. Maria breathed a sigh of relief and then winced against the pain coursing through her entire body. Thinking was the only thing she could do that didn't physically hurt, but that brought a different type of hurt. Thoughts of Tomas had been banished to the deep recesses of her mind while she had been fighting. Now they were free to bubble up to the surface.

At least she didn't have to worry about running into him tonight. His injuries were severe enough to keep him out for at least a week or so. She'd admit to not liking to see him hurt, but right now, it was better than running into him on the streets. She honestly didn't know how she'd be able to handle seeing him right now. Yet a part of her wanted to see him. She missed his touch and the way he seemed to worship her body with his hands.

Flashing lights out of the corner of her eye caught her attention, and she turned to see a police cruiser pulling up. Sure, now they show up. Five minutes earlier and she wouldn't feel like a punching bag in a boxing gym. Maria braced herself for the pain and pushed herself to her feet. She stood and reflexively put a hand to her right side. Of the two, the right hurt more. She knew she should go to see a doctor and have them bound, but she wouldn't.

She leaned against the wall while she waited for the police.

CHAPTER TWENTY-FOUR

Tomas shivered against the cold wind as he stood on the terrace. Maria was somewhere out there among the bright lights. No matter how hard he tried, his thoughts kept returning to her. Since that day in her office, he hadn't seen her, but he had received a few texts. She had even agreed to dinner tonight with his family but never showed. Not even a text saying she couldn't make it. He supposed their brief affair was at an end. Even though they had told each other it was merely a physical thing, his heart hadn't listened.

He knew he should put her in the past and get back to work. He hadn't done much in terms of work for his father during his stay in New York, and it was the reason why he was here in the first place. Maria had been a wonderful distraction and only that. Nothing more. Or so he kept telling himself. Maybe one day he'd believe it.

A gust of wind sent another chill racing through him, and he should go back inside with his family. Dinner with them had been pleasant enough, but they noticed he had been quieter than usual. The questions came, but he refused to answer. He couldn't answer.

Explaining it all proved to be beyond him right now. Maybe someday he'd be able to talk to someone about him and Maria.

A hand pressed down on his shoulder, and he turned to see his mother. Tomas forced a smile. After finding out about Tomas's injuries, she had come to New York and mothered him almost to the point of smothering. If he had to admit it, he enjoyed the maternal attention.

"You'll catch a cold standing out here without a coat on," she said.

Tomas put a hand on hers and gave it an affectionate squeeze. "You know I don't easily catch colds."

"True, but I still worry. Now, tell me what weighs on your mind."

Tomas turned away. "Nothing," he automatically said.

"Tomas, you should know better than to lie to your mother. Now tell me, what's her name?"

He looked at his mother. "Who says it's a woman?"

"A mother knows," she said with a smile. "What's her name, Tomas?"

"Her name is Maria Grayson," he answered. His mother wouldn't let up until Tomas told her, and it was easier to tell her. It saved a lot of arguing, and his heart wasn't into it.

"What happened between the two of you?"

Tomas shrugged. "Honestly? I don't know. We weren't serious or anything, but one day we stopped talking, and she accepts invitations to dinner, but never shows."

She squeezed his shoulder. "I'm sorry."

"It's okay," Tomas assured her. "It was fun while it lasted." It has been fun, and he enjoyed every moment he spent with her. He had hoped for more time.

"Perhaps it was more serious than you thought," his mother said. "It seems like you really cared for her."

Tomas shrugged but knew his mother's words were right. He had cared deeply for Maria, and maybe he had gotten too serious.

It didn't matter now. She had made it crystal clear that she didn't want serious, and Tomas didn't know how she felt about him. Sure, she had enjoyed the sex, so had he, but as for her feeling anything more in-depth than that, he didn't have a clue. "Maybe," he finally said.

"No maybe. You care a lot about her. I can see it. Have you told her how you feel?"

Tomas shook his head. "No. There's no point in telling her."

"Why not?" his mother challenged.

Tomas sighed, and he knew his mother meant well but wished she would leave him be. He needed time to process the turbulent emotions inside and to exorcise all thoughts of Maria out of his head. "Because she made it perfectly clear from the beginning that she didn't want anything more than a physical relationship."

"Maybe so, but maybe her feelings have changed," she said. "Have you asked her how she feels?"

"I haven't," he admitted. Maybe he should have asked her before things turned downhill. Maybe she did have feelings for him at some point. Even so, it was too late now. He got the message. She didn't want to see him. Even if he did see her, he had to tell her about Balestra and his costumed activities. If she did have feelings for him, they'd probably evaporate after those revelations. "I didn't have a chance."

"Perhaps you should tell her," his mother said. "I love you, Tomas, and I want you to be happy. If this woman makes you happy, go tell her how you feel."

He could, but he doubted it would make a difference. Maybe it was best if he avoided her and gave himself time to get over her.

Tomas turned and hugged his mother. "I love you too. I'll think about it." His mother released him and walked toward the door. "Mom," he called after her. "One more question." She walked back toward him.

"Yes?"

"Do you know what Father and Carolyn are working on? I asked Carolyn, but she won't talk about it."

His mother shook her head. "I do not. I've learned to never get involved in your father's business, and Carolyn has not mentioned it to me."

Tomas frowned. He had hoped his mother would have some insight into the secret project his sister was working on for their father. "Thanks."

His mother nodded and went inside the penthouse. Tomas turned and looked at the lights of the city.

CHAPTER TWENTY-FIVE

"WHERE HAVE YOU BEEN FOR THE PAST THREE DAYS?"
Gayle asked with her hands on her hips as she stood in the
doorway of Maria's bedroom. Maria never heard her come into the
apartment.

"Right here," she answered as she lifted her head from the
pillow where she had been curled up. "What are you doing here?"

Gayle's hands fell from her hips, and she entered the room,
taking care to step over and around the clothes scattered all over
the floor. As well as empty bottles. Gayle sat on the edge of the
bed opposite Maria. "Are you okay?"

"Got my ass kicked, hard, the other night," Maria said.

Gayle sighed heavily. "Please tell me you kicked their asses
harder."

"Of course I did," Maria scoffed, a little insulted at the remark.

"Good," Gayle said with a nod. "It wasn't Tomas, was it?"

The mere mention of his name was like a knife in her heart.
Her body hadn't been the only thing that needed time to heal. She
spent the last three days in bed to give her body time to heal and
give her the peace and solitude she needed. She tried as hard as

she could to forget Tomas and banish all thoughts of him, but she failed.

"No, it wasn't Tomas," she said, looking away. "Someone else. I had a few broken ribs and figured I'd watch a movie or two while I was healing." It was true for the most part. She did need to heal, but she hadn't turned on a movie. She had spent time going through the information she stole from Tomas's father's computer and listening to recordings from the bug she planted.

"Well, at least you had the sense to take it easy and heal," Gayle said as she shifted and stretched out on the bed next to Maria. Gayle rolled on her side to face Maria. "Have you talked to Tomas?"

"No," Maria answered quietly. Doubts and uncertainty gripped her. She knew she had to talk to Tomas at some point, even if it was to tell him about his father's criminal activities, but she didn't know if she could do it. Her heart already ached and seeing him would make it hurt more. There was a small chance he didn't know but she found it hard to believe he could not know.

"Why not?"

"One, I would have to explain my injuries to him, and I'm not willing to do that quite yet," she explained.

"Telling him the truth about who you are wouldn't be the end of the world," Gayle said.

"It would be if he went to the media," Maria pointed out. There had been times she wanted to tell him about her secret identity, but she didn't trust him enough. Secret identities weren't just to protect her, but they protected her friends and family as well. Anyone with a grudge to settle with Balestra, and there were quite a few of them, could easily go after the people she loved. Maria couldn't live with herself if someone she loved got hurt because of her.

"What else?" Gayle urged. She reached out and took a lock of Maria's hair and ran her fingers through it.

"He may be working for his father and helping him bring drugs into the city." Just saying those words left a bitter taste in her mouth. She wanted to believe in Tomas's better angels, but she was having difficulty doing it.

"Do you honestly believe that?"

"No. Maybe. I don't know," Maria said with a sigh. She pushed down the emptiness inside of her. She thought she had done a decent job of burying thoughts of Tomas, but clearly, she was wrong. Three days and a lot of alcohol weren't nearly enough time to get over Tomas.

"Don't you think the first thing you should do is find out if he's involved with his father's criminal activities?"

"I suppose," Maria relented.

"Then, if he's not, then you go have fun with that guy," Gayle said.

"No matter what happens, spending time with him is not in the cards."

"Why not?" Gayle asked.

Maria looked up at Gayle. "Because if he's involved with his father's activities, I have to bring him in along with his father. If he's not, he won't want anything to do with me because I brought down his father."

"But he won't know it's you," Gayle pointed out.

"What if he finds out?"

"Maybe he won't. Maybe he isn't involved and is against the things his father is doing. He would want to see his father pay for his crimes."

"That's a lot of maybes. If, and that's a big if, he isn't involved in his father's criminal activities, I would like to tell him the truth about who I am. I don't want to lie to him," she said. "If it's going to be something more than physical, I want to be honest with him, provided he doesn't hate me for bringing down his father."

Gayle's eyes widened, and Maria knew in that instant she said more than she should have. She braced herself for what was to come. "You have feelings for him!"

Okay, she had feelings for Tomas; she could finally admit that to herself. Out loud was a whole different story. Maria sighed. As much as she didn't want to say the words, she had to. Gayle would never let her off that easily. "Yes, I do," she whispered.

"I knew it! I knew it since the morning we had breakfast with the two of you at the diner. And you're admitting it stone-cold sober." Gayle propped herself up on an elbow and looked at the empty bottles sitting on the nightstand. "At least I think you're sober." Gayle lowered herself back down.

"I am. I ran out of alcohol yesterday. Are you done now?" Maria asked.

"Don't be so surly," Gayle chided. "You're acting like it's the end of the world."

"No, I'm not," Maria said a little more harshly than she intended. "It's only the end of the world if the media finds out my secret identity."

Gaye smirked. "Yes, you are. So what are you going to do about it? Did you tell him how you feel?"

"Nothing and no," Maria answered. "There's nothing I can do except bring his father to justice and then drink copious amounts of alcohol."

"That has never worked, and you know it. Go tell that guy how you feel about him."

Gayle had a point, and Maria had never successfully drank away feelings for a guy. Though it had been so long since she last tried, there was no valid reason not to try again. "Maybe so, but I'm going to try," she said, ignoring the second part of what Gayle said. It didn't matter if Tomas knew how she felt about him. Once she arrested his father, her feelings toward Tomas wouldn't matter.

"Is there anything I can do for you or get for you?" Gayle asked, putting a hand on Maria's shoulder.

"Shoot me and put me out of my misery already," she grumbled.

"Besides that," Gayle said with a small smile.

"Go buy me some more alcohol?" Maria suggested.

"Judging by all those empties in this room, you've had enough for a while."

"You're no fun."

Gayle chuckled. "That's not what Charlene says. Go take a shower, and I'll make you something to eat. If I know you, it's been a while since you've had any food."

"Okay, Mom," Maria grumbled. Arguing with Gayle was useless. Maria would do what the woman wanted, and it was easier to capitulate early. Maria pushed herself to a sitting position, as did Gayle. Maria smiled and then tightly hugged her best friend. "Thanks. Love you."

"You're welcome and love you too," Gayle said.

CHAPTER TWENTY-SIX

MARIA DUCKED, AND THE PUNCH AIMED AT HER HEAD whooshed through the air above her. Maria jabbed with her right and hit the man in the stomach. He doubled over, and Maria hit him with an uppercut. The blow lifted the man off his feet and sent him flying backward. He landed and collapsed into a heap.

Six down and knocked out without breaking a sweat. Damn, she was good. Now to see what was in the shipping container and the van. At least these guys were predictable with a van. It gave her a small sense of security to know at least a tiny bit of normal existed. She looked at the van and then at the shipping container. Van first; it was smaller.

Maria opened a rear door and looked inside. Empty. They hadn't had a chance to load whatever it was they were sent to pick up. It made her job a little easier. She shut the door and walked over to the shipping container.

One door stood ajar, and Maria figured they had just opened it. She grabbed the edge of the opened door and pulled it. The door moved with a protest of metal rubbing against metal. Maria froze and looked around to see if anyone had noticed. The late hour and the cold contributed to the lack of people. Even the few dockworkers on shift were huddled in their little outpost buildings.

Maria turned on a small flashlight and moved it around. Stacked wooden crates marked with the Dorrance logo lined the walls from the doors to halfway in. A vehicle sat beyond the crates. Maria set the flashlight down and looked at the padlock on one of the crates. She pulled a lock-picking tool out of her belt and set to work on the lock. A few moments later, the lock clicked and popped open. Maria removed it and opened the crate.

Five semi-automatic weapons lay nestled in packing material—nothing out of the ordinary for a security company. Something seemed off, though. Maria looked at the outside of the box and then at the weapons inside. She quickly removed the guns and set them aside. She dug through the packing material and felt around. The wood bottom didn't go all the way to the bottom of the crate as it should. Maria felt around the edges and discovered a hold in one corner. She hooked two fingers in the space and lifted the "bottom" out of the box. Packing material went everywhere, and she dropped the wood sheet on the floor. She reached in and pulled out a tightly wrapped package of a white powder. The files taken from Dorrance's computer, and these bricks, confirmed Maria's suspicions. Some small part of her had hoped she had been wrong, but this buried those hopes.

Dammit. She sighed and returned the package of drugs back to the crate. She replaced the false bottom. The weapons went in next, and Maria closed the box. Any chance of having something with Tomas also died. Time to call Rollins and hand over the stolen computer information and let the police bust Dorrance.

Maria exited the shipping container and looked at the unconscious men. She pulled out her burner phone and brought up the number for Rollins. The sound of footsteps behind her made her forget about the call. She dropped the phone and spun around, her hands up and ready to punch.

"What are you doing here?" she asked. Skanda, aka Tomas,

wasn't totally unexpected, but she had thought it would take him longer than this to heal from his injuries.

"Apparently arriving a little too late for fun," he answered, looking down at the inert bodies on the ground.

Maria didn't lower her hands. "You're too late," she said. "The police are on their way."

"I'm sure they are," he said, stepping around her and entering the container. "Though I'm uncertain why police would be needed for Dorrance employees picking up a shipment."

She dropped her hands and turned around to watch him. "There are drugs in those crates."

"Impossible," he said, opening the same crate Maria had opened. "Dorrance isn't involved in the drug trade."

"Someone is," Maria said. "There's a false bottom in that crate."

He shook his head.

"I have no reason to lie to you," she said. "Look for yourself." She flicked her hand toward the crates. He didn't verbally respond. Instead, he looked in the container. "Look beneath the weapons," she told him.

"Nothing but the bottom," he said, looking back at her after checking.

"The top right corner is cut out. Lift up."

He stared at her for a long moment and then removed the guns. He put his hand into the crate and lifted up on the false bottom. He pulled it out and stared at the contents.

"See? Kilos of Boost in there."

Tomas shook his head again. "This can't be right. This has to be a setup."

"It's not," Maria said. "Drug dealers across the city have been killed in the past few months. Mostly members of four of the five families. With them out of the picture, whoever is left has a monopoly on the drug trade here in New York."

He turned and glared at her. "It has to be," he insisted.

"Dorrance can't be involved in the distribution of Boost and the murders."

"You put on a good act," she said, ignoring the ache in her heart. "Making it sound like you didn't know."

"An act?" he asked. "Dorrance isn't involved in any drug distribution. I would know."

"You heard me," she said. Each word he said drove a stake through her heart and killed the possibility of them ever being together. The wounds he delivered would take a long time to heal. She should have known better than to get involved with him. Now she would pay the price. "Are you so sure?"

"Yes," he said after a slight hesitation. He crossed his arms over his chest and scowled. "This is a setup. You did this. After you found out who I am, you set this up to bring down my family."

"I did no such thing," Maria said. "I do not need to frame your father. He's done this all on his own." Maria opened a small pouch on her belt and pulled out a thumb drive. "I copied this data from your father's computer. This is how I know there would be drugs inside of those crates and which shipping container they're in." She tossed it to him. She made two copies, one for Tomas and one for the police, and kept the original.

"What is this?" he asked, catching it.

"Proof. Proof that your father is involved in drugs. If you don't believe me, verify it on your father's computer. There are recordings of him as well."

He looked down at the drive in his hand and then back at Maria. His hand curled into a fist around the drive. "Lies," he growled. "Nothing but lies."

"I'm not lying!"

"You are, and you're trying to destroy my family and me."

Maria shook her head and knew he'd never believe anything she said about his family and her intentions. She took a deep, cleansing breath and pulled off her right glove. The left one followed, and she tucked them into her belt. She removed her contacts and shoved them into a case in her pocket.

Tomas watched her, and Maria moved with deliberate and careful movements. Would this be considered a non-sexual strip tease? Whatever it was, she had Tomas's attention. His eyes never left her. She didn't even think he blinked.

"I never wanted to hurt you or destroy you." The bitter taste of losing him filled her. They could have been good together, but now they'd never have the chance.

She inhaled deeply and readied herself. Trusting someone came hard for her, and as soon as she removed her mask, Tomas would know her secret. She had to trust him to not go to the media outlets and to not hurt her.

She reached up to touch the sides of her mask, her hands shaking the entire time. "Quite the opposite, actually." As the words slipped past her lips, she pulled on the mask and removed it, delivering the death blow to any potential relationship with him. She didn't watch it fall silently to the ground, but instead, she watched his eyes follow the mask. Then he looked back at her face.

His angry expression drained away. Shock and surprise replaced it.

THE BREATH FROZE IN HIS CHEST, AND SHE LEFT HIM without the means to talk. A hit to the groin would have made less of an impact on him. He broke apart the same as any man, and she shook his faith like only a woman could. His brain scrambled to make sense of what he saw before him.

Maria. Maria Grayson, his pseudo-girlfriend, was Balestra, and he never caught on. Not even in the slightest. The signs had to have been there, but he had been blinded. His heart had taken control, and his brain didn't function as it should have.

It made sense now how she could keep up to him in bed. He always controlled his actions since he never wanted to hurt his partner, but he hadn't been so careful with her. She gave as good as she got.

He forced the breath out of his chest and inhaled another. Breathe. In. Out. Repeat. Maria stared at him, almost waiting for him to say something. Words refused to flow down from his brain. Even if he could say something, he had no idea what to say.

"I'm sorry, Tomas. More than you'll ever know." Maria turned and walked away. Tomas watched her for a few moments, and only one word made it from his brain to his mouth.

"Maria," he called.

She stopped, lowered her head, then turned around. Tears fell from her eyes. "I saw a future with you," she said, her voice wavering. More tears fell from her eyes. "When you finally believe me about your father, you know where to find me." She turned and walked away.

He stood there and watched her go, taking a part of his heart with her. He wanted to stop her, but shock kept him frozen in place.

She climbed on her bike, started the engine, and pulled out. Tomas watched the taillight disappear into the night.

Tomas sighed and looked at the thumb drive in his hand. Could she be telling the truth? If so, could this be what his father and sister were working on in private? It hurt his brain to even think of the possibility. His father and sister were good people and certainly not capable of this.

Sirens in the distance brought him out of his reverie. He had to leave. There would be too many questions he didn't have answers to. Even if he had answers, he didn't think the police would believe him. It was for the best he didn't put himself in that no-win situation. He picked up the mask lying on the ground and turned it over in his hands.

Shaking his head, he ran out of the dockyard. All of this was so surreal, and he almost didn't believe any of it. He didn't want to believe his father was involved in the brutal murders and the flow of Boost.

His mind raced as he made his way back to the family penthouse and a hollow feeling grew in his chest. Once he arrived, he went straight to his room and opened his laptop. He shoved the thumb dive into the slot and opened the drive contents.

An hour later, he just stared at the screen, his thoughts running in circles. She had to have had someone create this to frame his father. This couldn't be real. Maria was wrong and someone had given her false information, or she had someone create it. He'd prove it by looking at the real data on his father's laptop.

Tomas stood and walked into his parents' bedroom. They were out at the opera tonight and would be back late. Carolyn was out, but he didn't know where. He sat down at the desk and logged into the laptop. Thankfully, his father didn't change his passwords on a regular basis and had Tomas get information from the laptop on occasion.

It didn't take him long to realize the information on the laptop matched the information on the thumb drive. Physical hits wouldn't have hurt more. His stomach twisted up, and he logged out of the laptop.

Returning to his room and falling back on the bed barely registered. He stared at the ceiling wondering what he was going to do now. Maria had told him the truth, and he had been blinded by familial loyalty to believe her. He had to see it in black and white before his brain would even accept it.

Tomas sighed. Any chance of having a relationship with Maria was gone and members of his family were criminals and supplying drugs. The solid ground disappeared under his life, and he had no idea what he should do.

CHAPTER TWENTY-SEVEN

Maria kept herself busy with work, both jobs, to distract her from thinking about Tomas. She worked for ten hours at the office during the day. After work, she ate a quick dinner and then took a nap. Nine pm every night, she donned her costume and hit the streets.

A week had passed since she took off her mask in front of Tomas, revealing her identity, and during that week, she had managed to bust up five of Dorrance's drug shipments. The drive didn't hold any more mentions of shipments coming in via the docks, so Dorrance must have a factory in the city somewhere. It took a few days of hunting, but she eventually found the warehouse where the drugs were being manufactured. Dorrance had apparently stepped up the amount of Boost he was moving.

Maria perched on a nearby rooftop, watching the warehouse and taking note of whoever arrived. She waited for some time. No one came and no one left. She did a double check of her weapons. Her two mini crossbows were loaded and ready to go. The two pistols strapped to her waist were loaded with tranq darts—no time like the present to go in. Maria ran and jumped across to the roof of the warehouse.

She landed and went into a roll, springing to her feet. She looked through the skylight and quickly absorbed the scene. Tables were lined up and were loaded with wrapped packages of Boost. She dashed across the roof to the other end of the building. She looked through the skylight there and saw tables filled with laboratory equipment. Dorrance was producing Boost here in the city. Anger bubbled up. She thought of all the people hurt by Boost and wanted to hurt the elder Dorrance in the worst way. He had to pay for ruining so many lives.

Maria pulled out her burner phone and sent a quick text message to Rollins and slaughtered any chance of a relationship with Tomas. By the end of the night, his father would be in jail, and all criminal activities would be brought to light. Nothing killed a potential relationship like having his father and sister arrested. Maria was the all-time winner when it came to finding wrong men.

Maria wished she didn't have to do this, but there was no other choice. She took a deep breath in, held it for a moment, and then let it out—time to get down to business and kick some ass.

Pain erupted at the base of her skull, where it met her neck. White spots danced in front of her eyes, and Maria doubled over in pain. Wrapped up in her thoughts, she never heard someone approach from behind. She cursed her own carelessness. Another blow hit her on her cheek, smashing into her cheekbone. Maria stumbled and tried to keep her feet under her. She turned her head to look at her attacker and saw the masked woman, the one she suspected to be Carolyn Dorrance.

Maria stumbled away from her, but she didn't move quick enough. A foot slammed into her face, and the crack of her nose breaking filled her ears. Blood gushing out of her nose registered as a wave of blackness dragged her under.

Maria floated in the blackness until the sounds of people talking pulled her to consciousness. She forced her eyes open and willed them to remain open. Bright light flooded the room, and

Maria blinked against it. She moved her arm to put a hand up, but she found herself restrained to a chair. She pulled on the thick chains holding her, but they didn't budge. Someone had done their homework.

She looked around and found herself surrounded by six men in tactical gear, pointing semi-automatic weapons at her. The taste of blood filled her mouth, and she could almost feel it drying on her face. Pain throbbed on the right side of her face, and she knew it'd be swollen for some time. She wanted to shake her head and clear away the cobwebs and pain, but doing so would make the wrecking balls in her head move more.

"Welcome back," a voice said. Maria looked across the room to see Antonio Dorrance walking toward her. Carolyn walked next to him. Maria wanted nothing more than to knock that smug look off Carolyn's face. She placed that desire at the top of her list of things to do as soon as she got free. Right after she kicked the elder Dorrance's ass.

"I suspected someone had gotten information from my computer," Dorrance said as he stopped directly in front of her. "I figured whoever it was would eventually find this place."

"The police are on their way," Maria said. "It won't be long before they're here."

Dorrance smiled. "I suspected as much, so we will be leaving just as soon as I see who is under the mask and then have my men kill you."

"They'll be here sooner than you think," Maria bluffed. She hoped Rollins wouldn't waste any time getting here. She ran a little short on knights charging into battle lately.

"Maybe, but rest assured, we will not be here." He stepped forward and reached out toward her face. Maria jerked her head out of his reach and regretted the action as pain bounced around in her head. "There's no use struggling, my dear. Your mask will come off whether you're dead or alive."

Maria glared at him, and if looks could kill, he'd be a pile of goo on the floor by now. His hand darted out and grabbed her mask. He ripped it off in a smooth motion, and a small gasp escaped Carolyn.

"I will admit I'm surprised," Dorrance said. "I didn't expect a wealthy socialite who happens to be my son's girlfriend to be the thorn in my side."

"I try not to disappoint," Maria snarled.

"Perhaps," he said. "One question before I kill you. Does my son know about you?"

Maria looked Dorrance in the eye. He seemed the type to harm his own flesh and blood and admitting that Tomas knew about her could bring his father's wrath upon him. Despite all that happened between them and how it all unfolded, Maria never wanted to see Tomas come to harm. Maria would always remember the feeling in her gut when she dealt with a significantly injured Tomas. She never wanted to feel that way again, even if she apparently had moments to live. She pulled against the chains. They refused to give.

"No," Maria said. "He doesn't know."

Dorrance studied her for a long moment, as if trying to determine if Maria lied or not. Thankfully, moonlighting as a costumed hero helped her develop her ability to lie convincingly.

"He knows," Carolyn said. "How else would she have gotten information off of your computer?"

"No," Maria growled. "I broke into your penthouse and got the information myself. Tomas knows nothing. He was easy to fool because he is a fool, like all men. You kiss them and show some skin, let them fuck you, and they don't ask questions. They only think with the brain between their legs and are easy to manipulate." In general, yes, but not Tomas.

Dorrance backhanded her, and Maria's head jerked to the side. Either Dorrance had been insulted as a man, or he actually cared for his son. If she had to be honest, she'd place her money on the former.

"See?" Maria smirked.

Dorrance struck her again. At least he wasn't powered, or his blows would have hurt a lot more. The slaps stung, but Maria could handle those.

"Pity you are who you are," Dorrance said. "My son could have married you and had access to the Grayson fortune."

"As if I would let your son touch one penny of the Grayson fortune," Maria spat. He didn't know that she didn't even have access to her trust fund. Or ever would. She'd only inherit the family fortune when her father died, and even that wasn't a guarantee.

She strained against the chains. If only she possessed more strength, she could break them and make this sonuvabitch hurt. Maybe a different approach was required. Instead of pulling against all the chains, she maneuvered her hands so she could work on one link. If one link broke, the chain would come undone.

"Kill her and be done with it," Carolyn said, standing behind her father with her arms crossed over her chest.

Dorrance nodded. "Of course," he said. "We do not want to be here when the police arrive." Dorrance raised his arm and stretched his hand toward one of his men. The man lowered the automatic weapon and handed Dorrance a pistol from his side.

Dorrance turned back toward Maria and aimed the weapon at her head. Maria's mouth went dry, and her heart jumped into her throat. Yet, terrified out of her mind, she didn't flinch. If this was going to be the end of her, she'd face it like a woman. She could ovary up when she needed to.

She stared into Dorrance's eyes, almost daring him to squeeze the trigger. His eyes narrowed, and the breath stayed in Maria's chest. She continued to stare at him as she faced her inevitable death.

CHAPTER TWENTY-EIGHT

Tomas spent a week combing over all the information Maria provided and looking for something that would help him decide what to do. He found a mention of a warehouse in the files and decided to check it out. He just had to do it at a time when his family was distracted. An opportunity presented itself when his father and sister went out for the evening. He told his mother he was going to go see Maria, grabbed his costume, and left. His mother had to be the only innocent person in this whole mess, and he was extremely thankful for that.

Once out of the penthouse, Tomas suited up and headed for the warehouse. A few SUVs sat outside the warehouse, and the inside was brightly lit. It looked like the correct place. Standing on a rooftop of a nearby building, he watched the activity outside the warehouse. He watched his sister and father enter. He waited a little longer before going in. He gathered his courage and was about to leap off the roof when movement in the corner of his eye caught his attention.

He'd know that silhouette anywhere. Maria. His heart skipped a beat, and his mouth went dry. He supposed it was inevitable he would run into her on the streets. He just didn't know if he was ready for it. Emotionally, at least. Physically, well, that was a different story. He figured they would either try to kick each other's ass or end up fucking. Maybe a little of both.

She jumped from her perch to the warehouse. He held his breath as she jumped and let it out when he realized what he was doing. He shook his head. No matter how he tried, he couldn't stop caring about her. Even though he now knew what she could do.

He waited while she checked out the skylights and wished he could have had time to look before she showed up. Maria moved to another set of skylights and stopped. A figure materialized from the shadows and moved toward Maria. Tomas's gut twisted when he realized the shadow was female and probably his sister.

She hit Maria on the back of Maria's head. Tomas's stomach twisted more as he watched his sister repeatedly hit Maria until she went unconscious. Carolyn picked up Maria's inert form, tossed it over a shoulder, and disappeared in a rooftop access door.

Now what did he do? His father and sister now had Maria in their clutches, and saving Maria would mean confronting his family. Could he do it? He didn't have an answer at this moment, and he knew he'd have to decide soon.

In the meantime, he could watch. Tomas took a running leap and jumped. He cleared the street and landed on the warehouse roof. He raced over to the skylight and looked down.

Carolyn deposited Maria's unconscious form on a chair, and two of his father's men wrapped a heavy chain around her. They fastened it with locks. Tomas didn't know if she could break the chains or not, and he didn't have the foggiest clue to what his father and sister would do to her. Or what she would do to them for that matter. He didn't want any of them getting hurt.

Tomas continued to watch. His father's men, each holding semi-automatic rifles, surrounded Maria, and his father and sister stood in front of her. Maria moved her head, and Tomas knew she was regaining consciousness. He had to get down there.

He ran to the edge of the roof and jumped off. He landed and ran for the nearest door. He grabbed the handle, pulling the door off the hinges. He tossed it aside and rushed inside. Tomas ran as fast as he could.

He burst through a door to see his father pointing a gun at Maria's head. She had been unmasked and looked defiantly at his father. His heart leaped into his throat, and his stomach dropped. Time slowed and seemed to come to a stop. His sister and father turned their heads and looked at him. Surprise registered on their faces.

"What's going on here?" he asked, looking from his father to Maria. Her eyes widened in surprise, and he smiled behind his mask.

Tomas's father spun around and pointed the gun at him.

"Tomas!" Carolyn gasped.

Tomas ripped off his mask and looked directly at his father. His father's eyes widened, and his mouth dropped open a little. His father quickly regained his composure.

"You're just in time to watch your girlfriend die," his father said.

Tomas looked at Maria. Their eyes met, and his mouth went dry. He looked at his father and then at his sister. "Don't do this," he said.

His father turned and looked directly at him. "She has disrupted our business enough. She knows everything, and I cannot have her telling anyone."

"This is insane!" Tomas shook his head. "She hasn't disrupted the company's business," he explained.

"Brother, you are so naive," Carolyn said. "Now go away and let Father and I deal with this."

"I won't let you kill her," Tomas said. In that moment, he realized he had made his choice. He loved Maria and didn't want to see her get killed. But it wasn't only that. Killing someone in cold blood was something he believed his family was above, and he wouldn't let them go down that road.

Tomas moved to stand between his family and Maria.

"Don't be a fool, Tomas," Carolyn said. "Move."

"No," Tomas growled. "If you want her, you go through me."

CHAPTER TWENTY-NINE

MARIA'S EYES WIDENED WHEN TOMAS ENTERED THE room. She forced herself not to react and kept her face neutral. Her heart leaped into her throat at the sight of him in uniform, and her stomach tightened. At first, she thought he was here to stand with his family, but then he stood between them and her.

She struggled with the chain as she watched Tomas dealing with his father and sister. The metal refused to move, and she tried putting more force into it. She kept her movements to a minimum as she didn't want Carolyn and the elder Dorrance noticing what she was doing.

"Tomas, stop being foolish and get out of the way," his father said.

"Put the gun away," Tomas said. Maria pulled harder on the metal link.

"She cannot walk out of here," Carolyn said. "She knows too much."

"You mean too much about the drug smuggling and production?" Tomas asked.

"Honestly, it took you long enough."

"Enough!" His father aimed the gun directly at Tomas. "Now move. We need to get out of here before the police arrive."

"I'm not moving," Tomas said. His voice was even and didn't contain a trace of fear. Maria would probably be terrified if she had to stand against her family. Maria pulled as hard as she could on the link. The metal gave a little, and hope sprang up inside of her.

His father shook his head. "You disappoint me like always."

Maria blinked, and Tomas physically flinched from the cutting words. She never asked Tomas about his family relationships, but she would never have predicted such words could fall from his father's lips. She couldn't imagine having a family member saying something like that to her. Her family had their issues, what family didn't, but she never once doubted their love for her. Her heart ached for Tomas, and she wished she could comfort him. Maria pulled on the chain as hard as she could, and the metal gave way.

She froze and prayed the chain remained still. She didn't want anyone to know she had escaped her restraints.

"Move, Tomas," Carolyn urged.

"No!"

Dorrance flicked the fingers on his free hand, and the men surrounding them raised their semi-automatic rifles and took aim.

Time slowed to a stop. Despite the large empty space, the tension rose and coalesced around them. No one moved a muscle. The only sounds came from the hum of the large fluorescent lights overhead. Maria slowed her breathing, and her muscles tensed. She waited for someone to move.

Carolyn lunged for Tomas, and everyone seemed to move at once. Tomas stepped to the side and blocked his sister's attack.

With Tomas out of the direct line of fire, the elder Dorrance squeezed the trigger. The gunshot echoed in the cavernous space, and the bullet slammed into Maria's chest. Even though her costume was bulletproof, pain radiated outward, and the breath exploded out of her. She drew in another breath, and the pain spiked.

Maria threw her arms out to the sides, and the chain fell into a pool at her feet. Maria immediately went into a roll as shots from the men zoomed over her head. She rolled toward the closest man and sprang to her feet in front of him. She hooked an arm around his neck and spun him around, pinning his body against hers, using him as a shield. Another one of the men fired at her, riddling the man with bullets.

Maria removed her arm from around his neck and grabbed handfuls of the man's uniform in the back. She heaved him at the man who had fired. The body sailed the short distance and knocked the other man to the ground. Maria moved to the closest man and threw a quick jab at the man's head. He went down in a heap, and Maria launched herself at the next man.

Pain registered in her thigh as a bullet slammed into it. She collided with the man, and her momentum and weight brought them to the ground with her landing on top. Maria yelled and sent a fist toward the man's head. The hit connected, and the man went limp. Three down, three more to go, five if you counted his father and sister.

A bullet slammed into her side, and Maria winced against the pain. Tomorrow she'd be sporting quite a few bruises from this. At least they weren't bullet holes. Maria pushed herself off the man and rolled to the side. She looked around, doing a quick assessment. Tomas fought his sister, and the two looked evenly matched.

Another bullet slammed into her, this one on her side. Maria rolled and sprang to her feet. She charged the man who had just shot her and delivered a full-powered punch to his chest. The body armor kept him from being killed, but he went flying backward into a steel pillar. He hit with a thud and sank to the ground.

Maria didn't wait for the next shot to come, and she launched herself at the closest man, tackling him to the ground. She ripped the rifle out of his hands and threw it away. She delivered a punch to his face. His eyes rolled backward, and he went still.

Maria immediately moved and went after the last man. He regained his composure and aimed his rifle at her. Maria leaped into the air, above the shots he fired, and delivered a kick to his head as she came down. The man collapsed into a pile. She looked around. Only Tomas and his family were left.

Tomas fought his sister, and Maria watched, ready to act if needed. The two were evenly matched, and Maria figured they must have sparred together. Neither gained the advantage over the other, and they traded blow for blow. Until Tomas threw a punch, and Carolyn went flying backward. She smashed against a wall and instantly regained her footing. She charged toward her brother.

Carolyn kicked at her brother's head, but he managed to block it with his forearm. Tomas grabbed her in mid-air and slammed her on the ground. She laid there on her back for a long moment before pushing off and springing to her feet. Carolyn kneed Tomas in the groin, and he doubled over in pain. She grabbed him and threw him into a wall.

Sirens grew louder, and Maria breathed a sigh of relief. This was almost over. Just a few more minutes, and Dorrance would be arrested, and the flow of Boost would slow, if not stop. Movement in the corner of her eye caught her attention, and Carolyn slammed into her a second later. The two women fell to the floor with Maria landing under Carolyn. She shoved the other woman off her, sending her through the air. Maria rolled, and Carolyn crashed back down to the ground.

Maria sprang to her feet and put her fists up, ready for another attack. Carolyn didn't disappoint. She charged toward Maria, and as soon as Carolyn was close enough, Maria lashed out with a right. Carolyn ducked it and countered with a right uppercut. It caught Maria off guard, and pain ripped through her. The blow lifted Maria off her feet and sent her flying backward. Maria crashed onto one of the tables, landing on top of the packages of Boost. They exploded in a cloud of white powder, covering Maria.

Maria coughed and waved her hand in front of her face to disperse the cloud. Electricity coursed through her as the inhaled drug began to spread through her system. Her nerves were live wires, burning, and on fire. Maria couldn't remember a time when she felt more energized or powerful. The pain from fighting melted away in the rush of Boost. She wanted to take on all of New York City at this moment.

Maria rolled off the table and landed on her feet just in time to catch a charging Carolyn. Maria growled and grabbed Carolyn by the throat, oblivious to the blows the other woman was delivering. Maria lifted Carolyn off her feet and held her there.

Carolyn slapped at Maria's hands to get Maria to release her. Maria squeezed harder, and Carolyn struggled to breathe. Just a little more pressure and Carolyn's life would be snuffed out like a candle.

"Maria!" Tomas yelled.

Maria blinked and looked at him. She growled and tossed Carolyn across the length of the warehouse with ease, and Carolyn crashed against the far wall, collapsing into a heap.

Maria looked around for another opponent. With the energy and power coursing through her, she wanted more. The only ones left standing were Tomas and his father. Dorrance must have heard the sirens growing louder. He started running for the nearest door. Finally! Maria charged after him with her speed enhanced by Boost; she caught him just as his hand wrapped around the door handle. She grabbed the back of his shirt and yanked him away from the door. Dorrance spun around, brandishing a knife. He drove it forward toward her stomach, and it slipped through her uniform. It went into her skin, yet she barely felt it.

Maria grabbed him and threw him. He landed across the

warehouse on his ass. Even at this distance, Maria could see the murderous intent in his eyes. She walked toward him, determined to remove the stain of the elder Dorrance from the Earth.

Tomas stepped in her path and put a hand on her chest. Maria glared at him and grabbed his forearm. She squeezed, and Tomas turned into the pain. "Get out of my way," she growled.

"Let the police deal with him," he urged. "You had a large dose of Boost and aren't in your right mind. You're not a killer."

She stared at Tomas for a long moment and then looked at the elder Dorrance.

"Maria!"

Maria looked back at Tomas. "The cops are here," he said. "Let them deal with my father. He'll lose everything." Maria looked away. Tomas put his hand on her chin and gently turned her face toward him. "You're not a killer."

Maria blinked. It was as if Tomas was talking in slow-motion. His words took forever to reach her racing mind, but they slowly sank in. Maria nodded.

"Go," she told him. "You don't want the cops seeing you here like this. I'll handle this."

He looked at her stomach. "You're hurt."

Maria looked down at her stomach. She barely felt the knife go in and weirdly there was very little pain. She pressed her fingers to the wound and pulled them away. She looked at the blood on her fingertips.

"I barely noticed," she admitted.

"Go. I can deal with the police."

"What? No. I'll do it. They don't know you."

He shook his head. "I know, but I'll do it. It's something I have to do."

Maria looked at him for a long moment and eventually nodded. She understood. If a member of her family had done what the Dorrances did, she'd want to see it through until the end. She couldn't imagine how hard this all was for Tomas.

"Fine," she said.

"Go get that wound looked at. I'll catch up to you later."

That sounded too much like "we need to talk" and certainly no warm fuzzy feeling with it. She nodded. She stepped forward and placed a light kiss on his mouth.

Maria retrieved her mask and headed for the door. She looked back for a brief moment and then stepped into the night.

The sirens blared and red and blue lights flashed off the surrounding buildings. She hoped Tomas wouldn't be given a difficult time by the police. She pulled out her phone and sent a text to Rollins telling him Skanda is a friend and helped.

She climbed on her bike and sped off into the night.

CHAPTER THIRTY

FIRSTS HAPPENED ALL THE TIME, AND FOR MARIA, IT just happened to be her apartment being spotlessly clean. All the empty takeout containers disappeared from the kitchen, and the fridge and pantry were stocked. The living room had been cleaned, and no clothes littered the floor or furniture. Maria moved from the living room to her bedroom.

Clothes were the big issue. When Maria undressed, she let the clothes fall to the floor where she stood. The hardwood floors were barely visible. Clean clothes were in a basket near the closet, waiting to be put away for the past two months. Each time she did laundry, she put the clothes on top of the clothes already in the basket.

Maria saved the most formidable task until last. She put music on and grabbed a glass of wine, and charged in.

Halfway through, she picked up a shirt that didn't belong to her. Tomas. Maria closed her eyes for a moment and pushed back the ache in her heart. She opened her eyes and brought the shirt up to her face. She inhaled. His scent lingered in the fabric. The light musk scent mixed with the heady cologne made her dizzy.

The ache in her chest honed to razor sharpness, and she pushed it back.

He wasn't worth the hurt, or any of the tears. He wasn't worth the restless nights, but he had been worth it all. She had enjoyed spending time with him and getting to know him. She had been stupid enough to think about a future with him.

A week had passed since his father and sister had been arrested. The wheels of justice moved faster than normal as the two of them had already been indicted, and the arraignment was scheduled for next week. Maria suspected it was because Dorrance was such a high-profile person and a big case. Trying to keep busy failed, and Tomas's ghost haunted her waking moments. Every news outlet seemed fixated on his father and the coming trial. Maria couldn't escape mention of it. He intruded into her dreams at night, leaving her restless and tired. Not to mention extremely irritable. Gayle commented on Maria's mood numerous times during the week, and somehow Maria kept herself from snapping at her best friend.

She had spent a good majority of the week with her father and grandfather, coming down from the effects of Boost. The first two days were the worst. She had been stuck in high-gear and wanted to go out and beat up as many bad guys as she could find. The two men tag-teamed her and kept her still. They even had a doctor monitor her for any adverse effects. It took most of the week to get past wanting more Boost. Her father and grandfather finally let her return to her apartment at week's end, and Maria turned her attention to cleaning as a diversion.

A knock at her door provided a much-welcomed distraction from cleaning and from thoughts of Tomas. She tossed the shirt into the dark recesses of her closet to be lost forever. Maria wondered who could be visiting. Gayle had a key and would let herself in, as would either of her parents. No one else she knew would ever visit here.

She reached the door and pulled it open, not bothering to look through the peephole to see the person knocking on her door. Stupid thing to do, but she could handle whatever was on the other side of the door. Except the person who stood there. She froze and swallowed past the lump in her throat. Her eyes locked with his.

"Tomas," she said, barely able to get the word past her lips.

"Maria," he said with a nod. "Can I come in?"

"Why are you here?" she asked. Keeping him in the hallway was the safer bet. She wouldn't lie to herself; she'd fuck him if given a chance.

"I wanted to talk to you and see how you're doing. Can we not do this here in the hallway?"

For a long moment, Maria thought about letting him stand in the hallway, but she moved to the side, giving him space to enter. Tomas brushed past her, entering the apartment. Maria sighed and closed the door. She gathered her willpower for this and turned around.

She took two steps toward him and stopped. Keeping some distance between them was the best policy. One touch and clothes would be coming off. She'd bet money on it. She folded her arms over her chest. "Start talking."

He looked around. "You cleaned."

"You can leave right now if you came here to comment on my housekeeping abilities," she said, trying to keep her voice even.

He shook his head. "I'm sorry."

Maria blinked. He still possessed the knack for catching her off-guard. An apology was the last thing she ever expected. "For what?"

"I'm sorry for not believing you." He sat down on the couch, leaning forward with his elbows resting on his thighs. "I didn't want to believe you. It's my father, after all."

"I can understand wanting to believe in family members," she said. She'd never believe anyone if they told her one of her family members was involved in criminal activities.

He nodded. "I didn't want to believe it. Even after looking through his computer and seeing the facts for myself, I still didn't want to believe it."

"I'm sorry," Maria said. She couldn't imagine going through what he was going through. She couldn't imagine having a family member doing criminal acts and endangering lives. Maria unfolded her arms and crossed the room. She sat next to him on the couch and put her hand on his. She gave it a squeeze, thankful her trust in him hadn't been broken. He didn't go to the media to betray her. Eventually, with proof, he believed her about his family.

He rolled his wrist and interlaced his fingers with hers. He looked over at her. Maria looked at their entwined fingers and then at him. "Thank you."

Maria smiled. "Are you going to be okay?"

He shrugged. "I don't know. I don't know what to think, and I don't know what I should do. They're holding my father and sister without bail. My mother is a complete wreck."

"I'm sorry," she said. She didn't regret putting his father and sister in prison, but she felt terrible that he and his mother were going through this. The two of them didn't deserve to be hurt.

She slipped her hand out of his and stood. She walked into the kitchen and grabbed two glasses from a cupboard. She poured whiskey into each glass and returned to the couch. She offered him one of the drinks and returned to her seat.

"Thanks," he said, accepting the drink. "How's your stomach?"

"Healed," she said. Maria took a long drink from her glass, drinking half of it. "Do you have a place to stay?" she asked.

"I was planning on finding an apartment for my mother and me until the trial was over. Or an Airbnb. Then we'll go home. Thankfully, I have my own money."

Maria was happy for him. Tomas's father's personal money and the company funds and assets were frozen by the US government. Tomas would most likely take over the company if there was still a company to take over when this was done. Her stomach twisted at the thought of him returning to Brazil. She almost lost him, and she didn't want to lose him now. Somewhere along the way, she developed feelings for him. Her heart would break if he returned to Brazil.

Maria drained the rest of the whiskey in one long drink and held the empty glass between her hands. She wanted to tell him he could stay here if he needed, but uncertainty gripped her. She had no clue where they stood. Friends? Exes? Lovers? She distracted herself by standing and going for a refill. "Refill?" she asked as she grabbed the bottle and opened it.

"Sure," he said. "Though it's probably not a good idea."

Maria smiled. "I'm all about bad ideas," she said, bringing the bottle to him. Her latest bad idea sat on the couch. She refilled his glass, then set the bottle on an end table and lifted her glass. "Here's to bad ideas."

He raised his glass in return and then took a drink. "To bad ideas."

Maria lifted her glass, drank, and returned to her seat next to him.

"So how long have you been doing the whole costume thing?" he asked.

"A couple of years now," she admitted. Guess it was time to address the elephant lurking in the room. Definitely not what she had planned when she saw him standing in her doorway. "What about you?" She looked over at him.

"About the same," he answered.

"So, what now? We said never again in costume, and we didn't like each other in costume."

"I know we said that." He shrugged. "I don't know. We didn't know each other identities. How long do you think 'never again' was going to last?"

"Probably not long," Maria said with a half-smile. Libido and sexual attraction weren't problems for them. They had yet to spend time together without getting naked. "The masks complicate things, don't they?"

"A little," he said. "But they do make it possible for us to do the things we do."

Maria nodded. "And protect those we care about."

"Yes," he said.

"You know, I did feel guilty about making out with Skanda when I didn't know it was you," she said.

He nodded. "I carried some guilt as well. The good news is that we didn't cheat on each other."

"Yeah. Life is strange."

"You can say that again," he said.

Cue awkward silence for a few moments.

Maria looked over at him. Her racing mind slowed, and the world came into sharper focus. Dangerous thoughts turned into danger-laced words. "You can stay here if you want," she said quietly. She gripped her glass harder to prevent him from seeing her shaking hands.

He turned and looked at her. He tilted his head, and his eyes narrowed slightly. "Do you mean that?"

"Yes," she answered, barely above a whisper.

"I'm honestly surprised by the offer," he said. He took another sip of his drink. "I thought you were against anything resembling a relationship."

"I was," she admitted. She was now ready to redefine her life to include him in it. She remained herself, but she added another facet to the way she defined herself. She took another drink and then a deep breath. "I didn't plan on falling in love with you."

Tomas blinked and slowly smiled. He leaned over and dropped a light kiss on her lips. "I love you, and I want to move in with you, but I can't until after the trial is over. I need to be there for my mother."

Maria smiled, and the weight on her shoulders disappeared

with her confession. She nodded. She understood. She'd want to be there for her family if the situations were reversed.

She set her glass on the floor, then turned and put a hand on his cheek, leaning in to kiss him. The kiss was tender and soft, not demanding or intense as they had been in the past. He returned the kiss with equal tenderness. The kiss ended, and Maria pulled back.

She removed her hand from his face and stood. She offered a hand to him. He looked at the hand and then looked up at her. Her eyes held his, and he placed his hand in hers. Maria smiled, and he stood. With his hand in hers, she led him to her bedroom.

Maria stopped next to the bed and released his hand. She smiled and removed her t-shirt. His eyes remained riveted on her every motion, and Maria smiled. She slid her hands under the waist of her sweats and pushed the fabric down. Her underwear fell along with her sweats, and the material pooled at her feet. She stepped out of them and stood before him, completely naked, her eyes never leaving his.

He smiled and removed his shirt; his pants and underwear followed. He pulled his socks off and straightened. Maria wrapped her arms around his neck, pressing her body against the length of his.

Skin on skin never felt so good. Maria kissed him, but not as demanding as she usually did. Desire filled her, but not urgency and lust. She wanted to savor every aspect of him and what they were doing. He was a drug she couldn't get enough of, but tonight she could wait for the fix.

She put a hand to his cheek as she kissed him. The beginning of stubble prickled against her palm. She wrapped her arms around his neck, pressing her body against his. His arms slipped around her, and he caressed her back. Shivers chased over her skin where his hands moved, and the desire increased.

Tomas took a step toward her, and Maria took a step backward. The back of her legs bumped against the bed. He helped lower her to the bed and covered her body with his. Tomas was mostly muscle and heavier than her, and she savored the feel of his weight on top of her.

She thrust her hips against his as his mouth left hers to find an earlobe. He gently took the fleshly lobe between his teeth and applied pressure. Maria moaned and put her hands on his hips. She tried to take it slow and relish in the tenderness, but he made it more challenging with each passing moment.

He must have sensed her struggle and parted her legs with a knee. He entered her with a smooth motion, and Maria gasped before his mouth covered hers. He didn't move but stayed there with their two bodies joined. For the first time in a long time, a deeper connection to someone that went beyond the physical existed.

The kiss ended, and Maria put a hand on his cheek. She looked into his eyes. "I love you," she whispered. The words came easier after the first time.

Tomas smiled. "I love you," he said before kissing her again.

Slowly, he started to move against her. Maria removed her hand from his cheek and returned it to his hip. She matched his movements, using her hands to guide his hips, and her soul fell deeper into his. He set a slow, steady pace. Instead of trying to race to the inevitable release that awaited, Maria enjoyed the journey.

The tension slowly built inside of her as he moved. She put her hands on his back and curled her fingers, digging her nails into his flesh. It must have been a sign of encouragement as he thrust harder and deeper into her. He increased his speed a little, and Maria closed her eyes. Every thrust seemed to go farther in her and added to the building tension. Her breathing increased in speed as he moved faster.

The tension ratcheted up tighter and tighter until the dam burst. Waves of ecstasy washed over her, and she yelled his name. He kissed her with the force of a hurricane and swallowed her scream. She clenched around him, and he didn't change his rhythm. Maria held on while he continued to move, and she ground her mouth down on his. He ended the kiss and threw his head back as his whole body tightened. He groaned loudly as he reached his orgasm, and Maria smiled.

He slackened his body and kissed her mouth. He lowered and lay atop her.

"Mmmmm," Maria purred. Her body was physically satisfied, and her soul was one with his. Emotions coursed through her, and her heart swelled.

He kissed her again. "Mmmmm is right," he agreed. "I love you." He rolled off her to lie beside her. He wrapped his arms around her, and Maria draped a leg over his. She soaked up the warmth and security he offered.

Maria returned the kiss and then smiled. "I love you." The words came even easier the third time.

CHAPTER THIRTY-ONE

Tomas took a deep breath and knocked on the apartment door. It had been a long three months with his father and sister's trials and convictions. His mother left for Brazil yesterday, and now Tomas stood outside Maria's door.

He wouldn't blame her if she didn't answer the door. While they had frequently seen each other, he had focused on the trial and everything leading up to it. Not only that, but he also had to deal with what was left of the company. There had been so much to do. Most nights, Tomas fell asleep sitting on the couch with his laptop on his lap and papers all around. He barely had time to think, let alone spend it with Maria.

He hoped the offer to move in was still open. They had talked about it a few times during the past three months, but no definite decision had been made. If it wasn't, he'd look like a complete fool standing here at her door with his suitcases.

The door opened a crack, and he smiled when he saw her face peeking through. "Hi."

"Hey." She opened the door wider and stood in the doorway.

"Is that offer to move in still open?" he asked.

She blinked and remained silent. For a moment, he thought

she would say no, and he'd have to walk away with his tail between his legs and carrying suitcases. He honestly didn't know what he would do after that. He could always get an apartment here in New York, or he could fly back to Brazil. The latter was by far the least desirable option.

"Of course," she said as a smile stretched her mouth. Relief washed through him. She moved out of the doorway, and Tomas picked up his suitcases. At least he never got the chance to accumulate too many possessions during his stay here in New York, and it made moving easier. Tomas entered the apartment, and Maria closed the door behind him.

He set the suitcases down and looked at her.

Light danced in her blue eyes, and a smile played upon her lips. He reached out and took one of her hands in his. He pulled her to him and wrapped his arms around her. She wrapped her arms around him, and they just stood there, clinging to each other as time ticked by.

Maria put her head on his shoulder, her face toward his neck. Tomas closed his eyes and rested his cheek against her forehead. Peace and calmness enveloped him, along with a sense of belonging. This simple embrace did more for him than anything in the past three months.

Time slowed as well as his heartbeat. His turbulent emotions calmed, and his mind ceased racing in circles. The world narrowed down to thoughts of Maria and the feeling of her in his arms. Nothing else mattered at this moment. Not his father or his crimes. Not his sister. Not even the demise of the family company. Just her.

He smiled and slightly turned his head to press his lips to her forehead. He lost almost everything, but he found her. In that moment, she became his everything, and he wouldn't have it any other way.

Maria pulled away a little bit to look at him. "Everything okay?"

Tomas nodded. "It is now."

Maria kissed him lightly and then smiled. "Welcome home."

Thank you for reading! Did you enjoy? Please add your review because nothing helps an author more and encourages readers to take a chance on a book than a review.

And don't miss more from Sydney Ashcroft and Dani Nichols with IMMORTAL SECRETS available now. Turn the page for a sneak peek!

Also be sure to sign up for the City Owl Press newsletter to receive notice of all book releases!

SNEAK PEEK OF IMMORTAL SECRETS
BY SYDNEY ASHCROFT AND DANI NICHOLS

Joanna Shepard stood in the living room of her childhood home and looked around. Her stomach twisted into knots at the sight of the various boxes sitting around the otherwise empty room. She hadn't been here since her parents' funeral a few months ago and at the time never thought about what would happen to the house. While she would never live here again, it was still supposed to be home.

She had been living in Boulder, Colorado, since starting undergrad at the University of Colorado Boulder over four years ago. Once she graduated, she decided to stay in Boulder. If she could have avoided coming home to Maine, she would have moved heaven and hell. She told herself that if she didn't, somehow her life would reset, and she would find her parents alive. Now she had no more excuses. As executor of her parents' estate, Alex had handled the legal issues regarding life insurance, readying the house for sale, and guardianship of her younger brother, Ben. They would have been lost without her.

Alex Thorne, their family friend and honorary aunt, kept in contact with her and her twin brother, Mike, about every step and decision she made, but she wouldn't go through their rooms. Somehow Jo hoped no one would want the house, but then a buyer was lined up and ready to pay a fair price. Now they had to come home and get the remainder of their possessions, and anything else they wanted before the final renovations were made. Then the sale.

Ben, in the last few weeks of high school, had already taken care of his room. Alex and Ben had packed and stored most of their parents' things, with the idea that the three of them would go through them when they felt ready. Furniture and housewares were in storage, along with most of their possessions. There were a few boxes of personal things Alex would put in her attic for safekeeping once they'd gotten them all. She told Jo she didn't like the idea of irreplaceable photo albums, letters, and jewelry in a place where anything could happen. They could replace a couch or a set of dishes. They would feel the loss of pictures and journals.

Jo thanked the heavens for Alex. She couldn't imagine doing all that needed to be done while dealing with the overwhelming grief of losing her parents. She had spoken to her mother that fateful morning, never expecting it to be the last conversation she would have with her.

Ben seemed the most stable of the three when it came to dealing with the accident and aftermath, even though Jo had witnessed his sudden silences and furtive wiping of tears from his eyes. He'd lived with Alex for the last three months. His support system had been a physical presence. For Jo and Mike, it had been long distance.

Tears welled up in her eyes, and she furiously wiped them away. Three months later, it still hurt as it had the night Alex called her, informing Jo of her parents' deaths. The memory still made her sick.

She rubbed the bridge of her nose and took a deep breath. She tried not to see the room as she had known it. Tried not to mentally place all the pictures her mother had of the family hanging on the walls. Grief cut deeper into her heart. It had been a good life, a wonderful life to grow up in. She never imagined she would have to live without her parents at the age of twenty-three.

"Jo." Ben entered the living room with a box in his arms. "I think this is all Mom's pictures. She had so many, I don't think we've found them all. Do you want to go through it with me later?"

The word "No" wouldn't form on her lips or get past the lump in her throat. She shook her head and looked at Ben through tear-filled eyes.

She'd swear he was taller than the last time she had been home, which had been for the funeral. His hair was longer and hanging down into his eyes. Apparently he had been hitting the gym too. If she remembered correctly, he was going to the University of Maine on a football scholarship. Right now, it was hard to think about anything.

He set it on top of a stack of boxes near the door. "I'll go through it first. You and Mike can do it later. I think I saw Mike heading into your room."

Jo offered her younger brother a weak smile. Leave it to him to give her the nudge she needed to move. Otherwise, she would have been rooted in place forever. Ben smiled back. He looked so much like their dad.

Jo took a step, her feet feeling like lead, and then another. Ben gave her a small push to get her momentum going. She snorted a bit, sounding dreadful through the tears. She turned her head to say something, but Ben had moved off again.

She somehow made it to the doorway of her old room. Mike wasn't in there, but she could hear him moving about in the room next to hers. She took a deep breath and stepped inside.

Memories rushed back, and she struggled not to be swept under the wave. She put a hand on her old desk to steady herself. Footsteps behind her forced her to straighten up and regain her composure. She didn't want Mike to see her break. She turned to see Alex standing in the doorway.

Alex wasn't family by blood, but she was family in every other sense. She had been a constant in their lives, knowing Jo's parents since college, or so they had said. The woman was godmother and aunt to all three of them and had been there for every major milestone. Jo, Mike, and Ben would have never gotten through the past few months without Alex. Alex called Jo daily to check on her since Jo returned to Boulder after the funeral. She probably did the same for Mike. Some days Jo dreaded the daily call. Some days she feared Alex would forget.

As always, Alex's long, dark hair was perfect, and the makeup she wore was subtle. Alex wore jeans and a T-shirt instead of the flowing dresses she usually favored. She looked at Jo, and it seemed like those gray eyes felt everything Jo did in her soul.

"Need some help?" Alex asked.

At first Jo shook her head, but then she nodded. Alex stepped into the room and wrapped her arms around Jo. Jo clung to Alex and buried her face in Alex's shoulder. Tears weren't far behind. All she needed was a little help to keep moving. How was Alex so strong? She could use some of that strength.

At some point, the tears stopped, but the strength of Alex's embrace never lessened. Alex's heart beat in her ear, and in a way, it helped comfort Jo. She dropped her arms, and only then did Alex release her.

Jo wiped her eyes, and Alex brushed a lock of Jo's hair out of Jo's face. No words were exchanged. The need didn't exist. Instead, Alex kissed Jo's forehead and picked up a box from the floor next to her. She placed it on the bed and began removing books, most of which Alex had given Jo, from the bookshelves and placing them in the box.

Jo took a few deep breaths to orient herself. Once some of her composure came back, she opened a dresser drawer. She removed a stack of clothes and placed them on the bed. The two women worked in silence while they emptied shelves and drawers. Alex carried filled boxes out to the living room and returned with empty ones.

"Hey, Ms. Thorne." Jo turned to see Greg Sullivan standing in the doorway. She forced a small smile.

"Hello, Greg. I'm glad you could make it."

"I'm sorry I'm late." Greg smiled at her. "Hey, Jo."

"That's fine, Greg," Alex said. "I appreciate your offer to help."

Jo vaguely remembered seeing Greg at the funeral, but she had gone through most of the day in a haze and couldn't remember who she saw or spoke to. Greg had to have been there. He and Mike had been best friends since junior year of high school when Greg and his family moved to Good Harbor and opened a restaurant. Mike returned to Good Harbor for summer breaks, but Joanna had always remained in Boulder. It was another regret she carried with her. All that time she could have spent with her family.

"Hey, Greg," she croaked. Great, she sounded like a frog. She cleared her throat. "Hi."

Greg had changed since she first met him. He'd been cute then. He now had to be around six foot three and filled out to match the height. His dark hair was long enough to have some curls and was kind of tousled. She rather liked it.

"Did I hear Greg?" Mike's voice floated from the room next door. The next moment, Mike materialized in the doorway next to Greg. Jo realized how much taller Greg had become as he hugged her brother. Mike and Greg had always been around the same height, but now Greg had about five inches, maybe six, on Mike.

Mike's dirty blond hair was a mess, and it looked like he found the oldest shirt and jeans he owned to work around the house. His pale skin, the product of hours spent gaming and avoiding sunlight, showed the red splotches where he'd continually wiped his "I'm not crying, you're crying" eyes. Mike's coloring echoed their mother, while Jo's and Ben's dark hair and high cheekbones favored their father in looks.

"Hey, man." Mike released Greg. "Good to see you. What are you doing here?"

"Good to see you, Mike. Ms. Thorne said you might need an extra hand to move boxes. I said yes because she may have mentioned you and Jo would be here, and it's been a while since we got together. Seemed like a great time to talk while being useful."

"Well, she didn't tell us." Jo glanced over at Alex, and the woman had a slightly self-satisfied look on her face. Surprises and Jo never went well together, but she was glad Mike had a good friend to help with the task.

"All we need now is Carrie."

"She will be joining us for dinner at the house," Alex said. "Greg, you are more than welcome to join us, provided you do not have to work."

"Thanks, Ms. Thorne. I'd really like that. Dad gave me the night off as long as I show up in the morning to start the bread dough."

The thought of seeing Carrie helped lift some of the ever-present grief and help unwind Jo's stomach a bit. The two had a lot to catch up on, and it would help Jo not think about emptying out her childhood home for a few hours. Opportunities to think about something else were far and few in between.

"Why isn't Carrie here?" she asked. "It's not like her to miss out."

"She's minding the store. Work needs to be done here first. Then you can all catch up over dinner." Alex handed a box of books to Greg. "You can even have a house party if you like."

"Of course, Ms. Thorne." Greg stepped inside the room and accepted the box.

"The boxes in the living room can go in the back of my truck. The rest of the boxes will go into the rental truck."

"Yes, Ms. Thorne." Greg turned and slipped past Mike and out into the hallway. But not before Jo had a second to notice Greg's backside. Some men were meant to wear denim. She had definitely missed out on visits over her college years.

"Mike, your room," Alex said, reminding him of the task at hand.

Mike nodded and disappeared out of the doorway.

Jo scanned her old room. The bare walls looked strange. Jo couldn't remember a time before when they had been bare. She used to have posters all over the room, along with pictures she had taken. Alex had probably removed them and packed them safely away.

Her room and Mike's room were the only rooms that had remained the colors Jo remembered. She remembered when she had asked her parents if she could have her room painted. She must have been around ten or so. Mike heard her ask and wanted his room painted too. He picked a dark gray while Jo had picked a jewel-toned purple.

The other parts of the house Alex had cleaned out had been repainted, all the same light shade of gray. Some of the carpets had been cleaned, while the others had been replaced. Alex had taken care of it all. She imagined Alex already arranged for the remaining work. At least Jo didn't have to deal with those things.

"I'm going to go help Greg with those boxes and see what Ben has gotten into. Do you need any help now?"

"I don't think so." Jo sat on the edge of the bare mattress and savored the relative silence when Alex left the room. The sounds of Mike moving around in his room drifted through the wall. Jo didn't envy her brother. Mike shared the habit of never throwing anything out with their mother. Jo took after their father and had always been organized and didn't like clutter. They kept the things that were important and managed to let go of anything that wasn't. Ben landed somewhere in the middle of keeping things and letting things go.

Now it was time to let go of one of the major things tying the three of them to their past. They would never physically return to the house, but their memories would always take them back when they wanted to be here. Jo took a deep breath and slowly let it out. Inside, a part of her wanted to refuse and hang on, but logically she knew neither she, Mike, nor Ben could afford to keep the house at this point in their lives. Their parents wouldn't have wanted them to be stubborn about keeping it. She sighed and continued packing up her belongings.

Jo felt a million times better when Carrie walked in the back door of Alex's old Victorian and wrapped Jo in a bear hug. Jo held on to her best friend for what seemed like ages. Carrie held on just as tightly. Eventually they released each other.

"Hi!" Carrie grinned the biggest grin Jo had seen. Carrie's reddish-brown hair was a little longer than it had been at the funeral. Carrie wore the same style of black-rimmed glasses as she had worn in high school, her brown eyes sparkling with excitement. "I'm so happy to see you! When Ms. Thorne told me you were coming back for a few days, she was nice enough to invite me over for dinner. Thankfully I have a really short way to go."

"What do you mean?" Joanna tilted her head.

"I'm renting the apartment above the store. Makes getting to work so much easier."

"Really? That's incredible. She never rented it before."

"Yes! She took pity on me and rented it out to me at a really reasonable rate." Carrie danced a happy shuffle. "I think she did it because she was tired of hearing me complaining about still living with my parents and the kids still at home, or how I didn't have space or quiet to study. Or me moaning that I had to keep asking Mom for rides to work. I'm working in the store until I can find a full-time position at one of the nearby schools, and she lets me borrow her truck sometimes."

Jo was thankful she only had Mike and Ben to deal with, even if they were annoying. Carrie had three sisters and a brother, all of whom were younger. The second oldest after Carrie was Ben's age. Jo sympathized a lot with Carrie's situation.

After high school, Carrie stayed in the state and went to U Maine at Orono and completed an education degree with the hope of teaching history. Last Christmas Carrie mentioned the idea of going for her master's. Jo surprised herself by remembering that much.

Carrie wanted her master's. Greg worked for his parents at their restaurant and had earned a business degree at the local community college. Mike had a degree in computer science and learned about video game design. He had a job waiting for him as soon as he was ready. Ben was bound for UMaine in Orono in the fall. Jo completed a degree in journalism but had no idea what she would do now. She didn't have a plan the way the others did. It made her feel a little disconnected and unsure, but she'd figure out what she wanted to do with her life sooner or later.

Jo had forgotten all about the apartment over the carriage house shop until Carrie mentioned it. It would have been the perfect place to stay while they were handling all the details necessary to get the house sold. Still, it was ideal for Carrie, and that made her happy, if somewhat a little envious.

"I'm glad. You're in the right place."

Carrie smacked her own forehead. "What's wrong with me? You could stay there with me if you want. It has two bedrooms. Plenty of privacy unless Munchkin wants in, and he doesn't talk about what he sees."

Jo smiled through the threat of more tears. The people in her life were so good to her, and she didn't feel that she lived up to that standard as often as she should. "That'd be great, if you're really okay with it and Alex doesn't mind. I don't know how long Ben and Mike would live if I had to stay in the house with them."

"Hey now, we're not that bad," Mike called from the kitchen.

"Yes, you are!" Jo yelled back. "C'mon." She hooked an arm through Carrie's. "We have pizza, and we're planning on watching some movies. Alex bought dinner tonight instead of cooking. It's been a long day."

"I bet. That's another perk of living so close. She takes pity on me and lets me raid her fridge. She even brought meals to me when I was deep in studying for finals. She always says she cooked too much, but she's just nice enough to not let me starve."

Jo chuckled. That sounded like Alex. There had been many times Alex brought meals for her family over to the house. Usually Jo, Mike, and Ben's favorites. Alex's homemade bread was to die for.

They entered the kitchen where Mike and Greg sat eating pizza from a local place. Local in the sense that it was in the town of Good Harbor, still twenty minutes away from the house. Delivery wasn't even an option. She often thought a delivery service in Good Harbor during the tourist season would make a lot of money in the summer months alone. It was another reason Jo loved Boulder with its delivery options and availability of all kinds of ethnic foods.

The kitchen was a cook's dream. The house might have been built in the 1800s, but the kitchen was as modern as any house recently built. Alex had spared no expense in renovating the space, including black stainless-steel appliances, while still managing to make it feel warm and cozy. The countertops were dark granite and set off the white cabinets. The island in the middle of the kitchen had an eating bar and space for food preparation. The breakfast nook was large enough to seat an unruly family of six, yet cozy enough for one or two people to enjoy a meal. Like the rest of the house, the kitchen was spotless.

The antique table in the formal dining room could expand to seat eighteen people, but it was seldom used. Alex wasn't the hostess with the mostess when it came to entertaining groups, but small gatherings of friends and family were always well fed and entertained. Jo had always wondered why she didn't have more people in her life.

"We have meat lovers, pepperoni, and sausage and peppers," Greg announced. "Provided Mike hasn't eaten all the meat lovers by now."

Her brothers could eat an entire large pizza each, and it caused Jo's stomach to hurt just watching them. She always wondered where they put all the food. When she asked, they always replied that they were growing boys and needed as much food as they could get. Mike had five inches on Jo, standing at five foot ten to her petite five foot five. Ben was a different story. Ben had cleared six feet two years ago and had managed to grow another two inches.

"I didn't eat it all," Mike vowed. "But now I will."

"Like hell you will." Jo snatched a slice of meat lovers from the box.

"Hey!" he protested.

A bang at the back door halted what might have been the first cross words they exchanged in an emotional day. Mike's protest turned to a lopsided smile as he disappeared from the room. A moment later, a huge dog entered the kitchen and stopped all talk. Each one of them had to greet Munchkin as he made his way around the room to sniff everyone's shoes and get their adoring ear scratches and pets. To call the giant Caucasian Shepherd Munchkin had to have been a joke at one point, but Alex never told them how she'd come by the dog or why she named him something so tongue-in-cheek.

He settled down at Mike's feet and rested a huge paw on his foot. It was his subtle reminder that he, too, wanted his dinner.

Carrie selected a slice of sausage and peppers and sat in one of the empty chairs at the breakfast nook.

"Drink?" Jo asked Carrie.

"Water, please. Thank you."

"Certainly." Jo took glasses from the cabinet and filled them from the water dispenser in the fridge. She placed one in front of Carrie and one in front of her own plate.

"Are we going to do anything tonight?" Mike covered his mouth between bites so he could talk without spitting food at them. "Besides the movies."

"I just want to take it easy," Jo said. "I'm wiped after today."

"A movie night upstairs?" Greg smiled at her, and she swore her knees went a little weak. He had definitely gotten cuter in the last four years. "That brings back memories."

Alex's Victorian had three floors, and one of the bedrooms on the top floor had been turned into a gaming room for Ben. He slept in the bedroom next to it. It gave him the privacy a teenage boy needed. With him at a friend's house tonight, the giant—and only—television in the house was available for use.

"That sounds like fun," Carrie said.

"Yeah, we can do that."

"We are taking turns picking movies," Jo warned. She knew her brother. If left to his own devices, they would be watching movies with explosions and bullets all night. While Jo didn't mind them, she accepted the fact that other types of movies existed.

"Fine." Mike shot her a death glare with no heat or force behind it.

Jo laughed. Thwarting one's brother was never a bad thing in her book, and it had been some time since she had the opportunity to do it.

"When was the last time we were all together like this?" Carrie asked. "It feels like it's been ages."

"I'd say winter break. When Jo came home for a week, but Greg missed all those because he had to work."

"Oh yeah," Carrie said. "It still feels like forever."

Jo's chest tightened up. It had been the last time she had seen her parents alive. She swallowed past the lump in her throat and tried to force her stomach to unwind.

"Jo, you okay?" Carrie put a hand on her arm.

"I'm fine," she automatically answered. It was the same answer she gave whenever anyone asked her how she was doing. More so lately. She'd reached her limit of having folks ask about her current state.

Carrie lowered her chin and looked over the rim of her glasses.

Of course Carrie didn't believe Jo; she knew Jo too well. The best friends curse. Other people would accept Jo's answer, but not Carrie.

Jo waved her hand. She would. Eventually. With a lot of time.

"You know I'm always here to talk if you want to, right?"

Jo leaned over and squeezed Carrie's arm. "Yeah, I know, and I appreciate it."

Carrie smiled in return. "Good."

"Let's go watch some movies," Mike suggested.

"We need to clean up first." Greg picked up Mike's plate and his own. "How about Jo and I clean up while Mike, you and Carrie gather some snacks and drinks and take them up?"

"Sounds like a plan." Carrie went to the fridge for canned drinks. Munchkin hurried to follow the food when Mike left the room with the pizza.

Greg stacked the plates while Jo gathered the dirty napkins. She stuffed them in the compost bin and then collected the glasses. Greg had already started washing the plates.

Jo set the glasses on the counter next to the sink, and Greg turned and offered her a smile. "Thanks."

"Welcome. Thanks for washing. I hate washing dishes."

"I remember. I'm used to it. I wash dishes at the restaurant when we're running short staffed. Can't believe Ms. Thorne still doesn't use the dishwasher."

"I thought you'd be expediting by now. Like a polite Gordon Ramsay," Jo said.

"You honestly think Dad would let me polite him into hurrying a dish to a table? I like cleaning more than cooking. I can cook and do when we're that busy. I just prefer not to. Especially during tourist season."

"I can imagine." Jo grabbed a dish towel to start drying the dishes. Even though Alex had a dishwasher, four plates and four glasses weren't enough to run it. If she'd had paper plates in the house, they would have used those instead.

"It gets brutal," Greg continued. "We get a few customers from hell every week, and I can stay out of the line of fire. Not to mention cleaning means I don't have to remake dishes."

"Your dad is too nice. He doesn't have to put up with that crap. No way is a bad review from a jerk customer going to affect his business. He's too good, and Good Harbor adores him."

"It's better that he doesn't snap back. He can get hairy when he loses his temper. I'm better at the behind-the-scenes work. I like getting up at 3:00 a.m. to start the dough and get the sauces going for the day. I even made the bread dough for tonight's service before I left to help out at your house."

"I'll have to stop there for lunch one day."

"The family would love to see you. How's Boulder?" he asked, handing a plate to Jo.

"Still awesome." She accepted the plate. "Great food, always something going on, and the people are nice. I love the mountain air, but I miss the ocean, though."

Greg nodded. "Sounds like it really agrees with you. All but the no ocean part, of course. I understand missing it. I've only been in Good Harbor for six years, but the ocean draws you in, and Good Harbor makes you a part of it."

"Yeah," Jo agreed.

"How long are you going to be in town?"

It was a curious question for sure. Jo wondered why he asked it. He had never asked before during her visits.

"A week or two, I think. Mike, Ben, and I are going to start sorting through the boxes we packed today and the stuff in storage. See who wants what, and what can be sold or donated. Alex has offered to handle any sales for us."

Greg nodded and handed her another washed plate. He looked around for a second to see if the other two were paying attention and turned back to her. "Would you be interested in grabbing some ice cream with me?" he asked in a low voice.

Jo paused in the act of taking the plate. Did Greg just ask her out? It sure sounded that way. Her mind raced for an answer. An acceptable answer. He was her brother's best friend, and that alone could make it uncomfortable. But Greg was seriously one of the nicest guys she had ever met. He never said anything disparaging about anyone and always helped when he could. Not to mention he had grown hotter as he had gotten older. When Jo first met him, he had been tall and skinny. But in the past few years he had muscled out, and Jo rather liked it. An ice cream date would be just the thing to take her mind off her troubles for a while.

The plate slipped a bit. How old was she anyway? He was not the first guy to ask her out. She grabbed at it before it could crash to the floor.

"It's okay to say no." Greg chuckled, and Jo felt a shiver down her back. "I mean, it could be weird seeing how I'm Mike's best friend."

"No, it's fine. What I should have said immediately was I'd love to get some ice cream with you."

Greg smiled, and Jo loved the dimples that came along with the smile. "Great. I'll let you know when. Sometimes it can be hard getting some time away from the restaurant."

"I understand. Like I said, I should be around for a week or two, and you have my number. You do have my number, right?"

"Unless it's changed from high school, I still have your number. It's a plan then."

"It's a plan," she repeated.

They both froze when they heard a knock from the front door. Munchkin's bark from above carried through the house, followed by the thunder of four paws down the stairs. "I wonder who that could be. Alex usually doesn't get a lot of visitors." Or maybe she now did. Jo hadn't been around much in the past four years. Maybe she was dating, and it hadn't come up yet.

Greg shrugged. "Don't look at me. I don't know."

Jo dried and put away the last glass. She tossed the towel

aside. "Come on. There are movies to be watched. After we see who's at the door."

Don't stop now. Keep reading with your copy of IMMORTAL SECRETS.

And sign up for the latest news, giveaways, and more from Sydney Ashcroft at www.nicholsandashcroft.com

Don't miss more from Sydney Ashcroft and co-author, Dani Nichols, with IMMORTAL SECRETS available now.

Joanna Shepard knew her childhood home of Good Harbor wouldn't be the same after her parent's death, but she never would have associated it with danger. She returns to deal with the sale of her childhood home, but a sudden attack rips away the safety of a small town. The attack is the first of a series of events that expose dangers lurking in the dark. Lies told to her and her brothers by a beloved family member are revealed and they may be connected to the danger now threatening them. Jo finds herself a pawn in a struggle that is beyond her wildest imagination and she's not sure who she can trust.

Everyone has secrets, but Akantha, now living as Alex Thorne, has more than others. She put the conflicts in her long past behind her and focused on a quiet life on the coast of Maine with an adoptive family. The quiet she sought is shattered when she learns hostile forces are coming after her. She accepts help from her long-time love and sometimes enemy, Damianos, counting on him to keep Jo and her brothers safe from the danger now in their lives.

Secrets exposed. An attack in the night. Sudden betrayals. And a person determined to gain the secret of immortality at any cost.

Joanna has to find the strength inside to accept the new challenges, learn from Akantha, and come out of the other side alive.

Please sign up for the City Owl Press newsletter for chances to win special subscriber-only contests and giveaways as well as receiving information on upcoming releases and special excerpts.

All reviews are **welcome** and **appreciated**. Please consider leaving one on your favorite social media and book buying sites.

For books in the world of romance and speculative fiction that embody Innovation, Creativity, and Affordability, check out City Owl Press at www.cityowlpress.com.

ACKNOWLEDGMENTS

I'd like send thanks out into the ether to Jeffrey Cook. Maria and Tomas were originally RPG characters way back in the day. Maria was one of the most fun characters I've ever played and playing opposite Jeff's Tomas made her that much more fun to play. Thank you for letting me use him. I miss those days and I miss you. Please check out his books.

Thank you to Gail Simone for writing such amazing comics and such amazing characters. You are an inspiration to many.

Thank you to Amie Martin for beta reading and for being my NaNo co-ML.

Thank you to Amie, Wendy, Karri, Darcy, and Julia for being there for me and for listening to all of my ramblings about my books and characters.

ABOUT THE AUTHOR

SYDNEY ASHCROFT originally hails from Pennsylvania, but moved to New England over twenty years ago and has never looked back. She currently resides in Maine with a dog and two cats. During the day she works full time in the information technology field and writes by night. Tea, chocolate, and folk music fuel her through the day and writing sessions. When she's  not writing or working, she enjoys spending time with the dog and two cats, playing Dungeons and Dragons, seeing live music, and reading as much as she can.

www.nicholsandashcroft.com

facebook.com/SydneyAshcroftAuthor
instagram.com/authorsydneyashcroft

ABOUT THE PUBLISHER

City Owl Press is a cutting edge indie publishing company, bringing the world of romance and speculative fiction to discerning readers.

Escape Your World. Get Lost in Ours!

www.cityowlpress.com

facebook.com/YourCityOwlPress

x.com/cityowlpress

instagram.com/cityowlbooks

pinterest.com/cityowlpress

www.ingramcontent.com/pod-product-compliance
Lightning Source LLC
Chambersburg PA
CBHW020819260626
47169CB00003B/734

9 7 8 1 6 4 8 9 8 4 5 2 5